Praise for *The Empty Chair*

"Wagner meditates on our fundamental craving for connection—both human and divine—and meaning—both personal and cosmic—with wit, compassion, and a sharp eye for the lies we tell ourselves."

—*Kirkus Reviews* (starred)

"Remarkable . . . *The Empty Chair* would make a fine fictional companion to the Trappist monk Thomas Merton's writings on spiritual outrage. . . . The soul's cry beneath that rage is the gold Wagner has mined here, and he delivers it to us with a beneficent and magisterial touch."

—*The New York Times Book Review*

"*The Empty Chair* demonstrates Mr. Wagner's range as a writer, reminding us that he possesses a fluent ability to move back and forth between the satiric and the sympathetic, the scabrous and the tender."

—*The New York Times*

"The novellas are absorbing on their own, but what really makes *The Empty Chair* a gem is how two people from completely different backgrounds could tell two true stories that are extraordinarily intertwined."

—*Esquire*

"Few things make a story more difficult to tell than having a listener expecting to hear it. . . . It's this contradiction, among so many others, that Bruce Wagner captures so elegantly in *The Empty Chair*. The book, split between two novellas, teems with gurus and neurotics, martyrs and perverts, but whatever their differences, nearly all of them are storytellers, too. What a shame for them, then, that someone is always listening—and what a joy for us to read."

—Colin Dwyer, *NPR*

THE
EMPTY
CHAIR

Also by Bruce Wagner

Force Majeure
I'm Losing You
Wild Palms (graphic novel)
I'll Let You Go
Still Holding
The Chrysanthemum Palace
Memorial
Dead Stars
I Met Someone
A Guide for Murdered Children
The Marvel Universe: Origin Stories
*ROAR: American Master, The Oral Biography
of Roger Orr*
The Met Gala & Tales of Saints and Seekers

THE EMPTY CHAIR

(Questions and Answers)

BRUCE WAGNER

Arcade Publishing • New York

Arcade Publishing books may be purchased in bulk at special discounts for sales promotion, corporate gifts, fund-raising, or educational purposes. Special editions can also be created to specifications. For details, contact the Special Sales Department, Arcade Publishing, 307 West 36th Street, 11th Floor, New York, NY 10018 or arcade@skyhorsepublishing.com.

Arcade Publishing® is a registered trademark of Skyhorse Publishing, Inc.®, a Delaware corporation.

Visit our website at www.arcadepub.com.
Please follow our publisher Tony Lyons on Instagram @tonylyonsisuncertain

10 9 8 7 6 5 4 3 2 1

Library of Congress Cataloging-in-Publication Data is available on file.

Cover design by David Ter-Avanesyan
Cover painting: *Miracle #64* by Edward Ruscha

Print ISBN: 978-1-64821-131-7
Ebook ISBN: 978-1-64821-132-4

Printed in the United States of America

to Muni Araña and Julius Renard

I will die in Paris, on a rainy day,
on some day I already remember.
I will die in Paris—and I don't shy away—
perhaps on a Thursday, like today, in autumn.

—*César Vallejo*

The author wishes to gratefully acknowledge the National Endowment for the Arts, NPR/Hearing Voices, the Guggenheim Fellowship, the Lannan Foundation, and of course, the PEN/Faulkner Foundation, for their continued support.

THE EMPTY CHAIR

PREFACE

I've spent a good part of the last fifteen years traveling around the country listening to people tell stories. Each spoke voluntarily and without compensation; none were public figures. Sometimes I went looking for storytellers, other times they seemed to come looking for me. Regardless of our methods we managed to find each other. The stories that interested me most were those that described a pivotal event or time in the teller's life. My plan was to stitch together excerpts that moved me or made me laugh, until I had the proverbial American quilt.

My plan changed.

I decided to publish a book—the one in your hands—that holds just two narratives, unabridged. Both share a leitmotif of "diet Buddhism" (again, distinctly American) that serves as a backdrop for a variety of seekers slouching toward spiritual redemption. Though told years apart by a man and woman of divergent social classes, in many ways the tales are complementary. But there's something else, far more compelling: an extraordinary bridge from one to the other, a missing link whose apprehension came as a shock, a *coup de foudre*, an almost traumatic epiphany. From that moment of illumination, the idea of binding both together was non-negotiable.

Some of the material is a little dated. I had no inclination to excise or contemporize, so let once-topical references stand. While I tried to leave most repetitions, lacunae and narrative tics intact, editorial liberties were exercised under the flag of general readability. I am solely responsible for divvying up the transcripts, with the added benefit of being able to listen to the original tapes, into suitable paragraphs; for occasionally relegating parenthetical remarks to footnote status so as not to break the flow of narrative; for carving indents, spaces, and yes, parentheticals from the text (when doing so wouldn't break the flow), the better for it to breathe; and responsible too for inadvertent—and sometimes advertent—wholesale homogenizations. I'm certain there are times when I went too far or didn't go far enough, and if a heavy hand left too many fingerprints I offer my sincere apologies. I ask the persnickety reader to let narrative trump style. The "authors" here are vessels, not virtuosos. But you can't please all of the people all of the time.

Though if it *were* possible to hold all of the people's stories all of the time in one's head, heart and hands, there is no doubt that in the end each would be unvanquishably linked by a single, breathtaking detail, as are the two presented here . . . what I really wanted to write was "single, *religious* detail," but stopped myself. There's been so much sound and fury around that word these days that I hesitate to join the fray. At my age, one doesn't have too many fighting words left. Still, I wonder. Have I let myself be bullied?

I suppose if one needs to ask, the answer may be obvious.

Well, then. Allow me to clear my throat and revise:

If it *were* possible to hold all of the people's stories all of the time in one's head, heart and hands, there is no doubt that in the end each would be unvanquishably linked by a single, *religious* detail . . .

* * *

I wish to thank all of those who shared their stories through the years with such abundance and openness of spirit. Not incidentally, I want to give thanks to the unknowable Mystery that made us.

I don't wish to offend anyone this early on, but I call that force God.

There—I said it.

Why not go out on a limb?

There is a well-known story about the death of Marpa's son. The great sage was inconsolable. After a week of mourning, his grief redoubled. One of his students cautiously approached.

"Master, you have taught us that all of life is an illusion. If this is true, why do you suffer so?"

"Yes, it's true," said Marpa. "Most illusions are petty, without bravura—the phantoms of daily life." He smiled through his tears. "But *this*. This was a *great* illusion!"

FIRST GURU

A 50-year-old man told this tale. I shared a 3 a.m. hot tub with him at Esalen, in Big Sur. He had just finished a five-day gestalt workshop and now I remember that he touched on the phrase "empty chair work," in conversation. I'd heard it before because I'd done a little gestalt back in the day. Frankly, I was surprised the practice was still around.

A therapist of mine used to have an extra chair in her office that played an active role during our sessions. The idea was to project something onto it—a childhood nemesis, an old lover, a father long dead, even things like your job, your car, your depression, your ciga-rette habit—whatever was charged enough to engage. You'd begin a kind of dialogue, often bitter, that held the promise of catharsis. While suddenly notable, the gestaltian "empty chair" happens to be coinci-dental to the title of this work. But who knows? I'm not too proud to say it's possible that the phrase and its metaphor crawled into my brain for a nap and woke up just as I was wondering what to call my book.

The gentleman was staying across Highway 1 at a monastery I wasn't familiar with. Toward the end of the soak, I said I'd been on the road awhile, listening to people talk about momentous events in their lives in view of compiling an oral tribal history of these emo-tionally United States. He immediately volunteered.

It was almost a week before I heard from him again. (It isn't uncommon for initial enthusiasms to dampen or dissolve.) He was calling from the hermitage on the hill. He invited me to visit his room, *one of the Spartan trailers the monks rent out to guests. I was already a few hundred miles away but something told me to turn back.*

The sessions took place over a weekend. The storyteller demonstrated great stamina—our only breaks were for meals and when he took leave to pray.

Then Jonathan said to David,
Tomorrow is the new moon:
and thou shalt be missed,
because thy seat will be empty.

—*1 Samuel 20:18*

The following interview took place in 2010 and was redacted in the fall of 2013.

I'm a gay man who happens to have had a handful of relationships—"serious" ones—with women. The last of these partnerships was unique in that it was the only union to produce a child and a marriage certificate, though not in that order. I've never spoken of the events that caused us to separate (we never bothered to divorce) and for whatever reason, this moment in time seems to have presented itself as ripe for the telling. Bruce, I'm not interested in knowing why you stepped into my life. I should say, my tub! You know—the wherefores of the universe conspiring to provoke this "confession." I only know what I know. And what I don't know, I have learned to leave alone.

I've lived in the Bay Area for what, 30 years? My wife and I met on a six-week silent retreat at Spirit Rock, that's up in Marin. We were Buddhists then. She might still practice, though I strongly doubt it. Anything's possible.

I've always wanted to teach, but it never panned out because of my allergies—I'm allergic to getting up in the morning and going to work! Never graduated university. I'm self-taught, a bit of a pedant. A few people have called me that, more or less. I'm a perfect example of an autodidact. Isn't that the most horrid word? If I *had* matriculated,

I suppose my specialty would have been medieval literature but that's never going to happen. It's pretentious though I'm prone to use it as an icebreaker—I'm even using it with you! Playing the ol' medieval literature specialty card. The truth is, I've always gravitated toward the spiritual. So what happened was, I renounced my fantasy tenure to become a roving ambassador for my own brand of Zen. If the Buddhists call sitting meditation "zazen," I call my theosophy "vanzen" because I live in my van. I can't conceive of a life without the ol' Greater Vehicle.

My van is my Higher Power, as the alcoholics like to say, and my lower companion too. (Not as big as your SUV but I'll bet it's got a tighter turning radius.) I've actually converted it to a library because any self-respecting auto-*mobile*-didact needs his moveable feast. The bookshelves are *Brosimum paraense*—that's bloodwood—embellished by ornamental carvings commissioned from local artists along the way. I'd hunker down in whatever community, hand over a plank to the right artisan when he came along, and say: *Have at it.* I've got the handiwork of a monk from Tassajara, a skater from Morro Bay, and a docent at the Charles Schulz Museum in Santa Rosa. Cherished volumes are held in place by color-coded bungee cords: red for Bio, blue for Fic, orange for Relig, and so on. Honestly, I can't remember a time when I wasn't a reader. Books have always been there for me in my darkest hours. I'll admit my collection's a little biased. I have an estimable selection of San Francisco authors, oh yes I do. And a lot of the Beats. A *lot*.

You see, everyone knows Jack London was born in San Francisco and went to school in Berkeley but did you know his mother channeled spirits? Oh yes she did. Went nuts too. Shot herself and lived to tell the tale. Dante wrote about the suicides but there's a hell right here on Earth for those who botch the act. I believe the professionals put them in the "attempters" versus "completers" camp—like rescue versus recovery. She was so bonkers that the authorities gave him a foster mom, who just happened to be a former slave. Make a pretty good movie, wouldn't it? It's got the whole deal: genius kid, daydreamer dad, whacko mom, and ex-slave foster. Like one of those movies Leonardo DiCaprio used to star in when he was young. Leonardo'd make a pretty good Jack. Now *that's* a film I'd go to see.

Mark Twain was a cub reporter up here, wrote for *The Call*. Legend has it he dreamed up his stories an hour before deadline. Rather Hunter S. Thompson of him! Did you know Kipling came to America just to find Mr. Clemens? Not to San Francisco—to Elmira, New York. I believe that momentous rendezvous took place sometime between the writing of *Tom Sawyer* and *Huck Finn* but don't hold me to it. Lord, but Kipling was a fan! Just in complete awe. Came all the way from India to see him, can you imagine? I'd love to have been a fly on *that* wall. Now there's *another* movie . . . though this one might be better as a play. If I was a terrible playwright (which I would be if I ever tried my hand), that'd be one hell of a theatrical theme—Kipling and Twain in New York. There's the title too: "Kipling and Twain in New York." Readymade. Though maybe "Kipling and Twain in Elmira" would be better. Makes you a little more curious, draws you in.

I got all *kinds* of ideas today! Aren't you happy you came back?

He abruptly yet politely excused himself, leaving the trailer for half-an-hour before we resumed.

Did you ever have a love like that? Like Kipling's for Twain?
Starts as an *intellectual* love, then becomes something else?
Crosses over into something else? You read a book and *wham*—
Cupid's arrow goes right in. And suddenly you're compelled? To
make a pilgrimage. *Love* is what made Kipling travel all that way.

I had a love affair like that. Once is all you need! I must
have been all of thirteen. He was a monk, a Trappist monk
named Thomas Merton. You've heard of him? I think everyone's heard of Merton. Though all they usually know is *The
Seven Storey Mountain*. Or maybe about the terrible way he
died. But I wasn't as fortunate as Lord Kipling. By the time I
got the idea, my beloved monk was already dead. He was in
the Far East, if memory serves—was it Burma? or Thailand—
taking a bath when a fan fell in and he was electrocuted. Right
then and there he entered the pantheon of famously ignomin-
ious literary deaths. You know, Barthes and the bakery truck,
Randall Jarrell and W. G. Sebald versus automobile, Tennessee
and the frisky bottle cap . . . though some folks say it wasn't
a bottle cap that did him in at all, but rather what they call
"acute Seconal intolerance." Which is French for overdose.

Did you know that a lot of writers have been knifed?
Beckett was stabbed on the street, almost killed him. And
Sartre too, by a crazy man who was always asking him for
money and tried to break down the door of his apartment.
The door was chained but he nearly cut off Sartre's thumb.
Sartre never had any money! That comes as a surprise to most
people. It worried him right to the end. A few days, maybe a
few *hours* before he died, he was asking Simone de Beauvoir
how they were going to find the money to have him cremated.

Anyway, I was crushed—I mean, about Merton. Death
by fan . . . I guess we should feel lucky they don't keep fans

up there by the Esalen baths! And he was *handsome* too, like a movie star. At least *I* thought so. *And* a monk. *And* a poet. And a—oh! I was only however-old-I-was but boy that hit me hard. My first serious crush. And say what you will, but the root of crushed is *crush*. That's the human comedy for you. I suppose it would have been more romantic if Merton had been knifed like the others. Or shot, like Rimbaud. Anything but death by fan!

Father Thom struggled with celibacy all his life. I really do believe God made us that way, with all our base instincts and perilous urges, and out of His mercy bestowed conscience and shame. I'm afraid I failed Him early on! I was too young to understand God *knew* I would fail and I was already forgiven. The older I get, the more I subscribe to Tolstoy's views. You've read *The Kreutzer Sonata*? The later works? By that time in life, Tolstoy was opposed to sexual intercourse, he really thought the high road was to let the whole human race just die out. Life of the party, huh. Though I bet the folks at Esalen would give him a workshop! They're pretty much open to anything. I've got some *wonderful* books on the topic in my van. Did you know celibacy was *optional* in the first thousand years of the Church? O yes. "And when the thousand years are expired, Satan shall be loosed out of his prison"—Revelation 20:7. Don't get me started! Thom Merton was a Renaissance man, he had one of those far-reaching, magisterial intellects, good Lord. The man could toss off an essay on Zen just as quick as a raft of poems. He was a *marvelous* poet.

Here's a favorite of mine:

I always obey my nurse
I always care

For wound and fracture
Because I am always broken
I obey my nurse . . .

I have a book in the van, at least I *think* it's still in there—unless I've loaned it out, which I'm almost certain I didn't because mostly I lend my books to impoverished kids or homeless folk, and *this* one wouldn't be high on that list—it has the somewhat daunting title of *History of Sacerdotal Celibacy in the Christian Church.* How's that for pedantry! Now, I'm a Catholic but each faith struggles under the yoke. The *OED* tells us sacerdotalism is the assertion of the existence in the Christian church of a *sacerdotal order of priesthood,* having *sacrificial functions* and invested with *supernatural powers.* These were the Middle Ages . . . there is an absolute *profusion* of intriguing texts from that time by the so-called Christian mystics—Hildegard of Bingen (the monks here are completely gaga over Hildegard. Sinéad O'Connor would have made a *great* Hildie B), *The Scale of Perfection,* Pseudo-Dionysius, St. Teresa's *The Way of Perfection* (lotta striving toward perfection in those days), and my own personal fave, *The Cloud of Unknowing*—and O! Better not leave out Jacobus de Voragine's *The Golden Legend . . .*

Sorry to digress. I think I have a case of nerves, that's why I'm chattering away. I'm usually not such a motormouth. It's just that I guess everything's building up, all that's been unspoken for so many years. The whole kit and caboodle, as Mama used to say.

* * *

A break for lunch. As we settled in, he excused himself.
When he returned, he wore a sheepish smile. His face was
blotchy, as if from crying.

I had to "make my toilet." Splash some water on my face . . .

What was I saying?

The Christian mystics—

Kipling! Kipling *also* did his time in the City by the Bay,
oh yes. Mind you, there was no love lost between the two—
not between Kipling and Twain, but Kipling and the *city*. He
was a flinty, finicky man, and most decidedly "on the road."
What do you think the Beats would've made of him? Now
there's *another* play—my third of the day!—the meeting of
Kipling and Kerouac. "Kipling/Kerouac," *that's* what you call
it. Or maybe just "K2" . . . *K-squared! Yes.* I like it. *On the Road*
with Jack and Rudy. Stendhal said something marvelous, that
a novel was nothing more than a man holding a mirror as he
walks down a road . . . it reflects the sky above and the mud
below, and woe to the man who carries it in his rucksack and
captures nothing but the mire! For he will be pilloried.

I was saying. Kipling didn't care for San Francisco a whit.
If he didn't leave his heart, he certainly left his spleen, or
some other mess to clean up. Had a reputation for being a real
pisser. Thought everyone was rude, particularly hotel workers. Isn't that funny? I guess that's understandable, he was
used to India where the English were treated like gods. I have
an old Kipling in the van, I know just where, green cover,
introduction by Henry James. (Come to think of it, I've a very
pretty *Le Rouge et le Noir*.) There's a chapter in there, if memory
serves, called "American Notes," subtitled "Rudyard Kipling at
the Golden Gate." Apparently, the thing he absolutely could

not tolerate about our beautiful city was all the white people! Too many white people. Not enough blacks and *fellaheen*.
(Oh, the Beats were great fans of the fellaheen!) There was
just this *very* long list of complaints. The querulous Lord K
had no truck with the custom of the day, which allowed that
a fellow who bought a drink would get his food for free. The
man even hated cable cars! Moreover, he was of the mind that
Americans plagiarized English authors without compensation
or acknowledgment, and to make things worse, willfully perverted the pilfered texts. On the topic of copyrights, he was
apoplectic. A drooling hound from Hell . . . but we forgive
Genius its prickliness. And he *was* a prickly pear. Some of my
best friends are prickly pears.

Kipling actually wrote about the Cliff House. You know
the Cliff House, Bruce? You said you lived in the Bay Area
when you were a boy . . . *that* took me by surprise. The very
Cliff House I—we!—remember from our youth! We lived
south of LA, see, in Orange County, and would drive to Point
Lobos and Sausalito . . . our little unhappy family. Those
dreadful, benumbing, contentious vacations. Good Lord!
We'd go to the Cliff House and my big sis and me climbed
the hundreds of steps to that positively *Brobdingnagian* indoor
slide—remember?—made out of slippery, buttery blond
wood. I was so struck with fear, my tiny face all scrunched
up in tears, like I was heading for the gallows. I never looked
down, only straight ahead, at the ass of whoever was in front
of me, yet couldn't help but see from the corner of my eye the
sliders *whooshing* past, the joyful *screaming*, the chute wide as
a highway, like some monstrously tilted bowling lane waiting
patiently to strike me out. To avoid the paralysis of vertigo,
when I finally reached the top I gave my full attention to the

spreading out of my smelly burlap sack, the threadbare magic carpet that would carry me to Hell. You couldn't take *too* much time with preparations because a cackling crowd was endlessly summiting behind you, anxious to fling themselves down that bizarre man-made mountain. So you'd plunk yourself on that useless mat and—Geronimo!—off you'd go, hoping to catch up with your stomach at slide's end. All the while knowing I'd have to immediately begin the climb again, or be called a fag, and be publicly ostracized—

I know, I'm off-track. It's just the butterflies . . .

We're not in a *huge* hurry, are we?

I just need to work up to it. I'm finding my way. Promise.

All right, and do forgive: the Kipling/Twain rendezvous in New York. As it turns out, the two shared a common passion: copyrights. Ha! According to historical reports, Samuel Clemens had *lots* to say about this particular issue. Copyrights! Mania of the Titans!

Kipling was an absolutely superb reporter, even referred to himself as a newspaperman. (Jack London had his own view of the papers. Called them "man-killing machines.") Kipling was known as a human tape recorder, capable of flawlessly transcribing from memory. Capote used to say the same thing, but Capote was more full of shit than a sewer pipe. Lord Rudy quoted Twain, a little speech I spottily committed to memory, as it touches on a topic mentioned earlier and which I am certain we will soon explore, which acted as a balm at the time—

A conscience, like a child, is a nuisance. If you play with it and give it everything it wants—spoil it—it'll be sure to intrude on all your amusements and most of your griefs. Just treat it as you would anything else.

When it's rebellious, spank it. Be stern! Don't let it come out to play with you at all hours. That way you'll end up with a *good* conscience, one that's properly trained. But a spoiled one destroys all pleasure in life! I've done an excellent job in training my own; at least, I haven't heard from it for some time. Perhaps I killed it from being too severe. It is wrong to kill a child . . . though in spite of all I've said, a conscience does differ from a child in many ways.

Perhaps it's better off dead.

Wonderful, isn't it?

Sometimes satire is the only thing that does the job. All right . . .

Enough nonsense.

I began by disclosing that while I prefer men to women on the sexual front, I've had meaningful relationships with both. I told you I was married but separated, and that I—*we*—have—*had*—a child. A son. We had a son.

His name is Ryder.

(I won't say "was" because it still is.)

My wife's name is Kelly.

I haven't seen her for seven or eight years. She lives in Canada with her sister. On her sister's property anyway. I send money every month. The occasional postcard or email. She writes back now and then. Her sister worries, endlessly. "She's thin as a bone!" My frontal lobe seems to have taken that information and run with it, because whenever I think of Kelly I picture a haunted scarecrow piercing me with haunted, pleading eyes.

We were living together but hadn't been physically intimate for a long time when Kelly said she wanted a child. She was 35 or 36—I was 29—she'd had four abortions. Also had PCOS, polycystic ovary syndrome, so the doctors said the odds were slim. We were prepared to go another route if we didn't have any luck but never talked *exactly* about what that route would be. If I recall, adoption wasn't entirely ruled out. Kelly was certain motherhood had passed her by (I was certain too) and as a hedge against likely heartbreak she convinced herself that it wasn't possible, wouldn't happen. Made her peace. When the kit showed the + sign, it shocked her into bliss. Me too (into bliss). I was a little surprised by that. She said it was a miracle baby and I couldn't argue.

Back then, we had the understanding our physical needs would be met outside the partnership. I mean, sex was actually fun—for a while—but once she got pregnant, we were forever done. I knew Kelly was involved with various women over the years but had no idea she pursued men as well. I'm not sure if that would have bothered me or not . . . I mean, another man. I guess it would have, if she didn't invite me to share! At any rate, we were a "don't ask, don't tell" household. If you're wondering why we stayed together, that's a little predictable. Better to ask, What forces prevailed to bring us together in the first place? And for what purpose?

I said it before and I'll say it again: I only know what I know. And what I don't know, I've learned to leave alone.

Until now.

* * *

Kelly was an old friend of the Learys' and liked to tell people our son was named after Tim's goddaughter, the actress Winona Ryder. Kelly thinks *she* came up with the name—Ryder—but that's not how I remember it. And my ego has nothing to do with it. You see, our son didn't have a name until the very moment he was born. When he popped out, a name popped in: *Ryder*, from the Djuna Barnes novel. God, I loved that woman! The mad hermit dyke of Greenwich Village. Lived right across the street from e.e. cummings by the way . . . I know that sounds precious, to name your kid after a Djuna Barnes book—about a monster-dad!—but that's how it went down, as my biker friends like to say. I didn't realize it at the time but I think that when I mentioned it as a possibility, Kelly immediately thought it was some sort of ode to *Winona*—she had a soft spot for glamour and celebrities. She probably loved the idea of being tied into Winona and the Learys. When people asked about it she said she liked the karma of the name, as if our son's fate (and her own) was to be part of a famous clan. Oh, she *basked*. I was just happy she went for it. One of the things I love about "Ryder" is that it's close to *writer*. And *reader* too.

My wife—that still sounds weird to me, "my wife," and it's funny how it still makes me feel good to say it, that bourgeois part—has always been a serious Buddhist. Me, I'm a dabbler. I told you we met at Spirit Rock but technically that isn't true. We'd seen each other a handful of times before on skid row, at the mission in Alameda. Part of the do-gooder crew serving meals to the homeless over the holidays. I was surprised to find an attraction there, on my side anyway. I wasn't sure what she felt but had an inkling. My hetero radar isn't completely broken, you know. I guess it was karma, as Kelly would say—that I'd feel an attraction toward this woman that was *physical*, aside from anything else. We didn't talk much but there was definitely somethin' going on. We percolated for three years running until we bumped into each other at the retreat. Which brought things to a boil.

Like a lot of people who become interested in Buddhism, I was traumatized by religion, in my case the Catholic Church. My big sis and I were both victims. Cheryl got pregnant at 16 and confessed to one of the fathers. He told her there were special things he could do to make sure the baby would never come out. He said God would help, as long as she kept his intervention a secret. He tried "the cure" a bunch of times but the baby came anyway.

Oh, they did things to me too . . . that's why as an adult, I was lost. I drifted toward Buddhism, becoming fairly serious in terms of my meditation practice. But I was never as into it as my wife. Kelly went to all the advanced workshops, you know, the ones they won't let you in unless you've received the transmission of whatever obscure teaching from whatever non-English-speaking roshi. Like a lot of folks, she definitely set out to acquire a black belt in Zen. I just wasn't that interested—the minute prayer became work, I was out the door. I wasn't wild about the hierarchy thing either. Hierarchies bug the shit out of me. That smugness, the whole power-tripping, my-silence-is-better-than-your-silence deal. (Anyway, it ain't Buddhism's fault. "It's the people, stupid.") Oh boy, did we use to skirmish! Kelly called me a living master of "couch potato Zen" and I called her Brigitte *Bardo*. "Bardo" is Tibetan—have you ever heard?—it means the limbo or "in-between." There's a bardo between life and death, a bardo between wakefulness and sleep . . . a bardo of dreaming. "Brigitte Bardo" used to piss her off, though not completely, because remember, she was into glamour and celebrity. It was all pretty playful. The mood was still light.

Our little family moved from the Haight—from the same block Kenneth Rexroth once lived, he had these famous salons back in the day . . . everyone used to go, Ferlinghetti, Lamantia, Snyder and Joanne—Kyger—Whalen and McClure and di Prima and Anne Waldman, and of course Ginsberg and Jack—we got out of there and rented a bungalow in Berkeley. I clerked at a bookstore on Telegraph until my lawyer advised it'd be better for my case if I just stayed home and collected disability checks. (More about that in a minute.) I didn't like that but I do as I'm told. *I always obey my nurse.* So I became the house mascot, the flâneur who perfected his couch potato Zen. Kelly taught at junior high a district away. She was wrapped too tight—another phrase used by my Hells Angels friends, some of whom are *very* literate, you know, big readers, and I'm not just talking Stephen King and John Grisham, there was a 400-pound fellow with a swastika tattooed on his forehead who was crazy for Schopenhauer and Spinoza, good Lord!— whenever I hear about one of their weekend gatherings, I'll try to show up in the bookmobile and they're *tremendously* appreciative, though I suppose I took some getting used to— my dear wife was wrapped too tight and all that meditating wasn't fixing her. A month after we moved to Berkeley, I began to have the vibe that Kelly was staring down the double barrel of a righteous depression.

One of the larger things on her plate was Mom, a semi-invalid living back East. (Her father passed away years before.) The family business, Ballendine's Second Penny, a high-end antiques shop, had been a fixture in Syracuse for over 40 years; it only took Kelly's alcoholic brother three months to run it into the ground. Her mother had heart problems complicated by diabetes or maybe it was the other way around. The brother was living at home, doing more harm than good. Like all old people, Mom insisted she didn't need help even though she could barely make it to the john. The caregivers my wife managed to hire— she interviewed them over the phone from Berkeley, the brother being a useless piece of shit—usually didn't last the day, and for $4 an hour the best you could hope for was they didn't steal, at least not in front of you, or beat your loved one to a pulp. Like all daughters (the ones I've known), Kelly's relationship with her mom was deeply fucked up. Whole lotta codependency goin' on. Clara was a real pro at pushing Kelly's buttons, especially the one marked GUILT. She started flying back there every other weekend. Once she even took Ryder. He came home with a twitch; I made sure *that* never happened again. I used to have one when I was a kid and now there was Ryder, widening his mouth every 10 seconds like a fish scooped from its aquarium.

I was surprised when Clara died. I mean, shocked at the speed of it. The flying back and forth and whatnot, the hassling with the brother, all that, had only been going on for maybe three months and I was settling in—we both were— for the long run. The money drain, the emotional drain, the massive *inconvenience* of it . . . So when we got the call she was gone, I actually couldn't believe it! I was like: *You're kidding me.* I might even have expressed as much when Kelly gave me the news. Because how many times does a pain-in-the-ass parent die in a timely way, with relatively minimal fuss? Thanks to modern medicine, the death of a parent is usually protracted, more unnatural in cause than natural. And medical heroics aside, the old scumbags seem to willfully hang on! Like they're *invested* in not making an easy death—not for themselves, not for their kids, not for the caregivers, not for anyone. I don't mean to sound devilish but I thought she'd linger until she was 100 and counting. We *both* did, which has to be most children's secret fear. So in its own way, my mother-in-law's death was as surprising as Ryder's conception. A miracle death! I remember thinking about Clara—just a thought, no malice, hell, I was *grateful* to her—I remember thinking, "You go, girl! *That's* the way to do it—*bravo.*" There was even some money thrown in (another shocker), not a lot but enough for Kelly to take a sabbatical and go find herself.

Kelly thought it was a good time to get married. Mom always said she wanted to dance at her wedding and I couldn't figure out if Kelly's proposal to me was a sentimental capitulation to Clara's wishes or a posthumous Fuck You. Anyway, it was done. Nothing fancy. A backyard affair with a dozen guests and a Buddhist monk presiding. Ryder walked her up the aisle between rent-a-chairs and was the ring bearer as well. That was sweet. Kind of a funny fortieth birthday present for me. I think I was a pretty good husband though. Maybe it sounds nuts, but I was good husband material.

I thought that would chill Kelly out—not so much the marriage as her mother's death. The irony is that when she left her job at school things really began to unravel. Having both parties home at the same time is a game changer. The house was small. We kept bumping into each other, literally underfoot. You begin paying hostile attention, like cellmates . . . you get weirdly focused on the annoying habits, shitty sights, sounds, smells and general disgusting lameness of the other party. You start judging them in your head and your heart. Everything gets poisoned, paranoid. Contempt is the order of the day—and night.

* * *

You know, I consider myself lucky. I "found" myself a long time ago. And I'm grateful for that. I truly am.

I didn't say I *liked* what I found but the finding's half the journey. Jesus, probably more than half. When you think that most people are out there still looking. What's the definition of finding yourself, anyway? It really just means being comfortable in your own skin. That's all enlightenment is, isn't it? The Buddhists can do their crazy calisthenics, their marathons of Silence and devotion and ritual bullshit but at the end of the day if someone's happy in their own skin, that's the Buddha. That's an enlightened being. People think they need that perfect job or perfect inspiration or perfect spiritual practice but all anyone wants or needs is peace of mind. And you don't need a Nobel Prize or a million dollars to have it. It *helps* but it ain't mandatory. I've got my books and my van—it's a wonderfully nomadic life I wouldn't trade for the world. *[sings, robustly]* "Well I've got a hammer, and I've got a bell, and I've got a song to sing, all over this land!" Freedom's my landlord. The sky above and the mud below. I've got a mirror in my knapsack . . . sometimes I leave it there and sometimes I take it out and point it to the Lord Above!

By most standards I'm a wealthy man. I could buy a house tomorrow if I wanted. A *nice* house. Which surprises people. Not that I go around saying that because I don't. When you live the way I do, you can't be flashy. That's asking for trouble. You know, Bruce, I don't own a home or property by *choice*. Aside from the van and my books, I really don't have any personal possessions. Nothing to speak of. I'm unencumbered and I think that's what saved me. The one thing I sometimes yearn for is companionship. A human touch that isn't lurid. All in all, I'm at peace. I won't lie, there *are* days and nights when I feel alone, almost *insanely* alone—I don't think that's too strong a word—times when I feel abandoned by God and man. *Not*, incidentally, such a wonderful feeling! I've had to face certain truths. I can whine about not having a partner to share my itinerant life but the simple truth is I don't think I'm capable emotionally, maybe even spiritually, of a committed relationship. Not the happiest of insights but that's what hundreds of hours of therapy'll get you. (Most of it back in the '80s.) The last committed relationship I had and will ever have was with my son. Ryder. I'll never get resolution on that one, never have closure. After he died, a lot of friends told me I should return to therapy. But guess what—I already *know* the source of my supreme fucked-up-ness. It's called the Catholic Church. Whoop-dee friggin' doo.

Whenever I start to feel that *alone* thing, I look back over the last 24 hours to see what I've eaten because sometimes food'll make you crazy. I know I'm *really* in a bad place when I personify the Lord our God—play the blame game—because I happen to subscribe to the opinion of those Christian mystics, their elegant assertion being that God or the idea of God is beyond our ability to grasp. To speak of "atheists" and "believers" in relation to God is roughly the same as believing you can convince an ant that it might enjoy a cartoon in *The New Yorker.* Or getting a rat to read an illuminated text—

"Who has known the mind of the Lord?"

That's Job . . .

He splashed water on his face at the kitchen sink, then sat down and rolled a joint.

I come here to get centered. I call it Herman's Hermitage. It's lovely, isn't it? People pass by on the highway completely unaware . . . bit of a secret treasure. I was going to say no one knows about it but apparently that fellow Pico stays here, though I've never had a sighting. (A marvelous writer and dear friend of the Dalai Lama—lives near Kyoto but I believe Mum makes her home in Santa Barbara.) The place has been here since the '50s—can you imagine what this property is worth now? Oh boy! The woodcarving monk from Tassajara clued me in about it. And *cheap* too. Well, relatively. The oblates are Camaldolese Benedictine. St. Romuald, an 11th-century ascetic, founded the order. And here they are in Big Sur! Don't you just love "Camaldolese"? Like some kind of amazing candy or ice cream—"I'll have a scoop of Camaldolese Benedictine with my violet crumble." The monks live according to their founder's "Brief Rule" *[he quickly finds a scrap of paper on the bureau, reads aloud]*:

> Sit in your cell as in paradise. Put the whole world behind you—try to forget it. Watch your thoughts, like a fisherman watching fish. The path you must follow is in the Psalms. Never leave it. Realize above all else that you are in God's presence. Stand there as one who stands before an Emperor. Empty yourself. Sit and wait, at peace with the grace of God—like the chick who tastes nothing and eats nothing but what his mother gives him.

Tough to adhere to but the world would definitely be a better place. The services are just superb. I was in the rotunda this morning before it began to storm, gathering strength for our time together today. A group of visitors, casually dressed, tourists I think, were in the pews waiting for the hermits to arrive, which of course they always do, on the hour. They wore simple white robes with bunched-up collars, like cats taking naps on their shoulders. Before chanting began, the oblates made time for praying aloud, in counterpoint.

The visitors began, *"Lord, hear our prayers!"*

The monks said, "Let us pray for those in prison and for those who are hospitalized, and for those who are marginalized by our society."

"Lord, hear our prayers!"

"Let us pray for the children who are lost, for they abide."

"Lord, hear our prayers!"

Hildegard of Bingen is a rock star here, I think I mentioned that. I've always loved the woman myself. I went through a period of intense searching; it wasn't by accident that I was drawn toward the female mystics. I'd had enough of the men, thank you very much. I just adored the visions of Hildegard and the "showings" of Julian of Norwich—Julian was a woman—that's what they call them, "showings," like a new collection from Chanel! How can you *not* love divas having visions? How can you *not* love a reclusive anchoress and medieval feminist? They even referred to God as "our Mother" and I really took to that. Julian had a vision of God putting a sphere in her hand no bigger than a hazelnut. She asked God what it was and He said—*She* said!—"It is everything that is made. It lasts and always will, because God loves it." How *glorious* is that? And "the Three Nothings" . . . I can't remember what they are just now, which somehow seems appropriate. But I *do* recall one of these gals being of the mind that, when in the name of love, the soul becomes nothing—I'm not sure I understand exactly what that means—well, *that* was the moment it might at last rejoin She who made it. I'm telling you, Bruce, these gals would give *any* Buddhist a run for his money.

Nothingness . . .

For a while I was actually a bit obsessed with what they call negative theology. It's obvious only now what attracted me—I wanted to tear down the scaffolding of the macabre God Organization, I wanted to undecorate the "interior castle," to raze the diabolical diocese that terrorized me so. I loved the concept of being separated from God by divine darkness, better yet by a *cloud of unknowing*. I thought "Cloud of Unknowing"—the name of a famous anonymous work—was intensely poetic, even *erotic* . . .

> Lead us up beyond unknowing and light to where
> His mysteries lie simple, absolute and unchangeable
> in the brilliant darkness of a hidden silence.

(I know I'm riffing, but hang in. Something's telling me to ride this out.)

During the time I speak of, my 20s and early 30s, I was more interested in the devil than I was angels, with good reason. After all, the devil was *family*! See, I really *believed* in Hildegard's visions, *had* to. She had, what, twenty-six of them? Twenty-six "showings"! Julian only had *sixteen* but who's counting! I was channeling the whole gang. I guess it was my way of staying loyal to the Church by becoming an avenging anchoress, a superhero in penitential drag. I had showings of my own, enhanced by mushrooms and speed. I too saw the devil as a black and bristly worm, trolling for souls at the

farmers' market of *samsara*. "Some ran through without buying while others browsed at leisure, stopping to sell and to
buy." That's Hildegard. "And around its neck a chain is riveted,
his hands bound like a thief who deserves to be hanged in
Hell"—Walter Hilton, *The Scale of Perfection*. (I was born in the
wrong time, that's all, my friend. O, to be middle-aged in the
Middle Ages! Though *their* middle age was 18, 19 and 20, so
better to be *old*—somewhere in your 40s.) Richard Rolle said
the devil could put you in a cage whose bars were invisible,
and it wasn't just the avaricious or the lustful that went to
Hell, no ma'am. If you were an ascetic in the name of Christ
but *flaunted* it, you know, arranged it so folks would get the
tiniest peek at you mortifying your own flesh—off to Hell you
go! (The Buddhists say that too.) I was just reading a marvelous book called *Liberation in the Palm of Your Hand*. The rin-
poche refers to the Eight Human or "worldly" Concerns. The
toughest one of all to shake, even tougher than the desire for
comfort or the acquisition of material things, is the craving
for fame and reputation. The hermit who secretly yearns to be
the most self-deprived, so that he may become legend . . . Do
you know Francisco de Osuna? These aren't trick questions, I
swear. Francisco de Osuna said the devil whispers in our ear
while we pray or meditate. The longer the prayer, the greater
the danger. He was a Carmelite—doesn't that sound like a diet
candy? (I've got sugar on the brain.) Osuna warned that Hell
slumbered in a too-avid gaze or too-attentive ear . . . in other
words, anything touched by pride is insidious and if you aren't
careful your heart will fly off like little boys after butterflies.
He actually *said* that, isn't that so awesome? "Like little boys
after butterflies"! Very *Suddenly, Last Summer*. *His heart followed
his eyes* . . . that's Job again.

Our Miss Julian said that a person who doubts is like a stormtossed sea and the only thing that tormented the devil was human tears. Then why can't the sea itself be made of tears? That's what *I'd* like to know.

* * *

Kelly was a frustrated artist.

(Join the club.)

I think her idea was she'd somehow come into her artistic self during that six-month recess. Which may have been too ambitous. Kelly was deeply afraid of failure. What if in the end she had nothing to show for her efforts but a painting or two or a shelf of unfired ceramic pots or a notebook of mediocre koan responses and haikus?

Her resentment toward me was palpable. I totally understood. There she was having a dark sabbatical-sabbath of the soul, and there *I* was, the housebound blob who bore witness. She was naked and vulnerable, hard-bodied and weary from too much desperation yoga, waiting like a trembling innocent for the cosmos to provide order and direction—who wants to do *that* in front of the Pillsbury Couchboy? I became the court stenographer (I was already the jester) charged with meticulously keeping the minutes of her myriad creative miscarriages. Ideally, Kelly's struggle was of the sort best played out on Walden Pond or in a converted Nova Scotian lighthouse. Or maybe one of those forest lookouts on Desolation Peak that Kerouac and Snyder used to favor. I stayed as far out of her way as humanly possible, even pulling a teenage disappearing act whenever she was home—we kept separate bedrooms for years—and she was home a *lot*. It only made

things worse. To her, my conspicuous absence felt like a surveillance camera.

That isn't to say we weren't civil. We shared meals
together—my wife believed dinner with place mats and cloth
napkins was the last bastion of family life—and put up a unified
front for Ryder as best we could. But subtle and not so subtle
indications of household friction couldn't be avoided. At table,
she was spikey. She gossiped about friends and acquaintances,
the anecdotes always featuring what the boyfriends and well-off
husbands did for a living. X was a workaholic—"He spent three
months researching conjoint therapists!"—and Y traveled to far-
flung places yet always managed to bring his significant other.
"He goes to Europe every month for business and *takes her with
him*." I listened, friendly and wide-eyed, with the dumb, vicari-
ous smile of a freeloading younger brother fallen on hard times.

My only value was playing Mr. Mom, a role I happened
to relish. Finally, something I didn't have to apologize for. I
just loved being Ryder's dad. During holidays and school vacations we spent hours playing board games of our own inven-
tion, creating miniature worlds whose domains stretched from
hardwood floor to backyard grass and beyond. We rented
Cukor films and provided scatological commentary. I *adored*
taking him for bacon and eggs at the local greasy spoon and
he was thrilled when I allowed him a sip of coffee. Of course,
I couldn't resist dragging him to bookstores. The more rare
a book was—the more expensive, the more exquisite—the
greater his interest.

I look back now and see that time with him as an extraordinary blessing.

The result being that Kelly was free—to do, go, be whatever. I know that she used that opportunity to flush a few

trysts from her system, consummate a few flirtations. But it wasn't enough to *be*, Kelly needed to *become*. She got deeper into her practice. Went on retreats to gain esoteric knowledge from visiting *tulkus*. She was of dedicated service to the sangha, spearheading a fundraiser to repair the zendo's leaky roof. She taught incarcerated women how to meditate and got certified in Ashtanga. Began chanting and singing— kirtan. (Everyone said, "That *voice*. Where did it come from?") I watched her body continue to grow lithe, long, sculpted. Her yoga for underprivileged women class became so popular it was written up in *The Chronicle*. Ryder squealed with delight when he saw the above-the-fold photo of his mom.

But still, she languished. She complained that everything was busywork—everything a distraction. She thought she'd had lift-off from the lip of the void but there she was again. Then, in the middle of her leave, something shifted. A friend of hers from the Zen Center visited elementary schools, teaching Buddhist fundamentals to kids from Richmond, Larkspur, Millbrae, Palo Alto, San Rafael. He was a very sweet guy— Kelly had once introduced us at a Metta Hospice lecture—very hyper, very personable. His shtick was to make Buddhism accessible, to spread the dharma and make it fun. The gig he created for himself filled a niche. When Kelly asked if she could tag along, he was delighted.

She was captivated from Day One. She couldn't believe how these kids were *getting* it. They were jacked up, dancing around and playing music, shouting "Impermanence Rocks!" and generally strutting their crazy kid-wisdom stuff. Toward the end of each class, her "dharmabud" led them in guided meditation, which they took to like ducks to water. They even got the concept of Nothingness and the death of the ego, sitting like little fortune cookies in perfect lotus position. The guy would play "Nothing Compares 2 U," remember that? Well, Kelly just bawled like a baby. She said the experience put her in touch again with that feeling she'd almost forgotten, the joyful spirit of beginner's mind. She got blown back to those early days of study and devotion, when the magnificent, irrefutable logic of the Four Noble Truths cracked open her head. (I always tell people in AA that once you work the *Steps*, move on to the *Truths*.) See, Buddhism's like anything man puts his hand to; one day you wake up and everything's turned to shit. The magic's been replaced by cliques of assholes with policies, slogans and gibberish, empty rituals. I think Kelly might have been feeling some of that, the emptiness of it, the is-that-all-there-is-ness of her practice (though not in a good way), and the kids reset her clock. God bless the children. *[sings]* "God bless the child who's got his own! *Who's got his own . . .*"

Still, I wondered how this fellow managed to slip Buddhism into the curriculum. Wasn't that a violation of church and state? As liberal as folks tend to be around this part of the country, you'd have to be naïve not to expect resistance from *some* of the parents, right? But Kelly said that Dharmabud was very careful not to push Buddhist doctrine, at least not directly. He wasn't converting anyone. He just wanted to share the concept of compassion, to convey the preciousness of life. He covered his bases: meditation equaled nothing more than the traditionally vaunted "quiet time." Probably his strongest message was how Mother Earth needed respect and taking care of. (I suppose a Republican might have a problem with that.) He made the Buddha into a generic but dignified cartoon character who carried the message.

The pediatric Magical Mystery Tour—which suited *this* Namaste-at-home dad just fine!—came along at the perfect time, giving my wife some much-needed juice. As the licensed in-house observer, I sensed the groundwork for something being laid. Suddenly, Kelly got *very* busy. (Which was great, in that she was no longer crawling up my ass on an hourly basis.) When she wasn't "managing" the zendo, teaching yoga or doing her jail thing, she tagged along with Dharmabud, auditing his classes. She started missing our mandatory suppers and made up for it by "intensives" with Ryder just before bed. Whenever I stood by the door to listen, it was all bell, book and Buddhism. She even gave pop quizzes. It reminded me of those awful movies she used to watch over and over—*Little Buddha* and *Kundun*—starring the once and future Dalai Lama and his tutors.

I don't want to sound bitchy. The truth is, she was completely devoted to our son. Things were chugging along famously until I learned that Kelly was keeping something from me—my codependent, beleaguered, overachieving wife had been tutoring at the women's prison for months, and now was poised to continue the work.

At San Quentin.

* * *

The next day he was late for our session, and entered hurriedly.

Sorry—ran into the Gossiping Monk. We had an exchange of information . . . please omit from final transcript! I don't want people identifying him.

Oh, before I forget, something popped into my head when I was up the hill that is weirdly amazing. You've read Gary Snyder, the poet? He's extraordinary, far better for my money than Jeffers. He's still alive—Snyder not Jeffers. (Jeffers had a place up here in Carmel, Hawk Tower. Built it himself. A real he-man. And I understand Ferlinghetti still owns the cabin Jack wrote about in *Big Sur.*) Snyder and Ferlinghetti are pretty much the last of the living Beats, at least the ones I consider to be of any pivotal importance. You know, historically. Ginsberg and Burroughs died just a few months of each other, back in '97; Huncke went the year before. I would have loved to have met Lucien Carr,[1] the one who killed the teacher that was stalking him. Carr and Burroughs were friends from St. Louis, I think—the tangled web of all these folks, the *genealogy* of it blows the mind. You knew that Kerouac helped cover up the murder? There's supposedly a book about it that Burroughs and Jack wrote back in the forties, but no one'll publish it.[2] Now *that* would make a wonderful addition to the bookmobile! I would've wanted to meet Carr before Neal Cassady . . . Friggin' Ferlinghetti's outlived 'em all, he's older than these hills, but'll probably go to Snyder's memorial. Tough old buzzard. And no estimable talent whatsoever! When I think about the Beats—Lamantia, McClure, Corso, Whalen, and some of the marginal women . . . *all* the Beat women were marginal, all of the women and *most* of the men! Except Carolyn—Cassady—who's *never* going to die, not as long as

---

1   Lucien Carr died in 2005.
2   *And the Hippos Were Boiled in Their Tanks* was finally published in 2008. As current as he was on the Beats, I'm not sure why he missed it.

she's pawning Jack's and Neal's bones for cash money. What a piece of work! There's Joanne Kyger, Snyder's ex (I think she still lives up in Bolinas, a lot of them did, Creeley and Whalen lived up there, Lewis Warsh, a whole slew), there's di Prima and Annie Waldman . . . anyway, what popped into my head when I was up on the hill was, Snyder's pseudonym in *The Dharma Bums* is *Ryder*—"Japhy Ryder," remember? And all this time I've been thinking Djuna Barnes and her novel when it almost *had* to be Japhy *Ryder* who gave my son his name! Well, how do you like that? Which just *shows to go you* the fallibility of the proverbial eyewitness. Makes you really start to wonder. It's all a dream, anyway, no? A broken mirror-puzzle. We just reshuffle the pieces. Who was it that said, "Reality is a possibility I cannot afford to ignore"? Leonard Cohen? Or maybe it was Lily Tomlin.

Kerouac and Snyder were close. Jack looked up to him. Snyder was older and became Jack's mentor in all things Zen. I haven't thought about any of this in a *long* time, Bruce, you're bringing it all to the surface . . . You know, Kerouac's a god of mine, that's why I go on about him. And I know my Kerouac! What's disgusting is when the fancy literary folk write their essays for the Sunday book reviews, bloviating on how *in love* they were with Jack *when they were kids*, how *On the Road* changed their lives, yadda yadda—or should I say Yaddo Yaddo! You'll notice how they usually grace us with their perfect opinions on the anniversary of the man's death or when *they* have a new book out, and you're reading about how much they loved him and thinking it's a tribute when suddenly they *turn* on him. These tributes to the man who changed their lives suddenly become snarky critical *refutations* of his work! O they confess to loving and emulating him back in the day when they were feckless undergrads or during their own bullshitty rucksack *moment*—but then they grew up and put away childish things and destroyed whole forests so as to grace us with their neutered, mannered, irrelevant oeuvres. Their hors *d'oeuvres*. Five paragraphs in they cut this giant down to size as a mere folly of their youth. See, with me it was the reverse! Exact opposite. Do you remember Capote saying that nasty thing about Jack's methodology (he said a lot of nasty things), "That's not writing, that's typing"? In my *own* feckless youth, I happened to agree. Being the precocious kid I was, I'd have taken "A Tree of Night" over *On the Road* all day long. Because *On the Road* is rather terrible, kind of an awful book in terms of sheer writing, particularly if you measure it against his others, *Visions of Cody*, *Doctor Sax*, *Windblown World*, *Lonesome Traveler*. In a hundred years, *Visions of Cody* will be the one, that's his Everest. And the poems! Better than Ikkyu. And the paintings! Blake looks like a *child* next to Jack . . . But you see, I was a little snot, a classicist, and it took me the longest time to come around. Then *Big Sur*—Jack's beautiful, beautiful novel—sort of kicked the door down and in I ran. And I knew without a doubt this man will cast a shadow larger than Whitman, this man *is* Whitman. I don't care too much for the others, sorry to say, not to cast aspersions, even on Mr. Snyder. I was never cool enough for Burroughs or Jewish enough for Ginsberg. None of the rest really matter—except the strange case of Neal Cassady, of course. He's indispensible. I had a sort of divine vision once that if it were possible to exhume his body, one would find it transformed to vellum, in true Ginsbergian holiness, because at the end he was no longer human, Jack the princess had kissed Neal the frog and restored him to the original, magisterial state of what he was meant to be: a book, a book of *life*. If I could write, I might try a little Borgesian fairy tale along those lines . . . O, the Beats, the Beats, the Beats! If you took everyone away and were left with just Kerouac, you'd be just fine. All would be right with the windblown world.

All right. Okay. Good. Sorry.

I want to get back to my wife's preoccupation with incarcerated living.

I never had a wonderful feeling about it—her teaching there. Not even the women's jail. I've seen enough documentaries on MSNBC to know bad things happen on prison visits. You don't hear about every incident, that's all. Teachers raped in the prison library, raped and killed by lifers. Just because there's a bunch of guards doesn't mean a thing. These guys are barely making minimum wage. Most of them are crooks too, creeps and sadists. When Kelly was doing her thing at the Women's Correctional in San Mateo I didn't have too bad a vibe. But San Quentin took it to a new level.

Kelly hooked up with something called the Prison Dharma Network. The PDN went around the country giving meditation and mindfulness workshops to folks who were locked up. They called their teachings Path of Freedom. The Jewish mafia of the Middle Way sat on the board. You know, all the roshi–Rosh Hashanah *machers*—Ram Dass, Goldstein, Glassman, Kornfield, Salzburg. The PDN put Kelly through a fairly intense orientation but it was nothing like the one the staff gave her at San Q: what to do if a riot breaks out, what to do if you're taken hostage, that sort of thing. Part of the allure was ego. It was kind of a trophy gig—frontline bodhisattva service. It was *sexy*. That as a woman she had the balls to suck it up and walk straight into the belly of the beast . . . *for the enlightenment of others.* I think she dug people at the Zen Center knowing too. Gave her a major uptick in the incestuous world of the sangha, where competition for humility was dog-eat-dog.

> *The tape recorder stopped but new batteries didn't help.*
> *I had to go into town to buy a replacement so we broke*
> *for lunch.*

* * *

I was raised in Santa Ana, California.

An altar boy.

You can see where this is going.

I was one of the plaintiffs in a lawsuit filed against the Roman Catholic Diocese of Orange. That's why I was on disability. I had panic attacks for years, sometimes ten in a day. If you've ever had a full-blown panic attack, you know that means ten times a day you are *one hundred percent certain* you are going to die. Like, *immediately.* Don't have 'em anymore, thank God, and I'm not on meds either. When it comes to victims of child sex abuse, PTSD is pretty much guaranteed. You can set your watch by it. That means night terrors, bed-wetting, cutting, bulimia—the whole package. We had wonderful lawyers. From the minute they filed, they made sure we had top-flight care, that we saw the best of the best. I got put on a prescription cocktail that settled my nerves. One of the side effects was weight gain (and excessive cocksucking). Hey, I'll pick weight gain over night terrors and panic attacks all day long.

That's what I was waiting for during the couch potato Zen years—the settlement. Took about five years. We had a few suicides along the way, oh yes. Some of the man-boys were just too damaged to hold out. *Their hearts flew off like little boys after butterflies.* You'd think it'd be easy to sit at the depot and wait for the money train. It wasn't. The lawyers went for the gold but for all we knew, we'd get the call one morning telling us the gold had turned to brass, tin or dogshit. And there wouldn't be a thing we could do about it. Settlements were coming in from churches all over the country, seemed like every day it was on the news or in the papers. And some of these payouts came in low, I'm talking *very* low five-figures, which was *not* the outcome our guys were shooting for. No one knew the formula, how they arrived at the numbers, it seemed so random. One fellow from Cincinnati used his money to go to Club Med—five times in one year. They found him in the bathtub of his room in Cancún. Overdosed. After he took the pills he slit his wrists and wrapped a plastic bag around his head. What they call overkill.

I was in the choir with a boy named Ramón. His family moved from Santa Ana after only about six months so I didn't get to know him that well. But I'm sure the heavenly fathers got in their licks. O they were jackals! Ramón's family settled in Covington, Kentucky, God knows why, must have had relatives there because *no one* moves to Covington, Kentucky. And that's where the *real* damage was done—the diocese in Covington. They fucked, sucked, diced and sliced that poor little Mexican kid to an inch of his life. When he was of age, he was *pissed*. It's good to get angry. It's healthy. He sued the shit out of 'em. But the trouble with Ramón was he jumped the gun. I don't know how he found his lawyers. Wound up settling in '93, before all the public hue and cry. At that time, see, people still were saying it couldn't be true. That it was all hyperbole or plain bullshit. I think he got $25,000. What's that, 15,000 after the lawyers get theirs? Good representation—*stellar* representation—is essential. An attorney has to know his way around these lawsuits, it's become a very specialized area. The attorneys learned from the mistakes of those who preceded them. Poor Ramón! Goes and hires a fellow who's an expert in marine law! How about that! And they just sue too early. See, back in the day anyone who made an accusation got tarred with being fringy or perverted. The Church had the total upper hand. They were moving priests around like musical chairs, we only found this out later, it all came out—to Mexico, Scotland, Manitoba . . . hell, they were moving them around in *California*. To Fresno and Riverside from LA, what have you. The early bird most assuredly did *not* get the worm, not with these lawsuits. The *priests* got the worm, boy did they ever! Sucked the come right out of it. So you see it literally didn't pay to be too far ahead of the curve. Failed suits like Ramón's paved the way. They were the pioneers. The "visionaries" who went blind to spite their face.

Ramón tried to sue *again* but got his case thrown out. That was just a few years ago. Waited too long! No, that wasn't it . . . there was a double jeopardy issue. A new lawyer promised he'd find a way around it but didn't. We still keep in touch, sporadically. He sends me these wacky, hypersexual novelty postcards, the type you can buy in a porn shop. He doodles tiny hearts and cocks on them—oy. I never had the heart to tell him I walked away from the courthouse a wealthy man. If he *does* know, he's never mentioned it. That kind of discretion is actually typical Ramón. He's never asked me for money, anyway, though if he did I wouldn't deny him. It'd make me feel good to help. The last I heard (it'd be comical if it wasn't so heartbreaking) was that one of the guys who was a part of my settlement who loves to follow this stuff said that Ramón's been suing the Church, acting as his own counsel. He said they were going to nail him on vexatious litigation, but Ramón doesn't give a shit. I have to admit, the kid's got heart. The diocese in Covington eventually forked over $200,000 per plaintiff. It ain't the lottery but it's better than whatever Ramón got. But he seems to land on his feet. I won't start worrying until I get a postcard from Club Med.

* * *

Can you hear the rain?

There—hear it now?

A big storm's coming.

How grateful I am to God for making Big Sur!

Big Sur took me back, you know. Spit me out once, and broke me too. But took me back . . .

It's really the strangest place. You can *not* come here to be healed.

That's the mistake most people make. Big Sur does *not* feel your pain; it doesn't even notice your awe. It's easy to leave here worse than you came. Those who do best are the ones who allow themselves to be erased.

The waves were tall as buildings today, did you see them? Before we met, I parked the van on a turnout near Bixby Canyon, a half-mile from one of the dizzying, drizzled bridges, towering and hallowed, jaundiced and strange—forgive my poor poetry, but the topic always gets me talking

like a fool—their stony span and scope otherworldly, like
something from a Piranesi etching. I sat and meditated on the
place—Big Sur—and had the revelation that something about
it was *wrong*, which I suppose is the normal human reaction
to the unknowable. The sea *distorted* everything, and set off a
chain reaction that charged and changed the very molecules
of the air itself, the landscape too, until nothing resembled
anything ever seen before . . . you couldn't put your finger
on it except to say it was *wrong*. Those waves: at times they
rolled north to south, contrary to God's order, like mischievous ghosts running alongside the shore instead of crashing into it—rats through a witch's wet hair! And there I was
stuck staring, like a child hidden in the shadows watching the
forbidden rites of some malevolent cultus supervised by the
impetuous, unforgiving, predatory chorus of those waves, the
whole scene so majestically wrong, a sacred, supererogatory
mess, and *me*, struck dumb by an unnamable, eons-old sorrow . . . the permanent impermanence of water engaged—
enraged—in ancient, secret activity. The waves took the shape
of hunchbacked buffaloes, bristle-foamed brides and grooms
in tumbling betrothal, spewing and spuming their vows,
exchanged in a cauldron of blackness, each driven in succes-
sion by the taskmaster moon to spawn upon the shore then
freeze upon reaching it—sudden death upon sand and rock.
If that membrane of water could speak it would plash *"I go no
further no further I go,"* slipping back to primordial jellyfish'd
infancy, hibernating in Silence before rearing up again, slowly
then speedily, all gaudy and cocky, imperious, thundering its
bouillabaisse of white noise! Then: all business again—always,
again and again and again all business—the business of predatory indifference—in poised, crashing lunge, snatching what

it can of my comfort. Endlessly watchable, I watch, *we* watch, so easily mesmerized by artful anarchy, the mindless, mindful in-and-outness of it, for what else is there but in-and-outness, anarchy, death and indifference? But Jack already said it all, didn't he? In the "ocean sounds" poem at the end of *Big Sur*. "One day, I will find the words, and they will be simple." That's Jack too, from one of his letters . . .

I looked up at the Heavens, supreme and resplendent with dark latticed clouds and found nothing truthful in Dr. Williams' neatly turned phrase "an excrement of some sky." For the smallest part of this one, the only one we'll ever know until those *other* unknowing clouds come, could make nothing but midnight blue Silence—

I know.

The words are just a defense.

I promise I'll step up the pace.

You've been so patient.

I suppose I *am* finding this more difficult than . . . anticipated.

I keep saying that.

It's hard to focus.

Too much sadness.

* * *

Know who I was thinking about when I woke up just now? Bashō the poet. Do you know Bashō? Have you read the haikus? Bashō was the absolute god of the Beats—they all wanted to *be* him. Kerouac came closest but I suppose Snyder's taken the crown, out of sheer longevity. In sixteen-hundred-something, Bashō's house burned down. That's when he went on the road. I have it somewhere in the van, a chapbook, a lovely limited edition of Bashō's *The Recordings of a Skeleton Exposed to Weather*. Beat *that*, Beats!

Can I talk about my affair with Carolyn Cassady?

I know I'm skating around. Are you sorry you got yourself into this, Bruce? *[laughs]* I just can't seem to approach it head-long. I suppose I *could* get right to it—the full catastrophe—I just don't want to be rude and take too much of your time. But I promise I'll get to it. *Soon.* First, let me tell you about this thing I had with Neal Cassady's wife. It's guaranteed to amuse. Then I'll talk about . . . all the rest.

So there I was, falling for Kerouac head over heels—mind you, this wasn't all that long ago! What can I say? I was a late bloomer. The book that knocked me out, as I was telling you, was *Big Sur*. That novel's actually become more of a draw for me to come back—here—than my Camaldolese hermit friends. When I make my pilgrimages, it's to Jack's spirit and the book that I come. To the beginner, I'd recommend *Big Sur* first . . . *On the Road* isn't even on my shortlist! I know that sounds terrible. Did you know there are *Madame Bovary* haters? *Mais oui.* They're of the opinion—people have *beaucoup* opinions out there!—that Flaubert loathed his own creations, from the *Madame* on down, and his contempt bleeds through and ruins the text. Corrupts his achievement. Another group considers *Gatsby* a novel that fails in its prose but triumphs in evoking a world and a time, a kind of ghost book that lingers like a scent made from flowers pressed *between the lines*, all fairy- and fingerprint dust. I'm in agreement! Oh, those F'd-up similes that fall so trippingly off the tongue! The glibness gets treacly once you've had your fill—which for me was around Page 2. Vomitous! I have a *fitzsimile* of my own, if you please: at his best, which is most often his worst (at least in *Gatsby*), Fitzgerald is like a too-congenial whore, wearing too many perfect gossamer gowns. Take that, Mr. Jazz Age! And you heard it here! (I actually believe I'd have made a pretty good critic. I really do think about books all the time and have formed my opinions with great care. Eventually, I may try my hand at an essay or two. Wouldn't it be marvelous to publish a monograph with the "Vanzen" imprint?) To do what Fitzgerald did is an impossible trick and I'd put *On the Road* in the same camp. Does it evoke the ineffable? Does it evoke lost youth? Does it evoke the sights and sounds, the promise and magic of a time, an era, a world on the brink, of something mysterious and noble, numinous and *new*? Without question! Good Lord. *Yes.* Is it a wonderful novel? A resounding no! It's an *experience*, not a novel. It's a mess. *Gatsby* and *On the Road* are like owner manuals for products that can never be delivered. And yet, how beautiful! The spell they cast is diabolical, untouchable. The *genius* of it, to create a text, an *illuminated* text of words that somehow alchemize—*atomize*—into fragrance and music, that kick up the dust of the future and past, and the present too! Good Lord! Perfect mystery-tumbleweeds emitting the warm odor of nostalgia and the cold ardor of timeless, terrifying *Silence* . . . skeletons exposed to weather.

But enough about that.

I was telling you about my affair with the ancient widow of Neal Cassady aka Dean Moriarty, that square-jawed beefcake—*Beat*cake—bigamist fountainhead, automotive contortionist and cuckolded sex addict, that douchebag writer manqué who was Jack's woman as well, his muse and creator. Jack's *man* . . . who died on the wrong side of railroad earth's tracks.

When I reached the end of *Big Sur*—"Sea: Sounds of the Pacific Ocean at Big Sur," the great heretical coda—when I finished reading that end-poem, awash in the *Term Term Klerm Kerm Kurn Cow Kow Cash Cluck* and *Clock* of it, oh what a *staggering* thing it is!—which, by the way, like wine and wafer, is no *representation* of Jack, but the very blood, body and brain of him, in those stanzas the man truly dug his own deathless, unintelligible, operatic, watery grave—when I got *finis* with *Sur*, I went straight to the Internet and found a website for the estate of Neal Cassady. And there it was . . . a *real-time contact* for Carolyn! I have no memory of the emotions that compelled me to send what I believed at the time to be a short, sweet, wryly seductive e-note. It was late, and I was actually *here*—at the hermitage—of *course* I was, on a star-tossed mercilessly typical Big Sur night. After firing off my communiqué, I went outside and stripped naked, delirious with joy, got my skin tasered by stellar wind while listening to the rapturous offstage massacre of waves being their usual demure, assassin selves—warriors unlike Arjuna, with never a moment of doubt.

Within an hour, I received a reply.

From *her* . . .

I was stunned out of my skin. *Gob-smacked*, as Carolyn would say, for she'd written back from England, where she made her home. 'Twas mid-morningtide in Blighty.

Now *please* keep in mind I had just finished that wonder of a book in which Carolyn is portrayed as "Evelyn" and I had a bit of a—no, I had a *massive* crush on the gal I came to know as the fag hag Iron Lady. So, I write *back* and she writes *me* and before you know it we are *corresponding*. Her emails sounded young, Bruce, young, smart and *with it*, and suddenly I get paranoid. As if maybe I'm unwittingly participating in some kind of Web thing someone wrote code for, you know, being duped by a promotional goof the publishers use to hawk new editions of *The First Third* or *Off the Road* (fag hag Iron Lady's memoir)—half of me thinks I might be playing the fool for one of these newfangled interactive artificial intelligence ad campaigns getting written up in *Wired*. Remember too that in the initial throes of it, I was most likely drunk and had probably smoked a little, partaken of the *chronic* as my younger friends would say . . . *plus*, I'd *just* finished this glorious, glorious book and was so full of the Beats I was practically the fifth *Beatle!* I was *horny* for them, and lo and behold there I am having a sudden chat-fest, basically *flirting* with Neal Cassady's *wife!* In my mind she's not even his *widow*, all of them are still *alive*, and it's all happening *now*—like something out of Philip K. Dick! But I'm still paranoidly thinking, you know, uhm, okay, if this isn't some slick viral campaign then maybe someone hacked into the website, it's a *rogue program* merely *drone-responding* to the pathetic battalion of geeks that have Roman candle crushes on "Carolyn Cassady"—*who's long dead.* Of course! She's dead! What was I thinking! I was swooning so hard, I hadn't even bothered to check if she was still alive . . . all I had was a "contact" proving otherwise. I'd been "corresponding" with a rudimentary A.I. program that held up its end of the conversation with sad, schmucky groupies before eventually diarrhea-ing the humiliating contents all over the Web. Because how could it be possible that the *real* Carolyn Cassady, a wizened old woman, got it up for emailing—*immediately responding*—to strangers?

    This went on for a month or so. (The Internet informed that Mrs. Cassady was alive and well.) I didn't mean to imply there was anything sexual about it, of *course* there wasn't, not that *I* didn't feel sexual, Lord, I had a hard-on whenever I wrote her! Nope, nothing remotely immodest, in terms of content. I'm sure she sent the same incisive, vivacious emails to other fans but *no one* could take away from me what I considered to be fact: I was now, by definition— mine!—having a *ménage à quatre* with Neal, Carolyn and Jack. I'd have been the Ginsberg in the group. See, the miracle of Jack is that, from everything I know, from everything I *intuit*, he was a mess, and a not too *friendly* one. Kerouac was drawn to women but was so awkward around them, so deeply uncomfortable, so needy and nasty that he was a faggot by default. He was really kind of an alien, an extraterrestrial. The way he treated his poor daughter Jan! Shitting on her when she came to visit that first time—that *only* time?—she was just a kid!—disowning her to the end, can you imagine the pain of that young girl? Jesus, it'd have been more merciful if he'd killed her with his own hands. Both those boys—Jack Sundance and the Cassady Kid—had *serious* mommy issues. *Ti Jean*'s trouble was that he always felt like he was cheating on his mother. Gabrielle was his enduring love, his true wife. And Neal, well, the minute he got a gal pregnant, the minute she became a *mom*, he'd have to marry her on the spot, even if he was already married to someone else! Gotta do right by Mom! *R-e-s-p-e-c-t.* (Find out what it means to me.) Neal liked pimping his women—wives—Moms!—to Jack (to an extent). And the only real way Jack got off was sleeping with women who were "taken." That was the pathology. You don't need to be a therapist to figure *that* one out. Incest ruled the day. I've always thought of Carolyn as the Mother Superior of the Beats . . . Mother Superior—that says it all, don't it?

After a few months, the emails tapered off. Carolyn was pushing 80. I started to worry that her health might be an issue. So I resolved to do something bold. I decided to travel to England to meet my pen pal. Why not? Money wasn't a problem; anyway, I'd always wanted to visit the Lake District and see where Wordsworth and Coleridge hung out. Wordsworth was born in *Cockermouth*, imagine being a homophobe and living *there*! But I was actually thinking in historical terms, literary history mind you, albeit *minor* literary history, and my idea was to write a piece about the whole experience for a journal or a magazine. The notion of how we met and my flying over to meet her struck me as just the sort of thing that might also be turned into a wonderful little independent film. So I wrote to her and said that it happened I was going to be in the Commonwealth—I never told her that she was the only reason I was coming—and would she be amenable to receiving a visitor? She said she would and that was that.

Have you seen photos of her? I mean, when she was younger? They're in all the Beat biographies. There aren't so many, nothing "iconic," she wasn't really a looker. I think probably no one really *wanted* to take her picture, she was kind of a Debbie Downer. A pain-in-the-ass snob with a stick up her ass. There's nothing worse than a dumb snob, and prudish to boot. It seems like the same few photos are reprinted, over and over. She always looks like she had gas or was being forced to watch dogs copulate—that would be Jack and Neal! Or Neal and Allen. Or Allen and Jack. What stands out the most, in the shots I've seen, is her *male energy*. She looks stern, almost mannish. Which makes total sense, knowing all we know now. Of course the Bell's palsy didn't help the overall look.

When I called from London to confirm our appointment, I was beside myself. Welcome to Phil Dick's Match-dot-com! It was the first time I'd actually heard Carolyn's voice. She pleasantly offered directions to her place. She said she knew nothing about the "motorways" and the only route she could recommend was the approach from Windsor Castle. Which I thought was apt, because she *was* royalty—it didn't matter that everyone but Neal thought she was a pill and a sonofabitch. She was still the Queen and always would be. And boy, did she let you know it!

She came to the door like a movie legend expecting her biographer, a cross between Barbara Stanwyck—there it was, that male, Stanwyck energy—and Doris Day (the latter-day Doris, the one I've seen in pictures with her doggies in Carmel Valley). She had a throwaway elegance, an aggressively pretentious modesty, as if her role model was Queen Elizabeth in those "rugged" shots in the Land Rover at Balmoral. After all, Carolyn had decades of experience being the grail, or the next best thing anyway, for thousands of fanboys like myself. She'd outlived her men, and in direct bloodline to the gods, had gained immortality herself—

She asked me in for "a cuppa and nibbles" and it wasn't long before she turned on the poison spigot. I'm no Kipling, but I'll do my best to give you a *flavor* . . .

[*A hilarious impersonation of an American dowager followed, his voice taking on a sporadic, contrived "English" inflection*] "By the time Neal was with the Pranksters, he just wanted to die. The trouble was, he no longer believed in suicide. His religion was against it. So he *rolled* busses, he kept 'rolling' busses. I told Kesey it was terrible what was going on but he didn't want to hear it—Kesey stopped talking to me. They *all* stopped talking to me, heaven knows why. One day Neal showed up at my house without shoes, looking dreadful. I said, 'Why are you still with Kesey?' and Neal said, 'Honey, people look at me and expect me to perform.'

"Allen was very close to my son. And Allen was lovely—
for a time. But around 10 years before he died, he decided he
wanted nothing to do with me. We named my son John Allen,
after Jack and Allen. When John was a boy, he *loved* playing
with Allen. When Allen was dying, John asked me what he
should do because it'd been quite some time since they'd spoken. I said, 'Call him!' So John did and the person on the other
end said, 'You know, Allen would have loved to talk to you
but he's in a coma now.' I'd go see Allen before he decided not
to talk to me, he was in London all the time. He'd come for a
reading or to do this or that, see one person or the other, and
I'd go see him whenever he needed *a pair of hands*—he loved
applause. He even went to Venice on a stretcher because they
were giving him some kind of an award. As long as Allen was
being honored, he'd show up! I told him years ago, if you can't
learn to accept the plaudits for what they *are*, it'll never be
enough, you'll never be able to get enough praise. Right up
to the end he thought he was worthless. He thought he was
worthless when he was young, and he thought as much right
before he died.

"Ferlinghetti decided to dislike me because I said his
manager was ripping him off. He didn't want to hear that. I
was owed a *lot* of money and they finally paid *something*, like
$500—they wrote me a check. I told him the fellow was *steal-
ing* from him, but he liked the fellow and didn't want to hear
it. He's got a *different* manager now. *[He pretended I'd asked him
a question]* What do I think of *whom*? Joyce Johnson? Oh, *her*.[3]

3   Johnson's critically acclaimed memoir of her relationship with
     Kerouac was published in 1999. Her biography, *The Voice Is All:
     The Lonely Victory of Jack Kerouac*, would not come out until
     2012, a few years after this interview.

She's, well—*ugh*—I won't get into that. They're all whores and hangers-on. They slept with Jack *once* and all of them want to write about it. *[Again, he pretended to be engaged by an invisible interlocutor]* Who? Oh! *That* one *always* liked Burroughs—which probably explained why he stopped talking to me, and why I stayed away."

They *all* seemed to stay away from Dame Fag Hag Iron Lady! I'm really *channeling* that cunt . . . What else did we talk about? Allen Ginsberg's visit to Ezra Pound in Italy—Ginsberg *and* Pound must have been hungry for a pair of hands, no doubt! And Peter Ackroyd. I'm not sure *how* Mr. Ackroyd came up, but dear Carolyn had an opinion!

"Oh yes, he's a *wonderful* biographer. I used to stay in his house in London whenever I was in the city. He's written some marvelous books—the big one about Dickens—that's the one he's known for—I haven't read the last few—he stopped drinking and now he's *so fat*. We don't talk anymore, I used to know *why*, but I can't remember just now. Don't care, really . . .

"*Joyce Johnson and I do not speak.* She's jealous! My God, how those women lived! Sleeping around—with *anyone*. I never did that—

"The fact is, I *never* liked most of their writing much—the Beats—*none of them*—never did. Jack wrote a few good ones. But you see, I went to Bennington. I was a *discerning* reader. I was disciplined, I had a classical education. Do you know that's what Neal was seeking? Classicism and a traditional life. He wanted *respectability*. That was how he wanted to *live* and we *did* that. Neal was able to get along with people of all classes. And I had respectable friends. That was all Neal really wanted. Neal never had a mother. That's what he was looking for in me.

"I make good money now, they come and pick my house clean as a bone! I call them the 'Archive People.' The Archive People come and comb. And wow, do they know what they're looking for. In one of my memoirs, I wrote about a book Jack liked, by Sri Au—Sri *Audi*-something—like the car—no, hold on, let me look . . . I've got one of his over here somewhere—*Sri Aurobindo*. I don't know what the 'Sri' is all about, maybe it's supposed to be 'sir' but someone got dyslexic. He was a sage, from India, one of those holy men who appealed to Jack. I wrote somewhere that Jack made notes in the margins of books—even *I* forgot, but the *Archive People* didn't! They asked me if I still had it and I said I didn't know so they came over and we looked, and they *found* it. O there's quite a market! I sold a sticker, and this was a *tiny* 'Can You Pass the Acid Test?' signed by Neal, I think I got 75,000 after commission. You know, that was the little diploma they used to give . . . or maybe I got the 75 *before* commission. Gave it all to my son, told him to *use* it, because he was destitute. *Don't wait till I'm dead*, I told him. See, he's out there selling cars and no one's buying.

"My money manager invests *everything* and my account is getting *fat*. There's a Swedish rock star, the Elvis of his country. A friend told me she'd been to one of his concerts. She said that, behind him, right onstage, was an enormous picture of *yours truly*. Because this Swedish Elvis was influenced by Jack and everybody and even wrote some books, about *ten*, that became bestsellers over there. My friend saw that picture and said, 'Carolyn, you should be making money off that.' So I rang up the singer and said, 'You need to pay me NOW.' So we made a deal where he printed up a few hundred of these things and we both signed them and I'd get the money. But he was dragging his feet. I looked at his schedule and said, 'Well I see you're going to be in Stockholm. Wouldn't that be a good place to meet up?' So we did. And while we're signing the posters, he asked if I wanted to go to his concert—they're booked for *years* in advance—and I said, 'Sure, can I bring a few friends?' I wound up bringing a whole crowd! He announced me from the stage. There I was in the VIP section and 25,000 people roared and turned their heads to look at me. I asked my friend if she got a picture of all those people's heads turning and she said, 'No, Carolyn, I was taking a picture of *you*.' The next day I was told that when it was announced that I was in the stadium, it was like some kind of religious experience for the audience. I said, 'Well, if it was a religious experience for *them*, what do you think it was like for *me*?' Anyway, we signed the posters but I started to think those things were probably going to take a *long time* to sell. I mentioned that to the Swedish Elvis and he told me to ring up his man, to settle the accounts. When I got the fellow on the line, he said, 'Would you like it all in one? Or in two?' One lump or two. I said, *'Let me have it all in one.'* They cut me a check right there, for 18,000 pounds. O, the world is having a tough time, but not *me*!

"I always felt shy and worthless. Didn't get over it till I was 65—that's how long it took for me to speak in front of crowds. Because, of course, I was invited all the time. Ginsberg was just *needy*. At least I *knew* why I felt worthless. It was because my brothers molested me when I was 10. Took me 55 years to get over . . .

"Jack wrote *Big Sur* up in Larry's cabin. And I'm in the book. A few years ago, some people made a documentary about it. They interviewed me for an hour-and-a-half but I was in the movie about *two seconds*. When I finally watched it, I almost fell asleep. Had to pinch myself it was so boring. They filmed me walking on the beach but it was the *wrong* beach. Why, I don't know. I *told* them it was wrong but they didn't seem to *care*. I guess they were going to fake it. But what's the point of faking it if you're making a documentary? That cabin isn't even up there anymore. In Bixby Canyon. It's a posh home now. There *are* a few buildings or whatnot where it used to be— but *nothing* in that film is authentic. I just don't understand why people avoid facts! There I was walking down the wrong beach . . . and everyone they decided to put in the movie was so full of *opinions*. You see, I don't have 'opinions,' I have *knowledge*. Jack wrote to me that he *had* to write that book. He felt good about it. The *one* thing I liked about that documentary was they flew me out from New York on EOS. I don't think it exists anymore but it was all First Class—the only way to travel. My son met me there and we had a fabulous day in New York. Then we took the train to California and it was *horrid*."

* * *

One day at San Quentin—she'd been doing her thing up there, and had managed to extend her sabbatical another six months—they told Kelly that a prisoner from the East Block had requested study time. The East Block is Death Row. Kelly thought that was a good omen. The great Buddhist teachers had always said the dharma was best practiced in the shadow of death-awareness. What better a pupil than one on Death Row?

It took some wrangling between the prison and the ACLU because the powers that be weren't all that excited about the prospect of "Dead man meditating!" It was a control trip, that's all. A few months went by . . . my wife didn't have a clue what was going on. Then a friendly soul at the ACLU called to say their argument was a constitutional slam-dunk and the warden had capitulated.

Kelly told everyone she didn't want to know the man's crime or even his last name. "Half are probably innocent, anyway" was what she said to me. The prisoner was brought to a special room with a glass partition. (In her usual jail class, there were sometimes half a dozen inmates, and a guard but no barriers.) She described the condemned charge as "big and rough, sort of handsome, darty paranoid eyes, bookish glasses, big head of grayish Brillo pad hair, biker moustache." His name was Ricky. The first thing he wanted to learn about was the Noble Truths. When he pronounced "noble" as in Nobel Prize, Kelly was touched. She said his nervousness was poignant; it'd probably been a while since he'd seen a woman, let alone spoken to one. Kelly was certain this kind of teaching would strengthen her own practice.

They met a handful of times. He was an eager student— meditation is popular on Death Row because it dangles the popular out-of-body-experience carrot of astral projection. Kelly began keeping a journal with an eye to writing something for one of the Buddhist magazines, *Tricycle* or *Shambhala Sun*. The subscription dharma rags *love* that shit; growing the sangha in Sing Sing is a perennial. Then she got more ambitious and set her sights on a book. A memoir (dual memoir, actually), part about her, part about Little Ricky. Well, mostly about her, but still, a kind of we're-all-on-Death-Row type of thing. I thought the framework was immensely compelling: a condemned convict and a middle-aged Berkeley Buddhist engaged in the ol' impermanence dialogue. *Very* cool.

I knew it was only a matter of time before she found out the nature of his crime—his crimes. She was making it too much of a thing *not* to know, which never works. The *No!* thing never works. I think she was being somewhat naïve. She *was* naïve, which happens to be her nature. But if she were really serious about writing a book, she'd eventually need to learn. She'd eventually have to ask. Their evolving intimacy alone, so to speak, would force the issue.

As it happened, her caged songbird was a child killer.

Do you remember Polly Klaas, the girl from Petaluma who was kidnapped? Well, Little Ricky was the monster who snatched her. Richard Allen Davis . . . remember him? If you're from around here, you probably do. You're certainly old enough.

Can I remind you of the case? Polly Klaas was having a slumber party. Twelve-year-olds. Around eleven at night, Little Ricky waltzes in with a knife and ties up the girls. Polly's parents were home when it happened, how's *that* for survivor guilt? If you're a mom or a dad, you've got to be saying *Kill me now*. Swoops in and swoops out, Polly under his arm. Classic unthinkable bogeyman shit. Mrs. Klaas didn't know anything was wrong until the morning, when she came in to see who wanted pancakes.

The weird thing is (in terms of the Winona connection) that Winona Ryder went up there after the murder—I want to say it was '93—she went up to raise money for a reward. Because that's where she's from. Winona's from Petaluma. And she did, she raised a lot. I want to say the final tally was $350,000. I don't know the numbers, maybe fifty from the community, three hundred from Winona. Winona was awesome. A very kind thing to do, everyone appreciated it, you

know, local girl made good, she didn't come with a movie star
vibe. None whatsoever. It hit her hard, hit *everybody* hard.

Little Ricky was of that genus of killers who begin their
careers by torturing animals. Now imagine what the man-
version of that boy would do to a lamb like Polly, a lamb who
barely has its fur. A little lamb can certainly bring out the
worst in a Little Ricky. A fellow just did the same thing down
in Florida to a gal who was a few years younger than Polly.
Went right into the house and grabbed her. Took her home
and raped her, then wrapped her in garbage bags with her
stuffed animal and buried her alive. I think about her. I think
about Polly. I think about these things . . . Polly's with her
friends, they're doing their girl-talk popcorn thing, playing
music and dancing—safe. Maybe he punched her head to
shut her up as they left the house, she's under his arm, limbs
slow-moving like a drugged crab, his adrenaline's surging, he's
wasted, invincible, can't believe he's pulled this off. Drenched
in alcohol, pot and meth, barely feels the lamb-crab moving
on his hip, a pirate's pride and booty—I'll stop. Not from
lack of candor, that's one thing I've never been accused of. It's
more, well, you can't know how far I go into thinking about
these things, of *inhabiting* that sort of evil, *examining* it from
every angle. Particularly of a child's. It's just so unpleasant,
Bruce, but that's how I'm wired. My "lingua franca." If there's
a terrible place to go, I tend to be there. See, that's what they
did to *me*. I know it's dreadful but that's what I do, I conjure
the details because *I* was killed, right around Polly's age too.
And I've had lots of time to think about it, I'm a student of
murdered children, I *inoculate* myself. I know that's selfish . . .
well, the reasons I study them I suppose are twofold. One is
to honor and grieve for them—and honor and grieve for the

child *I* once was before those monsters . . . I suppose *another* reason I go so deep is to celebrate that I made it through. That I survived. Because I believed for so many years beyond a shadow of a doubt that I'd be killed by those men. That God could not—*would* not save me. Because it was He who put me in harm's way.

It was God who was intent on destroying me . . .

And if you're wondering why Kelly didn't recognize Richard Allen Davis when they met—I mean, from being in the news—well, her mom got sick right around the time of the abduction, that was when she started flying back east. Massively distracted. Plus, she had to stay out there whole hunks of time to deal with the hospice and the home liquidators, and with her brother. She knew about Polly's murder—we never spoke much about it—knew from the Learys about the Winona fundraiser. But it all happened during this period of difficulty for her and never really landed on her screen.

> *He looked as if he was going to continue, but grew quiet. He stared out the window. After what felt like 10 minutes, I quietly left to use the restroom. When I came out, the door was open; was he gone? No—just letting in fresh air.*
>
> *He smiled at me as he brewed some tea and smoked a roach. I declined his offer.*

Pardon my trance.

Needless to say, the crimes and misdemeanors of Little Ricky put a dent in Kelly's mood. But it was more than a fender bender. It was a full-on karma crash.

Suddenly, she didn't have the stomach for it—who would? But her pride was tangled up. How could she reconcile the mandate of sharing the Buddha's teachings, of campaigning for the enlightenment of *all* beings, with the horror and rage she felt toward the animal that slaughtered Polly Klaas? And what about her project? I know the book was on her mind. She didn't dare broach it because she didn't want to sound narcissistic. I *know* that in her hour of the wolf, my wife still thought the book was essential (which I think it was), not just as an expression of her creativity and development as a Buddhist and a woman but as a tool to work through this terrible dilemma. It seemed to be one of those classic at-a-crossroad crises. You know, what doesn't kill your practice makes it stronger. *But how can I face that monstrous piece of shit?* That was her most pressing concern. She couldn't seem to build a bridge from where she was to where she needed to be, knowing what she knew. So she went back and forth between abandoning the book and resuscitating its high hopes.

Kelly sought counsel from her teacher, who, like most roshis in the Bay Area, was a late-sixty-something Jew from the East Coast. He said that her work with prisoners was a gift. She wanted him to talk about Richard Allen Davis *specifically* but he deliberately wouldn't, invoking *all* prisoners instead. You know, "the dharma doesn't come with strings attached." That was the teaching. I thought it was smug and heartless. To *me*. No compassion, just bullshit. I'm just saying.

My wife continued her lessons with Davis. She was losing weight, puking before *and* after she saw him. And Little Ricky knew something was wrong. Kelly said she had a parasite, which made her even more disgusted with herself. That she didn't have the balls to say something, *anything*—even *Go fuck yourself!*—was eating away at her. And Little Ricky was *concerned*, he was filled with *metta*, he was genuinely *worried* about her! He told her to make sure she saw a doctor and maybe she shouldn't come back until she was better. Finally, she got too sick to handle it. She never returned, not to San Quentin or any of the jails. I remember wishing at the time that she wouldn't go back to the zendo and that phony roshi either.

I read in *People* that Polly's favorite book was *Little Women*. Winona starred in a film adaptation. It had a dedication to Polly at the end.

To all the murdered Little Women—

* * *

The halfway point in her sabbatical had been reached.

Kelly decided that her path was to teach "secular" Buddhism in the schools, like her friend. When she told him she was striking out on her own, Dharmabud said he was thrilled. But I learned through the grapevine that he was stung (don't get me started on the whole sangha jockeying-for-power thing). My wife was on the rebound from the trauma of San Quentin, a colossal failure in her eyes. Now she had other fish to fry. She knew she was encroaching on Dharmabud's territory, co-opting his shit, and struck a kind of warrior pose to justify her actions. She walked around the house saying it wasn't possible for her to step on her friend's toes, how could teaching the fundamentals of meditation to children be a *negative* in any way? Her argument kind of boiled down to "this town and the job of enlightening it is big enough for both of us." Dharmabud did a slow burn. He got mad at her, then mad at *himself* for being so proprietary—*attached*—in the first place. His teacher (some other Brooklyn-transplant roshi) told him that an assertion of Self was the cause of his suffering. Hence, Dharmabud redoubled meditation and *seva*. What a farce! He ended the *Impermanence Rocks!* tour entirely, so Kelly won by default. She began with farther-away schools, ones that had been overlooked by her mentor because of their geographical inconvenience. Gave her time to gain self-confidence, like Sylvester Stallone in training. Impermanence Rocky!

She ran into an old editor-friend at a party. After a few mysterious meetings in the city, Kelly came home with a bottle of wine and an announcement—she'd been given a $20,000 advance from Chronicle Books for a memoir about being a menopausal, bisexual, Berkeley-bodhisattva. She would write about being adopted. She would write about her cancer (six years in remission). She would write about her affairs. She would write about our son. She wanted to write a *lot* about our son—what it was like to raise a boy with her gay male partner. She was even screwing up her courage to unravel the nasty Little Ricky experience . . . but she wanted the overarching theme to be Buddhist thought, practice and doctrine. That was where she *lived*, it was the landscape surrounding the long road that brought her to where she was now: introducing meditation and metta into elementary schools. Kelly wanted to expose herself, warts and all, the trials and tribulations, and the healing. She'd been asked to write a book! She couldn't believe her good fortune. It was as if the Universe rung a prayer bell, summoning her to put everything on the table for that sacred, invisible tribe—*readers*.

You go, girl!

Suddenly, I wasn't in the way anymore.

She was a thousand pounds lighter and the transformation was lovely to behold. Whatever troubles we had, I *always* wanted my wife to be happy. (I still do, though it's impossible now.) That was a constant. It was nice too because before the settlement, I was really marinating in my own shit. Waiting for Godot and the call from my attorneys. So any rays of light were welcome.

One night over dinner, Kelly said she needed to reach out to Dharmabud. She'd decided to call her book *Impermanence Rocks* and wanted his blessing. That came as a surprise because the working title had been *Nirvanarama*. (Which I rather liked, particularly because of the felicitous Rama pun. An alternate was *Divine Mess*, which she rejected as "too Bette Midler.") Kelly claimed that her friend wouldn't—*couldn't*—object. Plus, she contended that by removing the exclamation point she had rejiggered the phrase's entire meaning. Without the ejaculatory punctuation, it was no longer juvenile. *Impermanence Rocks* had a plaintive, stately quality to it, nearly ironic, as if reminding that one can be shipwrecked on the shoals of impermanence as surely as anything else. Though she *did* decide to reinstate the exclamation point for the chapter on how she brought kiddie dharma to a whole new level.

She already had a dedication in mind: "For Stewart [aka Dharmabud], who gave me the match to light the fire."
Nope—not Buddhist enough . . .
"For Stewart, who brought me to puja."
Naw. People might think Stewart and I are a couple.
"For Mother, who speaks to me each day from Silence."
No. Not light enough/too New Age cliché-hokey. And a lie.
"For my teacher, Maurice Epstein Roshi."
Right, that's it . . . keep it simple, stupid!

My wife informed the school district that she wouldn't be returning to her old teaching position. Instead, she asked them to consider appointing her mistress of ceremonies for the oldest established impermanent floating crap game in the Bay Area. The new, improved version now included yoga for the 2nd-grade set.

Get your ya-yas out!

A homeschooled Ryder was the precocious recipient of Mom's private intensives. He became a kind of proving ground (I guess you could say more of a living laboratory), not just for *Impermanence Rocks!* but Kelly's book as well. The whole *house* was a work-in-progress. We were incredulous at his sophistication in embracing some of Buddhism's more subtle concepts, and that made my wife think. It was common knowledge that when it came to learning foreign languages, kids left adults in the dust—so why not teach them ethics and empathy? Kelly began to see herself as a promoter of what she believed was a radical new way to educate children in the spiritual realm. Based on whatever Ryder sparked to, she burned CDs of herself narrating Buddhist texts for her toddlers to listen to at the end of class while powering down in *savasana*. Kelly became the de facto ambassador for the growing "Armies of Awareness," a phrase she trademarked.

Ryder hung out at the zendo and became a favorite of Kelly's teacher, who whimsically suggested we might have a *tulku* on our hands. That's someone of high rebirth. I never really knew if the teacher was serious but I think Kelly believed he was. Made her prideful. Ryder even "sat" and they just marveled at his focus. He was really coming along, under Kelly's tutelage. All the women had crushes (and the men too), they absolutely doted over him. He was a gorgeous kid. Handsome. And I have to say pretty amazing because none of it went to his head. For him, it was like swimming or playing the piano, he just took to it. Ryder was what they call a "natural"—I think he could've been a big guru when he got older, not the *bad* kind, but a true teacher, with followers. People would have followed him anywhere, he had an innate charisma. Ryder was one of those rarities, a born leader with a keen mind. And completely book crazy too. The apple didn't fall far from the tree. He went through that period boys do when they read with a flashlight under the covers.

One night I asked what he was reading. It was *Songs of the Saints of India*, a book Kelly gave him. But on any given night it was a medley of *Huckleberry Finn* and the *Watchmen* comic books and even Kelly's favorite, Chögyam Trungpa—Allen Ginsberg's and Pema Chödrön's teacher. He handed it to me. As I flipped through, I saw that he'd made annotations.

"Did you know that to *Ram*," he said, "everybody stinks? Ram said they stink like *pus* from *pimples*. Or *diarrhea* from your *butt*."

"Nice."

He laughed.

"But Ram loves us *anyway*, Daddy! Bodies are smelly, and it doesn't matter if they're alive or dead—they stink. Ram said *everything* was stinky, even *honey*. Even milk from a sacred cow stinks."

"Okay. Uhm yeah, right on."

"Ram said the only thing that made people untouchable was if they couldn't love."

As for my wife, she wowed 'em at the schools. Her reputation and minor fame preceded her. Plus, she was now duly certified; she'd acquired some kind of district license that Mr. Unenterprising Woo-Woo Dharmabud never got around to applying for. Which opened more doors because these days you can't just stroll onto school grounds, not even in Berkeley. Too many issues of liability.

She hatched a scheme to go national. Her plan was to visit school districts all over the country and provide a template of the Armies of Awareness "Compassion Revolution." At no cost, of course. The economic downturn was in her favor. Cities were so strapped for cash that teachers were paying for crayons and Kleenex out of their own pockets. (That's still happening.) She'd go into some of those lavatories—they were a disgrace. Hellacious places, toilets clogged with shit, in shards from vandalism. In order for their kids not to go without, teachers bought juice for homeroom with their own money. They bought glue and glitter for art class, lightbulbs and Scotch tape . . . Jesus. Some of the teachers told Kelly they were doing this back in the '80s and everything got steadily *worse* after the lottery was supposedly coming to the rescue. The lottery came and things got worse!

I audited classes at a few of the formerly Dharmabudless startups and have to say that Kelly was pretty fucking slick. She soothed the savage Ritalin beasts, made 'em into little *bhaktas* faster than you could say puff the magic drag queen. The tapped-out, stressed-out educators got a respite in the bargain . . . a little downtime to reboot, before making the next Safeway run for nutritious snacks and yellow Ticonderoga No. 2s.

Kelly figured the memoir would take a few years so in the meantime self-published a Zen children's book she'd been working on called *How It Can Dance!* It was filled with quirky koans—"Does an *Awfully* Messy Room Have the Buddha Nature?"—loved that one—along with Kelly's distinctively

THE EMPTY CHAIR 67

squiggly, faux-naïf illustrations. (I take full credit for sneaking in a poem from Kerouac's *Mexico City Blues* and an "upside-down" nonsense rhyme by Kabir, the cantankerous saint of Varanasi.) Mom drew Ryder à la Jules Feiffer—she stole from the best—as the prototypical great-grandchild of the Beats, and her sweet, fanciful narrative allowed him to surf from page to page with beginner's-mind alacrity and charm. He had a blast . . . though again I'm compelled to say that Ryder's exuberance remained sunny and pure. Not a prideful bone in his body. Don't get me wrong—all kids like to please their moms but he somehow struck a balance between the scholarly and the Oedipal. I've tried to do that all my life and failed! Anyway, I kept a close watch on that heart of mine—one of my duties as househusband, don't you know—and can proudly attest that our son's head stayed firmly on his shoulders.

Kelly went on a *How It Can Dance!* book tour that she organized herself, from Seattle to San Diego and every place in between. She arranged for local library readings and hawked it out of vitamin barns, co-ops and daycare centers. Sold it from her *car* for God's sake.

We were on a budget, notwithstanding the advance on the memoir and my disability checks. You know how the money thing goes. I admit I was getting a little wiggy. I must have gained, oh, close to 45 pounds. I put in a lot of time on the porch in a rocking chair that rumor had it once belonged to either Neil Young or Pigpen. (Got it at the flea market.) You know, my wife had an interesting relationship to my lawsuit. On the one hand, she said it was bad karma to be sitting on my ass waiting for reparations over something that happened as a result of karma *anyway* and that the case had turned all us plaintiffs into virtual eunuchs, which was the ultimate triumph of the abusers. Probably had a point. On the other, I knew she wasn't above dreaming of the Big Win. With enough Merlot, Kelly's thoughts wandered to India, a mainstay of her recurring encyclical money-pot grand tour. She *loved* to tease. She said that when my ship came in—always referred to as the *Good Ship Lollipop*—she expected no less than a first-class expedition. "And if that isn't convenient for your schedule, Ryder and I will have a perfectly fine time by ourselves." She always diva'd out when she drank Merlot. But no bullshit, Kelly considered the fact that she'd never traveled there to be a gaping hole in her CV. She desperately wanted to visit the cave where Siddhartha Gautama meditated; she longed to sit under the Buddha tree in Bodh Gaya. She wanted to go to the Deer Park in Sarnath where he gave his teachings, and to Sravasti, where he taught breath awareness meditation . . . and make the pilgrimage to Kushinagar, where the Buddha drew his last breath. Her fantasy itinerary for Ryder was catholic indeed, mixing elephant rides (like his beloved if recently outgrown Mowgli) with a visit to Varanasi to watch bodies burning on a ghat—a ritual for which Ryder, courtesy of Mom's bedtime stories, had already seemed to have acquired a small but persistent curiosity.

After the third glass of wine she'd crinkle her eyes and stare at the moon, archly whispering, "Or maybe I'll just bring a . . . *ladyfriend*."

She was a hoot.

Oh and look, Bruce, I don't want to give you the impression I had no *life*. When Kelly was on the road doing her book or teaching thing, I took breaks from the drudgery of the legal waiting game. I'd arrange for Ryder to have a sleepover at a friend's then ride into the city to buy crack in the Tenderloin.

Find a friendly porn shop with booths in the back for watching movies and get high. Kneel in front of the glory hole and wait for Mr. Right to poke his dick through . . . *Suck-A-Mole* not Whac-A-Mole, huh. Not exactly a self-esteem builder but you do what you gostta do. I acquired gonorrhea that way once, in the throat. *Nice.* Another time I got crabs in my eyebrows. You haven't lived until you've almost blinded yourself with A-200 before finding out that Vaseline asphyxiates the little fuckers. *Vaseline!*

* * *

I was in the yard. What was I doing? I have no memory.

I know it was a Saturday, three weekends before the news of the settlement—O happy day!—though of course at the time, I wouldn't have been surprised to learn that everything had fallen apart or the case needed to be refiled on a technicality and would take five more years to resolve.

I went back in the house. Why? No memory.

As I passed Kelly's meditation room, something caught my eye. A chair, overturned on the floor. I went in to right it. Something stank—my foot skidded—it was shit, right next to the chair—*on* the chair. How did a dog—*what* dog—

Then I saw him, hanging from a rope.

No clothes . . . he wore no clothes.

—*what's this?*

(My heart was racing but my mind was calm, observing.)

Rushed to lift—so heavy.

Dead.

Dead—

But *what* is dead? And what does dead *mean*—

I could smell him, and all manner of stinky things—that thing Ram said—actually the awesome poet Ravidas said it, or wrote it, anyway—about everything being stinky—emanating from the untouchable touchable body of my son—poo smells, horsey, germy, *sandalwoody* smells—a complete, fetid jumble. *The sky is falling*—the phrase came into my head and kept repeating—the sky is falling—so *this* is what they mean by that—he was a bag, heavy boxer's punching bag, and I, me, a freak stuck in timespace, slow-dancing with that cold nude weight—*How It Can Dance!*—and if you've ever confronted this sort of thing (there are more out there than you think, I went to a support group for folks who discovered loved ones hanging), there's an odd moment when you're *lifting*—later you wonder why you didn't just cut them down—as if that might have saved him—you're *supposed* to cut them down, but at the *moment*—dread moment of moments—it seems counterintuitive so you find yourself holding and *lifting* instead, lifting *up*—in that odd moment—*very* odd—you're just *stuck*, your instincts say *raise him up*, take pressure off his neck (the damage already done, windpipes ruined forever), there you are left holding the bag, no way to cut the rope even if you wanted, there's no *knife* and you can't let go, and besides, the angle's all wrong and your hands are full, so you're stuck holding the torso of him who was—*is*—always *was* your love and your light—like one of those exhausted marathon dance couples from that wonderful movie *They Shoot Horses, Don't They?* If you can't cut it then you need to undo the knot but it's too *high*, you'll need to stand on a chair—conveniently provided!—so you can lift him with one arm and loosen the noose with the other . . . you'll need to bend down to right the chair (now inconveniently laying on its side) but it's been kicked a few feet away so you need to do more than bend, need to literally *let go* of him to get to it—the very first of a letting go that will stretch into Infinity—which you do, you have no choice but to let him dangle—*have to*—and it's against the will of every cell of your body—body of father holding his son, every cell shrieking *no no no he'll choke . . . again!*—and you cannot, *will* not bring yourself to be party to a further hanging—oh Bruce! It's just a horrible, terrible bind—I found myself in—a wretched, killing, scum of the earth moment, alone with myself in the deadly *present*—and you feel . . . you're just *completely useless*, you're *beyond*, like some demon who never should have existed, why were you born? *He* wouldn't have been in this ludicrous predicament if you never had been, you've murdered him by definition. Your busy, useless arms won't let you dial for help—*where are your clothes, son?*—but eventually you do just that, blacking out all thoughts so as not to be party to an unspeakable second hanging—you let go of him as you shuffle over to right that dastardly chair. The seat is broken but you see a short wood plank (what's *that* doing there? Well, never mind for now), you lay the plank across the broken drum of the seat so you can stand upon it, a good, *proactive* move that suddenly vanquishes or at least diminishes other awful thoughts, our brains are so primitive, they enjoy ordering us to take action-steps, now suddenly face-to-face with Ryder's dead head, staring at the twisted hard candy features. And again the mind begins its metal machine Muzak:

Ryder?—

—son?—

SON!

You brush his penis with your arm, it's larger than you thought—

The mind metal-machines: Hmmm, when was the last time I saw it?

My son's penis—

—probably a few months ago when he was sick.

. . . right? Holding his head with a cold rag. He puked into the trash.

But he was a shy kid. Always modest about his body, at least more than his parents.

Ry? Why aren't you wearing clothes?

Ryder?

What is it you've done?

What's happened here—

In the unfathomable midst of it all, your monkey mind noshes on its usual bullshit buffet. But whose thoughts and emotions are these? They don't feel like yours . . . you're a thousand miles away, in the middle of a dream.

A daydream.

You even feel—*I felt*—silly.

. . . tongue herniating from mouth—impossible to untie Kelly's blocks, he used the rope from Kelly's yoga blocks—why did I think that would be an easy thing? To noodle a finger between rope and skin, like a steel wire under the jaw . . .

So I had to let him hang again—third hanging!—and run to the kitchen for a knife. Easier to let go the second time. Serial killers say that with each victim, the killing gets easier—

I cut him down.

Carried the birthday suit bag to a phone (no phone in Kelly's meditation room)—carried! As if to break the vigil of human contact would endanger him—endanger *me*—and dialed 911. I told them what happened and they said, you know, they were sending someone out, and to stay on the line.

Please stay on the line, sir. I've heard enough 911 calls on the news to know that's what they do, that's protocol, they ask you to stay on the line and be calm. I dropped the receiver on the carpet and just held him, pretending he was asleep. It half-looked like that . . .

. . . *from a certain angle.*

Angle of repose.

What exactly *is* an angle of repose?

The sky is falling.

I really do have blocks against certain phrases. Words too—like "abide." "The Dude abides." I can never remember what it means. And right after I find out, I forget. It's a biblical word but people use it in songs all the time . . .

Later I learned that the firemen broke down the door. I didn't hear them till they wrenched Ryder from my arms. One of them asked, Did you take off his clothes? *Uh, no, he was like that when I found him.* Metal machine mind said, *That probably sounds strange to them.* Hell, it sounded strange to *me.* I knew the police would want to explore further. Protocol. Cop work 101. In death of spouse, rule out spouse. In death of child, rule out parent. In hanging death of naked child, rule out creepy gay dad.

My head told me it was going to be a bit of a hassle but would ultimately resolve. I just hoped it didn't turn lurid, that the truth would out itself—quickly.

But should I use my church-suit lawyers to defend? (Said monkey mind.)

I rode in the ambulance. They made me sit in front while they worked on him in back. No real memory of it. They tried to start an IV at the house but I don't think that works when someone's dead. The veins collapse, no blood's flowing. Far as I know. But everyone played their part, they were all great. No professional likes to give up on a kid. I think they probably ham it up with kids, it's instinct, you know, you're trying to resuscitate a person who hasn't had a chance to fuck it up, someone who hasn't had the chance to break any hearts (until now). So they put in that extra effort, apart from the fact that a lot of 'em have kids themselves. If you work on a child who dies, grief counselors and an extended leave with full pay is a slam-dunk. *Earth to monkey mind! Now* I remember, the chief paramedic, head honcho, was an old pro. Very seasoned. Some of those guys are even D.O.s. You know, osteopaths. There was a woman trainee too, doing her best to not be distraught. Her very first call as an EMT, someone told me later. That had to be rough.

I kept redialing Kelly's cell, secretly grateful each time she didn't answer. I finally left a message. *Something's happened to Ryder, call back right away.* From the front seat, senses acute, I smelled the pet shop we'd visited the week before, bad, sawdusty, wire terrier puppy smells wafting up—*why?* His shit was on my pants.

They "pronounced" him at the ER. *I now pronounce you boy and Death.* Death and wife . . . They let me in the room, the room with the clickety drapes and someone always moaning on the other side, they let me in to see him, a cop was there, he looked me up and down then hardly looked away, stayed there the whole time, probably protocol again, because of the weirdness of Ryder's initially undressed body, now covered by two flimsy hospital gowns. God knows what ghoulish things they thought the suspect might have done and was still capable of . . . They never took the tubes out, not even the one down his throat. Machine mind wondered why. It would have been so easy. Maybe it was someone else's first shift too, a new hire, an LVN who was supposed to do it but fucked up out of nerves. *Everybody too distraught*———

Or maybe just a bad RN.

I always obey my nurse.

* * *

[the next day] Thanks for your patience—that was very, very tough. I know it took me a while, I'm sorry. I've probably taken too much of your time. I think just sort of plunging in wouldn't have—I don't know, all the stuff leading up to it was the only way it would have worked. I'm pretty sure I'll never talk about any of this again. I mean, in such detail. There's still a bit more—can you listen? Have I made you late for any appointments? I know you wanted to leave today . . .

I was thinking some more about all this before I went to sleep, and this morning too, when I sat with the monks for prayers. For some reason there doesn't seem to be a charge to the next few "items." I think I can recount them in an almost clinical way. Maybe that's just a defense mechanism. Probably I numbed myself up by going through it, you know, telling you about it, I haven't really thought about any of that for years. In passing, yes, of course, images come to me every day, but not with that kind of . . . narrative detail. Not even close. I hope the anesthetic doesn't wear off in the middle of this next little procedure!

Around five days after the *event*, a short article appeared in the paper. Not on the front page, somewhere toward the back. See, I'd had a few nagging concerns that Ryder would be taken up as the poster child for tween suicides, some sort of talking point for the usual bogus discussions on radio or television. I didn't want our son to become, you know, the lead-in for a *60 Minutes* segment either. I *definitely* stayed away from the Internet, which I considered—still do—to be nothing more than a Dantesque filing system for one's worst fears. But nothing happened. Now I see those small worries for what they were, a distraction from the cruel reality of his absence.

I won't bother to describe the details of my wife's collapse when she learned what happened. Nothing I could possibly tell you could come close to delineating her sorrow. I wouldn't even try, wouldn't want to, some things aren't ours to convey. A mother's sorrows . . . that anguish is forever hers and hers alone. Do you know the Fourth Book of *Esdras*? There I go, the pedant again, with his GED in pedagogy. (One of the youngsters I met in my travels had one and called it the "Good Enough Diploma.") In the Fourth Book of *Esdras*, it is written, "And it happened that my son went to his room, fell down, and died: and my neighbors came"—no, hold it—hold on—I think it's "and my neighbors came and *rose up* to comfort me. Then took I my rest. It was the second night and all the neighbors rested so they could wake up and comfort me some more, and I rose up by night and fled and am come to this field— hither to this field—*as you see*—and *will not go back*, but will remain here . . . and neither eat nor drink, but rather to continually mourn and fast till I die." Not bad for an old guy, huh? My memory's always been good in terms of recitation. I'm just rusty. But I still get the Mensa gold star for today. I assume you carry them in your trunk.

Kelly was admitted to a psych ward for a week. A full week of heavy meds. They wouldn't let me visit for the first few days and when I did, she was barely responsive. By the time

she came home, the detectives had finished their grim inter-
rogatories and I'd been cleared. They'd gone around asking
the neighbors what my relationship with my son was like, you
know, if they'd ever seen me smack him around or jerk him
off, that kind of thing, but after a while their hearts weren't in
it. I think it became kind of apparent that it was an anomaly.
His being nude. My wife alibi'd out, as they say on TV. She was
60 miles away at the time of the event, teaching. On television,
you either alibi out or lawyer up.

She slept on a futon in the room where he died. The
meditation room that used to be *her* room, her sacred yogini
space. The irony being that now it was *incomprehensibly* sacred.
Though maybe there's no irony after all . . . She ignored the
altar—she'd fussed for weeks over its installation—with
its incense and brassy representations of Amitabha and
Sanghamitta, color photos of her teacher, and black-and-white
ones of sundry cantankerous diapered *siddhas* from the last
century. You know, the usual suspects. She didn't talk much
and hardly ate the food prepared by a never-ending stream of
friends and neighbors—yes, as in *Esdras*, they rested, so they
would have the strength to come back and comfort her, though
no comfort was possible. It seemed like the whole world was
shaken by that boy's death. Folks circled the wagons around
us. They were protective and I appreciated that.

I understood why Kelly never left that room. In her emp-
tied-out postlapsarian state, bitten by all manner of plumed
serpents, her febrile obsession became to return to the Garden
at all cost. She wanted to breathe the same air our son had.
And who was to say his effluence wasn't present, that some of
his microbes weren't still in the room? He'd napped on that
futon and she wanted to nest in a bed of his skin flakes, her

body caressed by the ethereal snowfall of subatomic particles and microscopic motes, she longed to breathe Ryder-rich oxygen saturated by sloughed-off cells and bacteria exhaled from his lungs and sinus. She would absorb through mucous membranes anything left of him. He had come from her and so he would return, in soluble, invisible, ingestible form. Pitiably, she prayed for something of him to imprint itself on her very eyes—what a blessing it would be to know for sure!—it would sustain her if she could look at the world through a cold case filter of his DNA. She'd close her eyes and never open them again if that's what it took not to lose him, go blind if it meant being subsumed. She'd settle for anything, as long as it wasn't his extinction.

Kelly sat on a cushion in front of the broken, empty chair as if kneeling abjectly before a *new* altar, a sacrificial one honoring impossibly infinite, impossibly malevolent forces. She courted it, for her life . . . sitting with such helplessness, futilely waiting, not praying, for she knew that prayers were pointless, that such a thing would never respond to prayer, no, just waiting, *abiding*, for whatever it was that swallowed him to spit him out. Sometimes I positioned myself so I could watch her undetected through the open door (it was a house rule that it never be closed again). She was having a dialogue with that chair, with body and soul, maybe even her sex. Once I saw her sit in it stock-still—on the plank, rather—feet on the floor, back upright, eyes half-shut. Other times, she'd sit before it and lay her head on that infernal plank like an exhausted child in the lap of its mother . . . or a lover who betrayed her. Then she'd pace and circle, raging, an interrogator outgunned—

And one day, she was done.

She only asked one thing of me: to burn the chair.

Kelly used to love that chair, isn't it funny? She actually stole it—but I suppose that isn't fair. Let's say she borrowed it and never gave it back. She found it by chance, in a storage room at school. See, my wife's family owned an antiques shop and she worked there every summer until she was 18. Her dad had an amazing eye that he passed on to Kelly. They were very close. By the time her apprenticeship was done, she could have gotten a job at Sotheby's. So there it was, shoved in with a lot of other chairs in a forgotten storage room, only it was different. Very different. Not because it was bruised and battered—the canework seat was broken through—or because it was anachronous, out of time. All Kelly needed was one look to know what she had, she'd come across these types of chairs at her father's shop before. I remember when she brought it home. She sat it in the middle of the living room, poured us some Chablis and commenced a frothy little *Antiques Roadshow* routine, with yours truly playing the excited rube. "Sir, this is a very fine *elbow chair*, Edwardian, circa 1900, and as you can see it is made from mahogany. That's *Cuban* mahogany." With an appraiser's flourish, she informed that if put on the market it might fetch around $800. When I told her she was no better than a common thief (all in good fun), she assured me that no one would miss it. Besides, she said, it would cost a few hundred to do a halfway decent repair and the district certainly wasn't going to shell that out. Shit, she did them a *favor*. Kelly couldn't for the life of her deconstruct how it had come to be nestled among all those crampy, banged-up desks from the '60s, the ones with the tiny, graffiti-carved tables attached. So she stuck it in the Volvo and drove on home. She never got around to fixing it; as a temporary measure, she laid a short piece of wood across the busted seat. That was what Ryder jumped from.

I had very careful pre-incineration instructions: it was to be broken apart until its pieces were unrecognizable. The order wasn't given so it would fit into our fireplace, though that certainly helped. She just didn't want it to look like a chair when it burned. I knew what she was doing. She wanted to strip it of its identity, to humiliate it. She wanted it tortured— she wanted to hear it scream.

You ask how *I* was doing? Well, you may as well ask how I'm doing *now*, because it's kind of the same. I dissociate. Space out. I run from pain—to food, sex, drugs. The one thing I *don't* do is overspend. There isn't a shopaholic bone in me. I do bury myself in books pretty well . . . You know, talking about all this, Bruce, makes me wonder if I haven't even come *close* to the point of grieving. Or if I'm even capable. See, those wonderful experiences with the Catholic Church helped me learn to compartmentalize. Don't you hate that word? Did you ever hear of something called Compartment Syndrome? A friend of mine had it after an automobile accident. They wound up cutting off his arm, on Thanksgiving no less. Compartment Syndrome can happen after a fracture. A closed space gets created in your arm or leg—a little compartment—and for some reason the doctors can miss it. The pressure gets so bad in there that all the nerves and tissue and muscle die, it can get to where they can't do anything but amputate. I guess you could say that psychologically, emotionally anyway, I've found a way to create closed spaces that don't result in amputation. Though maybe I've lost more limbs than I think! When Ryder died, I busied myself with tending to my wife. I'm *muy* codependent, if you know anything about that. Then, *wham!*—the settlement came in. A million and change *after* the lawyers took their piece. (When I told Kelly, it didn't seem to register.

Since celebration wasn't an option, there wasn't anything for her to do with the information.) The windfall became one more compartment for me to chill in. Another room, and a well-decorated one at that.

I haven't told you about the note. It wasn't a suicide note per se—though the authorities referred to it as such.

Kelly's meditation room was her holy of holies. Unless we were invited, Ryder and I were instructed to stay the fuck out. The door had a kitschy *Gone Fishin'* sign on it at all times— now where the hell'd we pick that up? I want to say a yard sale in San Rafael. O, that little sign really tickled her! She said her dad used to hang one just like it on the door of Ballendine's Second Penny whenever they were closed. The man hadn't been near a fishing pole in his life.

Ryder took the sign and pasted over a handwritten edit:

GONE TO BOODAFIELD!!!!!!!

You can imagine how many ways I've looked at this.

The strongest theory was the one that hit Kelly the hardest: that for all the arcane knowledge he'd absorbed, for all her "Little Buddha" projections of our son's scholarship, for all the tutelage in *phowa*—transference of consciousness—for all the cozying up to Maitreya's merry band of bodhisattvas, for all the instructions in the Great Embodiment of Impermanence *and* the Tathagata ("One Who Has Thus Gone") *plus* the Four Immeasurable Aspirations, the Eight Worldly Concerns, the 19 Root Downfalls and the 46 Transgressions, for all the rides thumbed on Greater and Lesser Vehicles, for all the picnicking with Vajra brothers and sisters, for all the comforts of the Six Mantras, Six Perfections, Six Gestures, Six Pristine Cognitions and Six Types of Bone Ornaments Worn by Wrathful Deities, for all the "mother and child aspects of reality," for all the protections promised by the thousand-armed Avalokitesvara, for all manner of Nyingma masters, lovingkindnesses, dream bardos and intermediate states of rebirth, for all the inherent existences, inner radiances, illusory bodies and causally conditioned phenomena, for all the songs of dualism and dream yoga, the burnt offerings and calm abidings, the apparent and actual realities—for all that, well, Ryder was just going to impress Mom (especially) and Dad with an unthinkably bold act of tantric precocity, a supercalifragilistic Peter Pan leap into the Void from which he could boomerang back to the welcoming arms of that dimensional continuum he called home—. . . to leapfrog the teachings, and rock the house of Impermanence.

There *are* a few pages of *How It Can Dance!* where Ryder's cartoon avatar learns about *tulkus*, modern reincarnations of dead Buddhist saints. I can't help feeling that's what he grabbed onto—the whole darkly mordant *Watchmen* superhero ethos married to that Hardy-Boy-with-flashlight-under-the-sheets thrill. "The great meditation of no-meditation," "the great training of no-training" . . . you can *hear* the woman on those CDs she burned for him to listen to as he fell asleep!

> *He grabbed an old tape recorder from the top of the bureau. It was already synched up; as fresh rain pattered the trailer's roof, the soft, slow-cadenced voice of his wife, Kelly, began. While we listened, he toked on a joint, and poured himself a glass of wine.*

"The most important dharma is to practice impermanence. *[long pause]* . . . To be at ease with impermanence is to open

the Golden Doors of dharma . . . The contemplation of impermanence cuts all ties to samsara, allowing all beings to reach
nirvana . . . As you train in the great training of no-training,
it will take root and light up your journey on the Path . . . As
impermanence flows through your heart, your discipline will
become diamond-pointed, but only if you *never stop meditating on it* . . . Befriending impermanence will allow you to see
the equal nature of all things and take you to a place beyond
falling back . . . Once you're certain you will die, you'll have
no trouble giving up evil actions and doing what is good . . .
Impermanence is the Golden Wheel of dharma . . . This is
the day! Turn the Thousand-Spoked Wheel! Turn it, turn it,
turn it!"

He shut off the player.

Impermanence *sucks*!

See, but I *knew* my boy wasn't a suicide. Weren't never a
doubt in my mind . . .

But why a hanging?

How come?

How comes it?[4]

No further questions, Your Honor!

[sings] "Big Thousand-Spoked Wheel keep on turnin',
Proud *Tulku* keep on burnin'! Rollin'! Rollin'! Rollin' on
the ri-ver!" *Golden Wheel* ever turning, tightening into a
magic ring around his neck—"To every season, *turn turn
turn*"—turning and turning in the widening gyre . . . to

---

4   He got stoned very quickly; my initial thoughts were to end the
day's session but I let it go.

every season in *Hell*—every *saison en enfer*. You know about Ouroboros, don't you? The serpent that devours its own tail? Right before you die, the sign of Death comes—your mouth forms a great O, those droll doctors call it "the O Sign." The mouth O-pens (and o-pines its last) and your eyes begin to flutter as they do in REM sleep—*RAM* sleep!—all roads lead to Rama, don't you know . . . that's what Gandhi said when he was shot, said "Rama" in his final exhalation. (And George Harrison, right after he was stabbed.) As the noose choked Ryder's neck, so the noose of his tiny anus opened (a lowercase "o" to be sure) to spill out the tainted, sacred contents of the Five Hollow Viscera: stomach, intestines, bladder, gall bladder, semen sac. Do you know the myth of the mandrake root? The medievals believed it sprouted from the semen that fell from innocent men who were hanged. And after the O, comes, as the drier wits like to say, "the Q sign," tongue lolling from mouth, the mouth's last vowel. Wagging . . . oh those wags!

But why? *[sings]* "Who by fire? Who by water? Who in the sunshine? Who in the night time?" . . . why *hang* himself?

Kelly and I had to focus on *something*. You can't just sit there *not* thinking—the mind won't allow it!—about every possibility, every permutation, every everything. Like his nakedness . . . I actually think I might have solved that mystery—maybe solved them both—with this memory. A few years ago we went camping by the Red River. We skinny-dipped in a hidden spring and there was a rope Ryder swung from way out over the river, then let go with a shiver and a huckleberry shout. Did that all day. I'll bet part of stepping off that chair was recalling that time.

Whatever.

Kelly blamed herself for putting the hanging idea in Ryder's head. When she was going through her prison dharma phase, she loved having a glass of wine at dinner and sharing Big House scuttlebutt. There were a lot of suicides in the penitentiary and the most popular method by far was hanging. The inmates went about it with trademark resourcefulness. A guard told her that a child molester hanged himself with his *shoelaces*, while lying down! Some went kneeling, as in prayer; you only needed a few pounds of pressure to do the job. Kelly became *obsessed* by the notion that she'd inspired our son through an anecdote, sort of a copycat death with a peppermint twist of *naisthika*. That's Sanskrit for nihilism. "That which denies the existence of objects and the laws of cause and effect." I guess in Ryder's case, the concept of cause and effect was certainly denied . . . *naisthika* also refers to the Great Vow of celibacy. One who never wastes his semen. I suppose Ryder spilled at the end, but didn't actually waste. It's just semantics.

Kelly hardly spoke a word in the beginning days of her sequestration, but one late afternoon started to murmur this very fear—the prison hanging anecdotes as virus fear—at first burbling the words under her breath, not really loud enough to hear, as if talking to herself, then eventually loud enough for me to understand. To be honest, it didn't matter *what* she was saying, I was just glad to finally hear her speak. I'd become one of those schmaltzy figures at the bedside of a comatose spouse, waiting for a sign, any sign. There was only one flaw in the theory. Being the superbly protective mom she was, Kelly *never* spoke about violent penitentiary stuff in Ryder's presence. To my knowledge, he didn't even know about Little Ricky. She was fairly assiduous about that. When I pressed her on that point, she insisted that he must have overheard.

That was problematic. First off, my son wasn't the eaves-dropping type. He wasn't a surreptitious character, not even remotely. But for the sake of argument, let's say he *had* heard something not meant for his ears. Well, Ryder's no dummy, he's impish too, my educated guess is that he'd have made a big guileless splash right away and sidled up to his mom to shake it out of her. See, he didn't have it in him to remain *hidden*, wasn't his nature. Too extroverted. And as I said, Kelly was extremely mindful of his presence in the house, moreso than her remorseful theory makes room for. Now if he *had* come into the kitchen or wherever while we were gossiping about some death, some *hanging* death, he'd naturally have been curious to know if Mom actually *knew* the deceased or was she at least there for the "discovery." Of the body. This is all a bit exasperating, Bruce, because I have to—I'm going to have to spend a little time talking about things that *never happened*! Theoretical things. Hopefully, you'll see why it's important that I do.

So I say it didn't happen because if it had we'd have known. Let me go further. Even if it had unfolded that way—Ryder furtively in the hall, lapping up a morbid mommalogue—it still wouldn't prove or mean a thing.

I knew what Kelly was doing. She was building castles of concrete instead of sand because sandcastles wouldn't do her any good. She needed constructs that were oblivious to time or tide, she was conjuring durable fairy tales that on completion could be hurtled into the past to provide Ryder with shelter that was at least up to code. Wasn't it sandcastles that had done him in? (Maybe.) Kelly's new spin on that old bugaboo impermanence was . . . *permanence itself.*

In permanence, lay liberation!

Too late, of course—

Fresh from the nuthouse, she sat her butt cheeks down on permanence and waited for it to hatch. Actually, it was her theories she was incubating. (More about that later.) First, there were a few things she needed to get rid of. A little housecleaning. She needed to banish the past *and* the present: too 3-D. The only survivor would be the future. The past was a quagmire, the present a nightmarish fraud. *Had to be.* The *future* was the promised land—the land of Maitreya, the Fifth Buddha, "The Future Buddha" . . . To save herself from the unbearable anguish of the present—present imperfect tense—*present impermanent*—Kelly had to take up residence in the future: *future perfect permanent.* The present, once venerated while she was an ecstatic, card-carrying member of the notorious All-We-Have-Is-This-This-Moment! cult, had been stuffed in the recycle bin along with its jealous, immutable, implacable shadow, the past.

My wife pulled the plug on the Power of Now.

I knew what Kelly was doing, Bruce. See, the future was the only place we could breathe. It was the only timespace that hadn't been compromised because it had never happened, never *would*, and we, its impassioned converts, became zealous phantom-footed soldiers in the world of what-will-but-never-will-be. The past needed to be erased, deleted, a heroic task that could only be accomplished by order of law—Ryder's Law. (The legislation bore his name but it was Kelly who pushed it through the house.) There was a certain genius to the idea . . . because how could we be *expected* to live in the past, that time in which our son would always live and always die? The past itself was always dead or dying and being reborn, it lived to be regurgitated by those unfortunates who were addicted to nostalgia—or worse, who chased after it in a castrated misery of rage, grief and hysteria, driven mad by the idea there was healing to be found if one could just pick through its vomit for a mirage of diamonds. The past was a bully-god, it *thrilled* to watch us fools throw fits onshore as it receded, dragging our sandcastles and unbreathing sons with it. The past put on an air of regal indifference yet was secretly boastful of its get-aways, its cowardice . . . the past was haughty and demented. And yet, the past was tormented too. The past was lustful and desirous, and had ambitions . . . the cross it bore was that it waited in futility to become the present, or at least marry it, each time getting infinitesimally close, unable to accept what it already knew: that its fate was of a bride doomed to be eternally jilted. The past was the angel fallen from the perceived para-dise of Now. (The real heaven—haven—was the future. But the past was blinded by its yearnings for the present.) Scorned, insulted, inconsolable, its monolithic, frozen-in-amber humil-ity inexorably turned to hubris, its acquiescence and sorrow to vengeful, perverted sadism. Its greatest strength—storehouse of all that ever was, seen and unseen—was its greatest weak-ness. For the past was vain. Kelly was of the opinion that the only way to annihilate it was by subterfuge. The past must be tricked into forgetting itself.

The present was defined solely by our son's searing absence. It felt like being on fire. A crush injury. You looked for him and he wasn't there. You'd hear him, smell him, *taste* him, but he wasn't there. You'd absolutely *know* he was but he wasn't. You saw children, children, children everywhere! An exquisite torture. Outside the window or on TV, being rude in the mall. Laughing and telling secrets to each other. (I always imagined they were talking about Ryder.) But my son wasn't there. You wanted to end the pain any way you could; always in the back of your head was that you could hang yourself too. For my wife and I, each second of every minute of every hour of Now was like a cold slap, a pinch to the cheeks of an unconscious prisoner who awakens only to realize he's about to be executed. Apparently, the human animal is poorly designed for mourning . . .

Erasing the present was a tall order because Kelly had been indoctrinated for years to believe in its power and relevance. She'd come to believe the New-Age Now was all there is, was, could be. This fresh idea of invalidating the present was antithetical to the thinking of her people, the Buddhists. It was heretical! Their whole raison d'être, as I'm sure you're aware, is the wisdom brought by living in the moment.

Obliterating the past was one thing—the numbness of serotonin depletion would help take care of that—but knocking the *present* out of the box required a bit of fancy footwork. For Kelly, the past wasn't really a problem anymore. She had bludgeoned it into amnesia and made it drink its own poison. Not only had the past forgotten itself, it had forgotten what forgetting was. Besides, Ryder hadn't died in the past, he was *continuously dying in the present.* And so, next on the agenda was to assassinate the Now. My wife did a little visualization. (Whatever works.) She saw salmon going upstream . . . the stream being the past and the salmon being the present, *but only while they were in the water*—are you following me?—the minute the salmon jumped into the sky, they were out of the Now and living in the future. *Frolicking.* Though that isn't really accurate . . . bear with me. What I meant was—what *Kelly* meant—is that when the salmon leave the water, they aren't just *in* the future, they *are* the future. Okay? Does that make it clearer? Try visualizing one of those Eschers with the braided flying fishes. As long as Kelly saw the fish suspended in air, as long as she held the *visual* of them arcing from the water, that was the future. If she could hold that image in her head then she could be in the future *with* them. She could stay in the future. I'm trying to let you—to convey what it was like to be in our heads. In *her* head, because I knew what was going on in there. Want a baseball analogy? Think of the future pinch-hitting for the past and the present. What we did was put the future up to bat—then froze the game. Called a permanent time-out. *That's* what we were going for . . . and the batter up was Ryder. Just do what Kelly did and picture a 12-year-old boy leaping from the water into the air toward whatever, toward *us*. He's on his way to us. Picture him in the air—*[mordantly]* not hanging, though, don't you dare!— picture him in the air, all goofy and sweet, and think: that little boy isn't *in* the future, he *is* the future. He's no longer a prisoner of past or present . . . *he's a child of Maitreya.* Maitreya, the Future Buddha, up there in a cloud of unknowing, await- ing his moment to migrate to Earth, that unforeseen yet immi- nent time when the oceans shall shrink so that he may walk from continent to continent. You see, Maitreya's next in line after Gautama and is prophesied to arrive in a time of great darkness—and boy, had that time come! It could not have *been* any darker, not for us—Maitreya is due when the teachings of the dharma have been forgotten and Gautama's lost his mojo. Legend has it that Maitreya will bring the promise of Oneness. When Maitreya comes, there shall be no more fathers, mothers and daughters and sons. When Maitreya comes, there can be no loss of parents *or* children.

That's the legend of the Fifth Buddha . . .

. . . the salmon-catcher Maitreya.

But Kelly wasn't at peace. She kept noodling back to ground zero, obsessed that Ryder had to have overheard one of our Merlot-fueled, sardonically tabloid conversations about a San Quentin hanging, our death gossip mixing with his esoteric *anicca*/impermanence training like a bad drug combo—potentiating it—until it pushed him over the edge (of the chair). No point in trying to dissuade . . . I understood this was her *process*. Hate that word! I think that what she *really* needed was communion. See, in the weeks that followed our son's death, she'd wished him too far into the future, banished him too thoroughly. Whenever the anesthetic of grief temporarily wore off, she missed him desperately, unutterably, brutally, needed to see him again at any cost, even if that meant enduring the sumptuous torture of parsing her "involvement" in his death through the forensics of mental masturbation. It was totally nuts—like doing a crime lab spatter analysis of a Pollock painting.

So she walked and talked us through. We sat on the floor of the living room, lights low, as in a séance. As she began to speak, Kelly set the scene, placing us in the kitchen like figures in a diorama. Laying out the bogus scenarios . . .

"Okay, let's say we were in the kitchen talking about one of the hangings. And I've had a few glasses and I'm telling you how amazing these prisoners are, how *resourceful* they are—about the one who did it with an itty-bitty shoelace. Maybe Ryder was on his way to ask us something. And he hears something *provocative* and just stands there listening where we can't see him. Who knows for how long. And maybe it sounds like I was *complimenting* the suicide on his ingenuity. Let's say it happened, for argument's sake, that one of us saw Ryder out of the corner of our eye but didn't really pay attention. Saw him standing there but we're blocking it out. That's possible, isn't it? That something like that might have happened and we're blocking it out? That's why I'm saying we *really need to concentrate*, like those people they hypnotize who suddenly remember all the details of a crime. You know, what the suspect was wearing or the license plate of a car . . . You have to admit it's possible, Charley, isn't it? [I agreed that it was. What's a husband to do?] Let's say he maybe even walked in and *asked* about it and we're blocking *that* out too. Or maybe the phone rang and you went to answer and that's when Ryder walked in and I got distracted too, maybe poured myself another glass of wine . . . [She closed her eyes as if she was being hypnotized] And when I'm trying to picture—I can *see* him in my mind and I'm wondering how much he heard—but I'm still distracted . . . maybe he asks about—about that shoelace thing— and if he *did*, if he *did* ask, Charley, what do you think I would have said? What would I have told him? I've been thinking about this and I believe I know. I *know* what I would have said. I would have seen it as a teachable moment. I'd probably say something like—maybe I actually *did* say it—I'd have said something 'real,' you know, like, 'Honey, sometimes people are in so much pain in their lives that they make a *choice*. It's not a good choice, but it's *their* choice, and we need to respect that.' I might even have used 'honor' instead of respect. Honoring the choice to hang yourself! Charley, doesn't that sound like something I would have said? Or *might* have, if the situation came up? What a stupid, stupid thing! Why would I *say* something like that? Because I think I *would* have."

She went on like that, rewriting a back-to-the-future history that never happened. The horror was that this berserk exercise allowed rare moments of peace, affording brief sanctuary for us both because it gave me respite from the agony of watching her suffer. It conferred a time-out from the storm of the *event*—event horizon of our son's death—and any kind of escape was welcome, any brass ring placed around the black hole of our hearts from which no light would escape again. During the grace time provided by these dramatic re-creations, his tiny, dense solar mass somehow lifted off of her, allowing her briefly to be free.

> *Charley made some tea, and ruminated. After a few minutes, he sat down again. Instead of a joint, he lit a cigarette.*

But it was all horseshit. Truth be told, my wife wasn't *capable* of a teachable moment, not even retroactively! No, no, *no*. What pisses me off is that she lied to herself (and to me), *even in theory*. Because if Kelly would have said *anything* to Ryder about Mr. Shoelace, it would have been closer to "He was ready to leave his body. Maybe he'll come back as the mother of a prison warden!" She was too cowardly to own up to the hypothetical implications conjured by her worst fears. She would *never* have stopped at the prisoner making a "choice." That's a liberal sentiment but not a mad one. No—she would have been *aggressive*. Jesus, maybe I *do* think she's responsible! Some little part of me, anyway.

Because truth be told, she was so far up Buddhism's ass all you could see were her feet dangling! The paradox of it, the hypocrisy—and I swear I'm trying not to be a cunt, Bruce, but I'm still angry about a lot of this, angrier than I realized—which is why it's good I'm rehashing everything, because it's probably going to be more helpful to me than I know—the hypocrisy was that the deeper she got in her practice, the more kudos the roshis and sangha threw at her, the greater her instincts were to blindfold Ryder to the realities of everyday life. A kind of insanity, to do that to a kid. But I was blind too . . . I was—*am*—culpable. Allow me to elucidate how that *teachable moment* (another phrase on my Top Ten Hit List) would have gone down. And I fully understand that what I'm about to say makes me a co-conspirator, a participant anyway, in her neurotic theorizing. There is absolutely no doubt in my mind that if given the chance, Kelly would have chosen to refract Mr. Shoelace through the lens of *maya*, that tiresome golden oldie. The ol' dance of illusion. She was up to her hips in prison dharmaworld, the "Path of Freedom," and whatever else her crafty Jewish rinpoches gave counsel. "Ryder, that prisoner has been *liberated*!" would have been more her style—a party line knee-jerk diluting of the depressing savagery of such a violent, hopeless act.

Her head was beginning to clear. A new voice—the voice of the quote-unquote "real"!—the voice of self-preservation—began to insist, *demand*, she cleave toward a revisionist Buddhist *weltanschauung*, that of permanence. Bald-faced, plain-dealing, square-shooting Permanence, a concept she once considered not just bourgeois but fascist. If she was going to find the antidote for the fatal damage caused by indoctrinating our little boy in the we-shed-our-bodies-like-old-garments shtick, she would need to dip more than just a toe in Permanence Lake. Like the time-traveler who changed the course of history by stepping on a butterfly, so did Kelly want to arrest Ryder's death by substituting a triple-decker reality sandwich for the wheatgrass and tofu of passive-aggressive homicidal

Zen platitudes. She had to flush out all the from-the-world-of-the-senses bullshit—"From the world of the senses comes heat and cold, pleasure and pain. They are transient. Rise above them, Grasshopper!" She no longer had the stomach for answering our son's (imaginary) thorny but simple questions about death—by hanging—with the bloodless, casual koans of an entitled urban sun salutator who paused during walking meditation to pluck Dzogchen daisy petals—*it's permanent . . . it's permanent not . . . it's permanent . . .*—until the whole random holocaust of the world was hushed up, tucked in, brushed under, sanitized and Shambhala'd away. My wife now needed to adamantly believe that her "teachable moment" had or would have conveyed the wisdom that life was precious and that she wanted him to live to a ripe old age . . . but knew that she *hadn't* or *wouldn't have* answered in such a way, and that gaping hole in his education could only mean she had killed him. So there was no alternative other than to alter everything that came before, tweaking her teachings, her memory, her very self, so at least she could draw comfort that she'd done no harm. *Do no harm*—that's Eightfold Path 101. Kelly had to submit to an Extreme Makeover because if she didn't, it would mean that Ryder, with his keen intelligence, would have embraced the corollary: Mr. Shoelace had rapturously shed his old garments and *Gone Fishin'* with all the other liberated beings—*not* snapped his own neck on the night he was gang-raped and sold!

Kelly stepped up her pitiful attempt to derail a train already at rest at the uncrowded station of its destination. She became a high priestess of necromancy. She put on proleptic operettas, as if Ryder could be kept alive—*was* alive—by their stagings. Variation upon variation of impossible possible

scenarios unfolded in the altered future of the past. She splin-
tered amber and bid the fossils dance to a tense, grieving,
bipolar shitstorm of tenses: past perfects were perverted,
bare infinitives laid bare, conditionals unconditionally loved.
So sad! In a Hail Mary, she staged a coup to restore democ-
racy, backing the impoverished, exiled leader that was her
old, has-been self: she would oust the ambitious, humorless,
dharma-thumping, girl-fucking Ashtanga dictator, and restore
to power the straight-up, samsara-loving woman of the people who got toppled in her mid-30s. She had a hunch she
could be saved—*he* could be saved—we *all* would be saved by
past-imperfect Kelly, she of the fine eye for antiques and other
permanent things, she who believed in mortal sin and taking
responsibility for the consequences of one's actions. She who
had no truck with the Ganesha in the room with its prayer
flags and banners of evanescence . . . the *old* Kelly had no
compulsion to acknowledge or worship that tired old circus
elephant, let alone sweep up its shit.

With sick, outlandish ferocity my wife composed a speech
she never gave, fantasizing that it might have had the power
to prevent him from stepping off the chair. As she began to
lose her mind, she paced the rug while votive candles burned,
reconstructing and reenacting, talking in articulate, disartic-
ulated tongues.

> *"People kill themselves, Ryder, they do, but it's a horrible*
> *thing! A taboo! They believe they're escaping the world*
> *but the truth of it is that they're actually going to Hell to*
> *be tortured by their enemies! Ryder, God punishes those*
> *who take their own lives or even try to! If I ever see you*
> *fooling around with a rope—listen: I know I gave you*

information that was challenging—'sophisticated'—but it was supposed to be theoretical, it was Buddhist theory and wasn't meant for everyday life! It was wrong of me, wrong, wrong, wrong! Now I'm going to give you another teaching, the teaching of all teachings! A powerful, secret transmission possessed by only the highest of Masters! Are you ready? Are you ready to hear? Because if you love your mother, this is the teaching you will follow—this is the teaching that is law! The secret teaching is that Permanence rocks! Ryder, do you understand? Permanence! Permanence is the right and natural cosmic law! Even impermanence is permanent! Do you understand? Permanence rocks! Say it, Ryder! Say it! Say it! Say it!"

Within her euphoric derangement—Dr. Bravo came to the house and gave her something for sleep, we were just about to commit her but she was a little better the next day and he said another stay in the hospital might not be such a great idea, he didn't like the idea of her getting acclimated to institutions and said we should try to put it off and I was actually glad we did, even though it was scary touch-and-go—in this fugue state Kelly thought that if she could only be stern, forceful, *parental*, if she could rewrite the indelible, just *maybe* there'd be a chance Ryder might be granted a stay, and allowed to be something other than dead. Even in diminished capacity— she'd take him anyway she could—

Please, Lord Buddha . . . I have failed the Fourth Noble Truth, for I suffer! I suffer so! I am attached . . . But Lord Buddha! Cessation of suffering is only attainable if my son should live!

She was moonstruck. A hair away from a 5150—that's a 72-hour hold. She told us that if Ryder was unpersuaded then at least maybe he could tell her—or *me*, or the *doctor*—*someone*—anyone!—*just what it was that he wanted*, what maybe *he* knew but no one *else* did . . . whatever the thing is that would allow him to live. To be alive in some way. She was determined to get resolution if it killed her. Which it already had. Would. Will?

Had . . .

O Bruce, how sad! How sad and unjust! In the day and the night she looped back to the living room to resume her hopeless, abstract disinterment: back to the future and forward to the past—I am telling you, it broke my heart. It was like watching a wildlife documentary of an elephant trying to nudge its stillborn calf to life with her trunk. Before she finally collapsed, the whacked-out musings came in a torrent as she fumbled and burrowed and downshifted, tenderly redacting her teachable moment . . . *Ryder, sometimes when people are in lots of pain, they—well, sometimes—if a person had cancer and was in a hospice—the Dalai Lama said that if the pain of a cancer or someone burned in a fire, then—then it's the choice of that person. But this is something very extreme. And irreversible! If Mommy or Daddy ever got sick, or even if you got very sick, this is not a path we would choose, darling! Because we have each other, and our love would see us through. And I know we've talked a lot about impermanence and rebirth but what is meant by that, what the Buddhists mean is that even a rock is considered impermanent, though a rock can live for thousands of years! I want you to know that life is precious and the main teachings of the Buddha are that birth in a human body—not animal, preta, Hell—is a rarity and a great privilege, and each of us have the sacred responsibility to live our lives joyously, to the end!*—suddenly stammering in recognition that she'd already been over this ground, feeling the weight of Ryder kicking at her stomach, not from inside, but from out, trying to climb back in so his rebirth could begin—again—wincing as she heard those imaginary words escape her doomed mouth—*no!* The contortions of her logic were already losing their power to distract and to numb, like heroin that'd been stepped on too many times. Everything was too much and too soon, death *and* life, wasn't there something between the two? (A bardo?) Wasn't there supposed to be? Because she wanted nothing to do with either of them. Only in deep sleep came the solace of pure, untrammeled conscious-ness . . . the house that gave shelter now sheltered no more, the food that gave sustenance no longer sustained, the glass of water once celebrated for its elegance and life-giving beauty was now a draught of poison. The crisp chimney-smoked air, redolent of winter, manna for breath meditation, had become sulphurous and mocking as the last gasp of her fanciful, pho-ney TMs—*teachable moments*—came crashing down around her without warning.

She was overwhelmed by nameless dread.

Words!

—the words of friends' and neighbors' condolences left her on the floor with multiple stab wounds, only made worse by words of my own, when *I* consoled with some random anodyne assholism, cool rag of banalities pressed against her mutilated forehead to help her through a rough patch. My poor, poor wife.

It was true. HRH 14—the Dalai Lama—*had* said that in certain instances self-murder was A-OK. So Kelly, engines failing, overthrew the notion of *reckless playfulness ending in tragic accident* and gave suicide a shot. Reluctantly embracing the monster rally factoid of it, she tried to accept sponsorship

of the idea that the highest of Buddhist authorities had ultimately condoned the act. Only trouble being, Ryder hadn't
been sick. Hadn't even been in any observable pain, psychic
or physical. Nope. Ryder was boyish, seraphic, rambunctious,
enthralled . . .

Gone Fishin'!

As I said, the shrink sedated her. She slept for 36 hours
and seemed much better. A postmortem honeymoon period
ensued. For a week or so, we couldn't stop talking, but in a
good way. Real chatterboxes. A freaky, hypomanic phase, like
being back in college taking speed to cram for exams. O, we
had mourning sickness (with a "u") for sure! We vomited, met-
aphorically and not, and when that was done, like after peyote—ever eat peyote?—that's when the magic began. Being
in our bodies, being in the world, was some kind of insane
kick. It was almost like we were discovering them for the first
time, no, maybe more like interlopers, those old Hollywood
movies where angels come to Earth and are amazed to have
bodies again. Or with psilocybin, when you get that insight
that the mushroom has taken *you* so it can see the world
through human eyes . . . It was *funny*. Even taking shits had us
in stitches! It was a way of being with Ryder too, as if the three
of us were already in the bodiless regions and Kelly and I just
came down temporarily, to revisit what a hoot and a comedy—
what a divine *travesty* it was to have a body, we were on spring
break but would return to our boy after a long carnal weekend. Good times! I think we had entered this weird labile stage
of loss where everything was so surreal it felt antic: we had
crossword puzzle showdowns, we painted little masterpieces,
we polished silver crap we didn't even know we had, cooked
dinner at 4 a.m. in formal dress . . . told forgotten, complicated

jokes and recited the first and last names of ancient homeroom geeks. We tried on distractions, competitive channel-surfed with dueling remotes, indulged in klieg-lit nighttime gardening, built ingenious Rube Goldberg devices. It felt zany and *erotic*—overheated teenagers in a seizure of shoplifting. In fact, it *got* erotic. We fucked again, just once. And that was . . . sad. For a while anyway and then it got funny again. *Really* funny. We were in a frenzy that we had no desire to name or explain. *Couldn't* explain. Just we happy two. And we had these—we experienced these *moments* of supreme, supernatural, grief-free giddiness! It was so awesome. In those fucked-up days, without knowing, my wife and I probably got pretty close to *getting* it—the formless form/gateless gate scam, the whole *bull-shitless bullshit*, "non-returning" Pure Abode–dwelling *anagami* rap—'cause something way outside of ourselves was forcing our hand. Talk about your unsolicited crash course in enlightenment! (And boy, *did* we crash. But that wasn't till a week later.) We got *out there*, like those airplanes that almost make it to space. Where the pilot sees the stars and the blackness just beyond the atmosphere?

The Theory of Relativity proved you would come back younger from a voyage to the stars, right? I think even when you come back from New York on JetBlue, you're technically younger. Infinitesimally so—but hell, I'll take it. Have to. It's like that old line about pregnancy—you can't be a little bit pregnant. You either come back younger or you don't. So we went through this phase, got our degrees in the jitterbugology of Death. We blew through verbiage, waving words like the man who waved his whisk before God, as the Sufi wiseguy once said. Danced our jive asses off to Motown . . . *how it can dance!* Had Ryder dancing with us too, we each held one of his little absent hands though that was tough because, see, the three of us actually used to do that, had our sweaty, popcorn'd *Soul Train–American Bandstand* Saturday nights. But Kelly and me danced through it, pretended Ryder was there, full-on boogie'd with and acknowledged him. I was the coach, Ryder the quarterback, and Kelly the head cheerleader for Team Zombie. O yes—the walking *and* dancing dead.

Dead man meditating . . .

Then one day it was over. Guess you had to have been there. You know, I learned a lot from Kelly. She was magnificent. I don't think that's been adequately conveyed in the few hours we've spent. Kelly was simply magnificent.

About a week after Ryder died, I spoke to a friend who lost his kid two decades back. He said the hard part came after the wake, when friends stopped bringing food and folks stopped calling, to give you your space. Or because they didn't know what to say or whatever. "These are the good times," he said. "Savor it."

The irony is that the death of our son was his teachable moment to *her*. But I think she's going to have to wait a long time to learn its lesson. Hopefully, she'll get it, at the TM of her own death: the lesson of Impermanence.

* * *

There's a marvelous little story that Sir Richard Burton recounts in his *Anatomy of Melancholy*. That book didn't leave my side for three years after we lost our son.

A young man, disconsolate over his debts, saw no way out. He went into an abandoned shack to hang himself. He'd already tied the rope on a rafter when something caught his eye. He went over to a caved-in closet to investigate and found a trove of gold coins. It was meant to be hidden but a rotting beam had broken under its weight. He couldn't believe his reversal of fortune. He crept away with the treasure chest under his arm. A while later, another young man entered the shack. When he saw that the treasure that he'd hidden was gone, he used the rope left behind to hang himself. Isn't that lovely? Like something from Boccaccio.

I hope you don't think it too strange, my telling that. I'll tell you why I did. Have you ever had a bad breakup? Or unrequited love? And when it's over, you keep thinking you see their car? You see it everywhere: on the freeway, in parking lots, in front of you, behind. You see it in your dreams . . . I did that for years once. I even knew it wasn't his car anymore, someone told me he'd bought a new one but there I was, trapped in time, still on the lookout for a yellow Corolla with a dent on the passenger door. Couldn't help myself. It's like that for me and hangings now. Whenever I read about one in the paper . . . I've got a book of clippings. Maybe that's carrying it too far. I don't do the tarot anymore. For some reason, I shy away from the Hanged Man, though I'm a real fan of upside-down crucifixions. St. Peter and all. Go figure.

What can I say? There's perverse comfort in it. I don't know the psychology. There's a hidden fraternity, you'd be surprised, of people whose loved ones hanged themselves. And folks like me, who *found* them. Thank God for the Internet.

He laughed, smiled to himself, then placed his hands together in his lap and closed his eyes like a guru who was done for the day. I took the liberty of boiling water for tea but in a few minutes he broke free of his thoughts and leapt

beside me. "No no, don't fuss with that. You've listened so
patiently that a parting cup of tea is the least I could do."
We drank in relative silence, with Charley resuming the
lotus position. A pleasant smile of what I took for catharsis
suffused his features. He asked me a few questions about
where I was going next, when I thought the anthology
would be published, and so forth.

I was in my car and halfway down the winding
hill when he appeared, out of breath. He looked not so
much anguished as startled. I asked what was wrong.
He said he'd left something out—"a rather crucial
last piece of business. I'd kick myself if I never told
you, whether you decide to include it or not." I told
him I would turn around but he said the afternoon's
talk had exhausted him. He apologized again for any
inconvenience, offering two choices: tomorrow—here
at lunchtime—or later on at 2 a.m. when the baths at
Esalen open. It appealed to me to end our encounter at
the place it had begun.

The superb night was cold and crystalline, and made
me think about his comment of the pilots who get so close
to the stars and the blackness—and about Big Sur being
a place where one cannot expect to be healed. Only one
other person was in the tub; she got out and nodded to us
in leavetaking, a cue to begin. Then she was gone.

I told you I wouldn't hold back and I meant it. What I'm about
to tell you may sound egregious or vulgar—TMI alert!

Here goes.

I think pretty much everyone knows that a hanged man
gets a hard-on. Most of us have heard it before, somewhere

or other. Wikipedia calls it "angel lust" but you never really know what's a bullshit Wiki entry and what isn't. Someone could have heard "angel lust" on *Grey's Anatomy*, which means it may or may not have been made up by smartass Hollywood writers. So pretty soon you've got fake entries in there that look real and maybe even *become* real if they catch on. Somebody could have put "angel lust" in there and it's bogus but the wikitectives haven't caught it yet or maybe never will until it's actually entered the vernacular. In which case, it'd stay on Wiki anyway. At any rate, it was true with my son. He got a hard-on. Or *had* one when I found him. The death erection, what they call a "terminal" erection. I've studied up on this a little—I mean, since. When a man is hanged, he gets hard and sometimes climaxes. Of course as his dad I saw his penis in every way, shape and form—you change the diapers and see an adorable stiffie, a *confection*, you want to take a bite! A terminal confection. Kelly and I would joke about it, I think that's probably something most parents do, you could see the purple vein, he'd pee straight up, oh do all *kinds* of things. It seems to me that in the delirium of the moment, my son hanging from the rope and me lifting him, hefting the weight of him, that infernal dance of ours frozen in time, tadpole thickened to anemonesized tentacle by the hanging trauma, its familiar now very *unfamiliar* purple vein not a rebuke but a wild reminder of God, that now Ryder wildly belonged to God—*I* wasn't aroused, Lord no, never, more like a frightened boy myself, making up for my shyness by clutching a tall girl at a cotillion dance, holding on too tight—what a simple heartbreak scene drawn in my head forevermore! His little balls made a horizontal 8, the Infinity sign, I saw *myself* as a boy just his age, see myself now as we talk, skittish child-victim of the clergy cotillion—there's my *son*, dead, hard—helplessly, *incognizantly* aroused by his yanked, roughshod transition to boodafield . . .

I've never told anyone that.

He wrapped himself in a towel and retrieved a cassette recorder from the backpack on a nearby bench. Back in the tub, taking care to hold it out of harm's way, he played a tape of his wife reading a Ravidas poem to their son. Her voice was lovely, carefree.

It's just a clay puppet, but how it can dance!
It looks here, looks there, listens and talks,
          races off this way and that;
It comes on something and it swells with pride,
          but if fortune fades it starts to cry.
It gets tangled in its lusts, in tastes
          of mind, word, and deed,
and then it meets its end and takes some other form.
Brother, says Ravidas, the world's a game, a magic show,
          and I'm in love with the gamester,
          the magician who makes it go.

He swathed the tape recorder in a towel and without getting up from the tub, set it on the ground. Then he resumed, with an enigmatic smile.

I was at a flea market in Sebastopol and came across an unusual item, the report of the Truth and Reconciliation Commission of South Africa. There's a lot of volumes and the three I laid my hands on now make their home in the van. There was a story in there of a young student the police detained. I can't remember why he was arrested, but I doubt if the punishment—injection of chemicals into his feet—fit the crime. After a few days, he was stripped naked and fitted with a hood so he couldn't see. Imagine his fear as they began pouring liquid onto his body! It was only milk and the policemen tried not to laugh . . . they brought in a calf that sucked the milk on his penis. One of the priests used to do that to me with honey, sans blindfolds. And I'd do it to him. On camping trips, he'd smear honey on himself and ask me to lick it off. (For some reason, he was in the habit of asking politely. Being polite probably turned him on.) Do you know what the sonofabitch used to say? That I should imagine his bunghole as Christ's wedding ring and the deeper I got my finger and tongue, the stronger was my marriage to the Savior. O, he was a great wit. He used to say, most *impolitely*, "It is easier for a little faggot to pass through the hole of a man of God than it is for a girl to enter the Kingdom of Heaven." When he went down on me, that hot mouth felt like the guts of some dying animal. Felt *great*. Awful to admit, but true. You could smell his dirty breath when he talked, right through his nostrils . . . hygiene was never a strong suit with the prelates. I have come to believe—no pun intended!— that the more flagrant the sacrilege, the greater the orgasm all around. I never let him know I was horny, always acted like he was hurting me. He knew I was putting on an act. He knew that I knew that *he* knew, which became our covenant. And that it felt good, his mouth, my mouth, our whatever, became a covenant between me and God, for how could there not be godliness in such a feeling? I remember so clearly the sound of the birds singing their indifferent song while he worked on me, I heard the scratchings of the leafless branches of court-yard trees as if the Lord Himself was at the door, impatiently waiting to be let in.

Now, my lust is *wanderlust*—I visit rocky coast and chap-arral, hermitage and open road, to reacquaint myself with all things beautiful that they tried to destroy.

You know the story of Saturn, don't you? Saturn castrated his father, oh yes, then married his sister. Talk about your dys-functional family. It was foretold he'd be dethroned by one of his sons. So what did he do? What any self-respecting God *would*: ate 'em all up at birth, like bonbons. Eventually, Rhea—his sister-wife—got a little tired of the drama. When it came time to feed him Baby Boy No. 6—that would be Jupiter—she swaddled a rock in blankets and he swallowed that instead. I guess gods know pretty much everything but still have trouble when it comes to spotting the difference between newborns and wrapped-up rocks. So the sister hid Jupiter away. You know, those oracles never made bum predictions. The gods were really dumb that way too. They never seemed to catch on that the oracles were always right.

There's a painting by Goya, part of what they call the "black paintings." They were done directly on the walls of his house, kind of in secret. None were commissioned or even meant to be seen. The most famous is *Saturn Devouring His Son*. Goya didn't name it that, someone else did. All the black paintings were untitled because they weren't meant for the public, they were for his eyes only. Well, it's an absolutely *fiendish* painting. He's just laying into this—Saturn's delightedly laying into this little *man*—taking big bites out of this—this *torso with legs*—the eyes are bulging in Daddy Dearest's head, I am telling you,

Bruce, it will make you shiver! Go online when you have a chance and take a look. By the time he did the black paintings, Goya was old and deaf. See, in the privacy of his own home he could just let it rip, God bless him. But here's why I brought it up, this is what most people don't know. You see, there were *photographs* taken before those paintings were transferred to canvas. Now remember, these murals were painted on plaster, on the plaster walls of his house and the experts took pictures before they moved them to the Prado. No one knows where the photographs are *now*, of course, but it's fairly common knowledge the government destroyed them. The thing is, there's still a few people living who *wrote* about what they saw—in the photos—and *they* say Saturn had an *erection*—Goya painted Saturn fully aroused as he ate his kid! Which makes perfect sense, at least to me. Which was totally suppressed, you know, for the "greater" good. Whitewashed. Literally. God *knows* how many hands those photos passed through. How many busybody committees, how many bourgeois arbiters of taste who ruled that such a thing would be too *scandalous*. Mustn't threaten tourism with a *scandale*!

By the time it got to the museum, the hard-on was painted over.

Ryder died in December, on a Saturday. That's a double Saturn. He was born in December too. Not favorable. Gloomy—bitter—cold—saturnine. None of which of course describes my son. Sometimes Ouroboros, the serpent that devours its tail, is a symbol used for Saturn. Ouroboros: the "O" sign. Remember that? The snakehead—or tail—even makes a little bulge in the "O," changing it to a "Q"—tongue lolling from mouth. Funny, huh? So Saturn devours his son, *deflowers* his son; Saturn eats his own tail . . . eats the thing he made, the thing-at-its-beginning, the thing-he-once-was. Everything comes full circle. Or so we like to think.

But wouldn't it be funny if everything didn't?

In the months after he died, I dreamt of waves, tall as buildings. Big Sur waves. I was drowning in them, with sick priests floating all around like goblins, or stuck to me like leeches, gobble-gobbling me up, licking my flat tits—

[recites]
And God did not make death
He did not make pain
But the little blind fire
that leaps from one wound into another
knitting the broken bones
and fixing the broken bones
and fixing sins so they cannot be forgotten.
I will obey my nurse who keeps this fire
deep in her wounded breast
for God did not make death—

* * *

As I said, Kelly's living on the edge of her sister's land, in Calgary.

A cabin; she lives in a cabin.

Her sister worries about her incessantly.

There is a field there, and I'm told she sometimes wanders in it.

But my wife never strays too far from the cabin.

SECOND GURU

*T*he next story was told to me in the desert of New Mexico, over five days.

Our sessions took place at night, under an ecclesiastical cope of stars. Queenie spent her days submerged in a profusion of journals and diaries (whose keeping was a lifelong habit; she revisited them in order to refresh her memory "so as to maximize our time"). Many of those writings were almost thirty years old. She made use of other source material as well and in the course of the story reveals how she came upon it. I make note of this to help explain what might otherwise be taken for superhuman powers of reflection. That said, she freely admitted she had no qualms extemporizing, if it helped her cause, i.e., advancing the story or to more accurately convey a mood or a message.

Before we begin, there are two things important to note. "Second Guru" actually preceded "First Guru" in the telling. The chronological order of our diptych has been reversed for reasons it is hoped will be clear to the reader at the end. Secondly, the storyteller had been grievously wounded in love, which was why she had taken to the road.

When I came across this formidable woman, she was traveling in an imposing black bus with a full staff and every creature comfort one could imagine (and some that one couldn't). In a droll tip of the hat to a storied bus of the '60s, the destination above the windshield read "Father" not "Furthur." Queenie wore kohl around her eyes *and elaborately tailored gypsy dresses that were as dark as her land schooner, with the occasional splash of tie-dyed color: half–Zaha Hadid, half–Stevie Nicks. She said she was in the midst of searching for a lost city that was rumored to have the power to reunite couples that had been separated by calamity, farce—even death.*

I hope one day to be reunited with her myself, for maybe that story too will one day ask to be told.

A single, massive *bhakti** movement had been gathering force in other parts of India for a millennium. A favorite Sanskrit passage personifies it as a lovely woman who was born in the south, gained strength and maturity in the middle regions of the west, grew decrepit—and was revived to experience her full flowering when she reached the north . . .

—*John Stratton Hawley*

---

* Passionate love of God

The following interview took place in October 2005 and was redacted in the summer of 2013.

How does a story begin?

    With the simplicity of situating it in time—anyhow, that's one way . . .

    Very well: it wasn't too long ago, in the fall of 1997. I was living in Manhattan in a triplex penthouse overlooking Central Park, on 110th Street. My humble abode came complete with ballroom, landscaped terraces (one with infinity pool) and a small orchard guarded by a rooftop of gargoyles I'd become quite intimate with, having become one myself. The property belonged to my grandfather—or rather, his investment firm— rumor being it was once in the hands of a shadowy Jewish cabal of financial consultants to the Vatican. I was 47 years old and going through the mother of all depressions. I'd been out to sea too long and washed up on impotent shores. In my youth, I was a voraciously curious girl, an exotic wild child who cut a swath through all manner of New Age modalities. At the time, my mind/body explorations were thorough enough to have banished the need (or desire) to learn anything more. It was my modest opinion that I'd achieved a hard-fought measure of wisdom. Unfortunately, the moment such a thing is impetuously declaimed in one's youth, even *sotto voce*, one acquires a nasty virus which lays dormant until awakened by the cue of that sometimes-fatal season, middle age.

I never thought I'd need access to that bewitching witch doctor world again. But there I was, all grown up and fighting for my life. It was *heal thyself* redux. I plugged in to the corporatized, kickass machine of Self-Help America, encompassing every spiritual, homeopathic, energetic practice known to man, goddess and horse (cf. *equine holistic healing*): magnetic therapy, tantric breath work, biofeedback, EMDR, Somatic Experiencing, marathon meditating, fungal scanning, sweat lodging, Adderall XR, Feldenkrais, Tensegrity, DBT, DMT, colloidal silver, craniosacral/chakra detox, Roman Catholicism, Reiki, Kabala and cancer-sniffing dogs, liposuction, ayahuasca, Watsu, What-The-Fuck, Qigong (it's been good to know you), polarity, ibogaine, candidal querying, Munay-Ki, angel therapy, singing bowls, flushing bowels, benzos and botulinum rejuvenation, Lyme disease dowsing, karma purification, cheap Thai massage, Third Eye vortexing, Lamictal, SSRIs, Christian Wholistics, Christian Louboutin, GABA, MDMA, AA, heroin, hypnotherapy, hysterectomy—

Then I ran out of time . . . or time ran out on me.

Yes, that's better.

I was jilted by Time.

It was with more than a little fear that I realized help was definitely *not* on the way. I confined myself to quarters, false messiahs having dwindled to hormone replacement therapy, 450 milligrams of Wellbutrin *q.d.* and a hundred mgs of Seroquel, PRN.

I read all the books on depression and came to the disgruntled conclusion they were just another venal publishing cycle perennial, always given a clever "fall release" (to capitalize on those legions with SAD—Seasonal Affective Disorder) and gussied up in literary clothing—when the smarmy truth of it is that "blues porn" found its way to the shelves and talk shows with the same calculated predictability as addiction memoirs and diet books. And why shouldn't it be so? Why did I think the genre was sacrosanct? Still, it rankled. The *quality* of blues porn always fell so far off the mark. Styron was the pioneer—*Darkness Visible* became the gold standard and I didn't like *his* book, either. The depression mavens just couldn't be trusted. It was my opinion that what the monks called "the noonday demon" was best served by my own customized definition:

> **de·pres·sion** : a feverish oscillation between sorrow and remorse, simultaneously inducing *grisly* numbness and the too-real sensation one is hurtling into the abyss.

* * *

It was a melancholy Monday.

I was doing my daily exercises, panting on the treadmill of obliteration fantasies that kept me sane. These included selecting which of the twelve terraces would be the one I chose to leap from after lunch. To keep myself interested, I pictured exactly *how* I'd make that jump, and what my body would be doing during the fall. In my imaginings, it might take the form of a clean corkscrew, belly flop or spectacular swan. Inspiration struck when least expected. My head would rummage around and surprise me with a long-forgotten defenestration from Pasolini's *Salò*—the piano player, having seen

enough perversion and murder, steps off the balustrade with
the eerie sangfroid of a maid dusting a sofa. I imagined one of
my housekeepers catching (or not catching) my fall from the
corner of her eye and promptly fainting. I saw myself flail-
ing, a silent film of windmilling arms, gravity rushing me into
the Lord of Pavement's arms. These musings never failed to
mischievously include a horrified gallery of sidewalk gawk-
ers, some of whom impossibly watched my leap from its very
beginning, and others whose heads whipped 'round at the
explosion of metal, glass and bone-spray.

The comic relief provided by those arpeggios didn't last
very long. I'd surface to the pitiless present fast enough to get
the soul-sick bends, a rotten cork bobbing on dead calm
domestic seas, mocked by the distant hum of vacuuming
armies . . . I wouldn't really *surface*, though, not entirely. I felt
like a *spelunker*. Let me be more specific. Think of yourself as
a spelunker—join me in my nightmare, won't you? One who
scubas through uncharted cave waters. Cave divers, they call
them. You're running low on oxygen—perilously low—you're
not sure how that happened, but there it is. A bad valve in the
tank or a bad whatever. And when you realize this, you've
been swimming for a quarter of a mile. Some of these caves
are completely sealed off from each other, the only way they're
linked is by common waterway . . . and let's say you already
swam a quarter of a mile to get from one to the other, there's
no in-between, only an implacably hard ceiling of lava above
your head. You're running out of air and on the way back to
your point of origin when your lights fail, even your backup
lights, a perfect-storm kind of thing. A perfect shitstorm. You
try to get your bearings. You *think* you're still heading back to
that initial manhole that you lowered yourself from at the

beginning of your little adrenaline-junkie adventure. You were supposed to come with a friend but they bailed because their kid got sick. You decided to go anyway. You didn't tell them because you knew they would think that was a bone-head move and would just try to talk you out of it. So today, you're extra careful about your prep: you've checked and double-checked the *equipage*. And everything was going so well but now you're running out of air and there are *no* lights and the water's dark as a moonless midnight. There's no way to surface—nothing to do but go along laterally until the tube ends. You marshal your energy and say: *Okay. This is shitty but I can do this.* You really *believe* you're swimming toward where you started but can't be sure anymore. One of your feet feels funny and you reach back—you've lost a fin. *Not good.* You acknowledge a devilish voice that tells you you're righteously fucked, but because you're a pro—you've been doing this for 20 years, been in touchy situations before and always gotten out—whatever panic that arises is quickly tamped down by a reflexive athlete-warrior's confidence that soon you'll be out. Soon be savoring late afternoon sights, sounds and smells, throwing your gear into the backseat and talking with friends over wine and dinner about the already-legendary anecdotal hairiness of the day. Laughing about it . . . You see something faintly illuminated—a hole? phosphorescent lichen?—something in the distance that you jerkflutter toward with your one fin. You understand it's not your destination but right now you're a pilot who needs to land, you need a run-way, a clearing, anywhere, before the wings and wheels come off completely. You close in . . . it *is* a hole! You break surface. Remove the mouthpiece and inhale deep, germy draughts, a literal second wind—and with horror realize you've merely exchanged one darkness for another—darkness visible! That creepy, slamming doomsday sensation as the eyes adjust: *it's only an air pocket.* By habit, you put the mouthpiece back in so you can get the hell out of there then remember the tank's kaput. Done. You're done. By perfect satanic design, the short-lived promise of escape—and sweet familiarity of breathing uncylindered air—jump-started your adrenaline, heightened your faculties. The full understanding of your predicament comes with nauseating certainty: *sealed off.* Your head just above water, elbows resting on the hole's rocky rim to more or less comfortably keep it there—the rest of you wading in the grave. Now the other fin drops off too . . . *finito.* Somewhere into the void. *That fin is lucky,* you think. *That fin is already dead, was never alive, and now, at least, is free.* A moment of panic before instinct forces you to arch back your neck to create more space between you and the low ceiling of the pocket. Instinct requires the organism to seek more space or the illusion of more space. Heart hammering as your brain fritzes in the effort to solve an insoluble problem, instinct/habit makes you grab that useless mouthpiece again. You even keep it in your mouth a moment, as if to give yourself "distance" to help gather your wits. Sadly, there is no instinct that cleaves to the extinction of the entity it protects, no natural cyanidal impulse that shuts down systems in the face of certain annihilation, to allow one an easy (easier) death—no. (None of it is easy.) Only that relentless, dumb, primal imperative to save the organism at all costs, brain ordering neck to lean back on the fatal pillow of a slurried shelf, a brief truce before you drown. Nature has thoughtfully—*so thoughtful*—provided a small comfort cushion for your head on the available silt, an ergonomic bolster that *instinct* kindly arranges for you to make use of on your deathbed . . . nature and instinct, working together! The irony! Because at its terminus, the organism supercharges the integrity of its mandate: to survive at all cost (including death), to keep eyes and nose above the water *until the end*. Just doing its job . . . as when, with lightning speed, the animal—you—assayed the pocket's height to be 14 inches and change, a sidebar left brain measurement made in the instant after you first exuberantly, accidentally smacked the top of the cryptspace with your skull. Unforgiving, non-negotiable instinct then bid you retreat and regroup. Come: lay your head on this silty pillow to sort things out. *Come stay awhile.* One never knows how one will behave at the end but *this* ending is so hopeless, so monumentally lonesome and grotesque that it comes as a shock that you're still capable of logical thinking. Soon, you reason, hypoxia (and the attendant) hallucinations will put an end to my suffering. Not only is this true but its wise reiteration has the effect of soothing the panicked organism. (It was instinct that orchestrated that thought in the first place—instinct *needs* the organism to be calm because panic is the harbinger of erasure.) Resting on your sad pillow, waiting for your buddy-system pal hypoxia, you remember seeing a documentary about a man who survived falling overboard in a storm-tossed sea. He said there was a point when every cell in his body told him to *let go* . . . you draw succor from his words, and await such a directive. In your vertical, phone booth–like coffin, you berate yourself for having foolishly dived alone but self-recrimination is soon replaced by thoughts of your husband, your baby, a trip you once took to Poland and other random things, then wonder how long it will take to find your body or if it ever *would* be found and for some reason the idea of never being found makes you yelp like a dog accidentally stepped on by a party guest, nothing more pitiful than a human yelp, this one has a gasp thrown in and the yelp-gasp robs most of the remaining air, hastening your end—*no!* You get a fourth, an eighth, an eleventh wind! *Instinct* won't let go—won't let you go—yanking you to full awareness again. It slaps your cheeks and wants you alert, still wanting to save your life! Like the old joke about the patient dying but the operation being a success. *Again*, instinct arches your neck and bids you rest your head on the pillow. Instinct rallies, like a drowsy fly on a corpse. Instinct stage-whispers: *Hey! aren't you wondering where the light is coming from?* From the beginning, a pathetic amount of light lit up the pocket, "lit" too strong a word, still, enough to draw you toward it from the waterway, to your phone booth grave, because the nearly invisible alteration in color—from below, it was a dime-sized deep grayness amid the black—was enough to catch your reptilian eye. It's the end of the play; in the middle of your big death scene, instinct keeps interrupting from the wings, telling you—politely *asking*—to *please* make an effort or at least *consider* making an effort to dig or even *think* your way toward wherever that light is emanating. But your brain understands the feeble radiance is seeping from microscopic fissures in the rock. The brain overrules instinct's clownish, crude, surreal fantasies of ascent and escape, and won't let you take the bait. Your brain at last provides what it rarely seemed to, in life: dignity.

Her eyes filled with tears—the metaphor had transported her back to that time of severe depression. We took a 20-minute break then resumed. She seemed much refreshed.

When I'm in a normal frame of mind (ho ho! normal!) I'm actually quite capable of reveling—or wallowing, anyway—in the serene dullness of a familiar domestic landscape. But in the condition I was in *then*, it was those very things—hum of vacuum, chiding position of sun in the sky, sound of Spanish soap opera on kitchen TV—that held my feet to the flames. The more routine the trappings of my life became, the more banal, the more exquisite grew the pain. As the entry in my personal Devil's Dictionary says, the sensation of speeding toward the abyss—insanity—is the thing that gets you. That unstoppable velocity before hitting your head on the ceiling of the air pocket . . . I was reading about a method of torture the *narcos* use called "bone-tickling." They shove an ice pick in then click-and-drag. That I tickled my bones in the sanctuary of my own home was truly the devil's work.

I was sitting there stewing about all this shit when my flip phone chirped. No one was on the line. I did that stupid thing we do and said "Hello?" over and over. Then:

"Queenie?"

I floated through shamanic dreamtime.

"Do you know who this is?"

It was almost 30 years since I heard that voice yet it was as familiar to me as any of my gargoyle friends. (The way I was feeling just then, I'd have been more than pleased to hear one of *them* speak.)

Knowing *exactly*, I still gave his name an interrogatory wisp.

"Kura?"

He laughed that laugh and my underground caves flooded.

I know it's kind of one of those clichés (I have the feeling I'll be using a *lot* of them during this story, apologies in advance), but *this man actually saved my life.* Back when I was oscillating between my own madness and another's—*oooh!* To even *think* of that time before I met him absolutely makes me shudder, and to think of the time *when* we met . . . well, the woebegone part of me, the part whose head had been stuck for weeks in its 14-inch airspace, couldn't help but wonder if the man behind the voice would save me. Again.

"Wowee zowee," he said. (I hadn't heard *that* one in a while.) "Stanley meets Livingstone!"

I'd been thrust into the way-back machine—Kura's—where the cultural references were always a bit fusty.

"Though I have to say I didn't look for you quite as long as Stanley searched for the good doctor, which was less than a year, I believe. I found *you* in a week's time. Five business days to be exact."

"This number is eight hours old! How in the world—"

"My *Queen*, you've been an endless presence in my thoughts. I was so happy to learn things turned out well for you."

"They did? Someone forgot to tell me."

"Ho ho! You've kept your wit."

"While those about me were losing theirs."

Ho ho, ha ha.

Okay, so we bantered. I always had a thing for *The Lady Eve.*

"You outlived your parents, which for many years was an *iffy proposition*, no? You *routed* the executors in court. All of the attempts to rob you of what was rightfully yours—and they were formidable—failed *dismally.*"

"True. But that's a matter of public record."

I wasn't really in the mood for *This Is Your Life*, or the psychic TV routine either.

"Yes, it is. For the last few years, you've been depressed."

"Tell me something I don't know."

"How about if I tell you something you dare not utter, not even to *yourself* anymore?"

"Go for it."

"A woman broke your heart."

The wit and wind went out of me.

And I won't talk about any of that—not to you, or anyone. You just have to trust me when I tell you this is something *no one* could have known.

"Dear Queenie, I must tell you that 'more die of heartbreak' is a phrase which only applies to myth and storybook. You, precious girl, are a *survivor*."

I always hated that word.

I masked my emotions best as I could and said, "Well, that's comforting."

Kura laughed again. His voice was a few registers lower since I'd last heard it, accompanied by an echo of phlegm that hovered just shy of unfriendly, blurring the border of good health. His accent seemed to have thickened too yet somehow had rendered his English simpler and more precise.

All at once I grew nervous about the motive behind the call.

"Queenie," he said, "I don't have too much time."

Though I took it to mean "at this moment," I absorbed the poignancy of the remark. Then his speech took on a certain brusque, still delicate formality, as it always did when he got down to "brass tacks." (Kura had a weakness for archaic American idiom.)

"I wish to make you a proposal. Do you have time to listen?"

Another thing came rushing back: whenever Kura had something "heavy" to *lay on me*, as they used to say, he asked his wild child (who'd grown into a louche woman) if she had the time to listen. I did then—or fancied so—and I did now. Though I have to admit, "proposal" triggered an absurd millisecond fantasy he might ask for my hand.

"Tomorrow morning, at a little before 7:30 o'clock a.m., a Rolls-Royce Phantom will pull up to the kerb outside your building. A *black* Phantom, I may add."

He sniggered over that small, deliberate touch; the black phantom's black Phantom, whisking away a white wraith.

(He was actually more of a mocha phantom.)

"I know it's a bit early for you, unless your sleeping habits have changed—I stopped my man short of delving further. If you agree to what I propose, I ask you to appear outside *no later than eight*. I grant you a half-hour's grace!" Came the laugh, again; no need to rub my nose any further into the epic, pathological tardiness of years gone by. "When the driver catches sight of you—most likely, he'll be having a morning smoke— he shall go briefly rigid in that timeless salutation of the servant class, then flick his fag to the street, gather up your things, and *whisk* you to Teterboro, depositing you on the tarmac beside a private plane. *My* plane, at least for this particular *hajj*."

He pronounced the already sensual word as a lover would an intimate act, drawing it out like an exhalation of *hasheesh*— stratocumulus of perfumed smoke.

"It will be a long flight but I believe you'll find it *quite comfortable*. I know how important superior comfort is to my Queenie!"

And by the way, I couldn't remember the last time anyone called me that. I'd gone back to my birth name, Cassiopeia, in my mid-20s—she of the constellatory skies—and, as Kura once enlightened, the namesake of the legendary black queen that hailed from a region called Ethiopia.

"There shall be three pilots and two stewards looking after you, and a doctor onboard as well, though I'm certain he will remain well-hidden—unless of course you get lonesome and wish to chat him up, for he is at your service. The gentleman walks softly but carries a big syringe. Actually, he's bringing me some medicine; a *godawfully* expensive courier. I strongly doubt that you'll require his ministrations . . . not to worry! He's *very* good at tending to that once in a blue moon in-flight heart attack. O, he's absolutely *keen* on it. You might say it's his specialty!" The honeyed laugh, then avuncular advice: "My Queen, if you accept your old friend's mysterious invitation, I encourage you to pack a *very small bag* . . ." No need to rub my nose any further into the epic, pathological overpacking that was—still is—my predilection. *Je ne regrette rien.* "Anything you may possibly need shall be provided upon arrival. Bring nothing formal, as there shan't be any galas or social fêtes on *this* end. Why don't you come in your pj's? Isn't that a fine idea?"

I've lived too long not to know the human animal's universal default is a humbling insecurity. Fearless and resolute as he was by nature, Kura was unaccustomed to initiating a game whose results were uncertain. Ringing me up as he did after so many years was a risk outside of his comfort zone. He was wily enough to know that to presume I would say "yes" was an excellent way to court major disappointment. There were just too many variables. He could Sherlock around all he wanted but to suddenly be face-to-face— voice-to-voice—with the flesh and blood of a thing—*me*—fudged any predictable conclusions. I imagined that in weaker moments, parsing the rainbow of potential responses before he called (or even while we spoke), he must have shrugged his shoulders, conceding that the only leverage he had was *la nostalgie*.

He had reached out in desperation (and not a little mad- ness, knowing what I now know) and leapt into the void. Though a good part of him must have been certain that he had me, as the dreaded phrase goes, "from hello," I still felt him take my temperature during his pitch; but perhaps the trem- ulous bravado, the quaver in his voice, was indicative of ill- health. I was in the dark in that regard, having in that moment no idea what the man had endured in the decades we'd been apart—what transformations had occurred on the physical, psychic and spiritual planes. When I didn't push back, he was palpably relieved that his fall had been arrested.

"Throw a talisman in your Goyard duffle, Queenie! Something for luck—a mysterious *truffle*—we'll need it. Yes, we shall *need* a bit of luck. And, ah! I should add that there will be no danger in our errand."

He was being courtly, for he must have known he was the single person on Earth that I trusted most. Maybe courtly is the wrong word—our bond had been forged under the most savage, nearly fatal circumstances.

"I wouldn't want you to be dissuaded for fear an old flame might catch you on fire."

"I could think of worse ways to go."

In my mind, I was already on the tarmac. It gave me great pleasure to know that in just a few moments, he would hear my *assent* to flight. I was suffused by the overwhelming feeling that so much had been hard for Kura of late and dearly wanted him—wanted us both—to believe that with this one call, everything would now go his way. He'd saved *me* once— maybe now, I could return the favor.

We could all use a little Hormone Replacement Therapy, no?

"Do you mind if I ask where this plane is landing?"

I didn't care. But like a teenager with a crush, I suddenly wanted to keep him on the phone. Besides, there was nothing to lose by asking a few questions; we were officially going steady again.

"Of course, I don't mind. That much you deserve! But first you must say *yes*. It is important—*energetically*."

I Molly Bloom'd a breathless "Yes I said yes I will Yes" and the most glorious thunderclap of a laugh shook the Heavens, and my heart.

"You'll be arriving in *Delhi*, late afternoon. But we shall only be there overnight. The next morning, we leave for points north—the second leg of your journey."

"How many legs are there?"

"As many as a scarab's."

"How many is that?"

"For this, you must tell the computer to *Ask Jeeves*."

"And you won't say anything more until we meet. Correct?"

A dead quiet: it sounded like we lost our connection. In the split seconds that followed, I panicked, wondering if he'd call back . . . and if not, whether the velocity of madness would return with speedier vengeance. Might it begin with a rumor the call was a black phantom of my imagination? No doubt the result of striking my head against the roof of that underground grave . . .

Perhaps when I opened my eyes I'd be balancing atop a ledge watched over by my beloved gargoyles, a crowd of people below urging me on—

I heard him inhale.

He said, "I've found him."

"Found who?"

"The American, Queenie! I found the *American*."

* * *

Kura means "guide" in Swahili, and my friend was aptly named.

His parents were Muslim—*Kura* is close to *Qur'an*, no?—but he renounced Islam, just as he renounced most things. His father was a diplomat, a Francophile who uprooted his family from a small African country (an act not without controversy in its day) to settle in a working-class Parisian neighborhood. After the move, Kura was inexplicably given a ludicrous new name: Pierre. "Lucky Pierre" is what they called him. By the time we met, in 1968, he was Kura again, the alias and its sobriquet long since relegated to the bits-and-bobs bin of dislocated childhood. (I should add that it was oddly retained as an occasional nickname, but mercy to those who added *Lucky*, because he thought that a jinx.) In truth, he was never comfortable with either appellation. At heart he was a refugee, a traveler in the shadowlands. The classic man without a country.

He was beautiful. O! He looked like a pharaoh. High cheekbones, aquiline nose, regal bearing. If he'd been raised in America, he was one of those men who would have been called "Duke." Thin, light-skinned, light on his feet . . . green, piercing eyes—sad, delighted eyes. He inherited them from his mom, a Brit. She was a brilliant woman but on the cool side. Emotionally distant. I think he'd have preferred she had a little "white mischief" in her blood.

We met at a club in Chicago. I just turned 16; he was at least twice my age. I can't remember why he was in the States but it would had to have been some monster dope deal. *French Connection*–sized. It was a terrible, self-destructive time for me. I wanted to leave the iron grip of my family's wealth and dysfunction but didn't stand a chance. I was in a vise.

I haven't showed you this, have I? It's probably time . . . *[Her right hand slowly emerged from its brocaded silk sleeve, a night-blooming flower in search of lunar light. She held it out for inspection. I looked closely, with curiosity, as if it were an exotic pet—and got the feeling the hand was looking back. The index and middle finger were stumps; those that remained, bejeweled in priceless stones. The skin was covered by graceful, black henna tattoos, extending to the crook in her arm]* I'm a southpaw, so it really hasn't been too much of an impediment. I don't parade it around, though I'm not particularly hypervigilant about concealing it either. I guess I favor it just a little. I'm as vain as the next girl but not so much about my hand, funnily enough. Anyway, my stock explanation is—or was, back in the day—that I was night-snorkeling along the Costa Smeralda and the propeller of our motorboat chopped them off. I'm going to tell you what really happened. *[The hand retracted]* So, back to Chicago, when Kura and I first met . . . I was in my wild-child phase. I walked around in a not-so-famous blue raincoat, a kid in a woman's body. It was a rough club, oh boy, I don't think it even had a name. No number on the building—a crazy hellish place. But *exciting*. I was a sick puppy! The only men I was attracted to were gangsters. (If you think that may have had a little something to do with my father, you better believe it did.) And I don't mean gangbangers, I mean *gangsters*. My Puerto Rican boyfriend was quick with a knife and I had a death wish—*not* a good combo. But *aside* from all that, I really wanted to bond with a killer. I had these warpy Caril Ann Fugate fantasies—remember *Badlands*?—they based that movie on her and her boyfriend—I wanted to meet someone who'd murder my parents without having to be asked! I wanted to ride off into the sunset with a soulmate sociopath.

We were in the parking lot of the club and my man was drunk. When he got drunk, he got very, very quiet. Never a good thing when that happened, nuh uh. Supposedly, I was the first girlfriend he'd had in years that he didn't beat the living shit out of. The other gals who hung around the club—all older, 19 and up—they couldn't believe it. Couldn't believe I wanted to be with him *or* that it'd lasted so long. They just shook their heads. "He must really love you, Cassie." (That was them being kind.) Mostly, they looked at me like I was psycho, which I was. I didn't care what he did to me. I actually started to goad him. There wasn't anything cute or courageous about it . . . it was ugly and degrading. He'd been in the penitentiary for murder, for like 10 years. He told me about two killings, contract killings he did while in the joint. That's what they call the penitentiary—the joint. If you were a junkie you were a *hype*, and your needle was a *harpoon*. I picked up a whole new vocabulary. I learned about *rigs* and *works* and *wolf tickets*, oh I learned a *lot*. Quite the sentimental education. I thought he was afraid of me! Which probably he was, a little bit anyway . . . We were in the parking lot, standing next to his car. I said some stuff I knew I shouldn't have. I was horrible, Bruce!

I needed a shot—had a bad habit, an *expensive* one, and he wouldn't give it to me. All part of our little S and M game. I was out of my skin. I think I probably called him—no, I *did*, I *remember*, I called him a fag. Nice, huh? Because he couldn't get it up a hundred percent of the time and I thought I was the Fuck Queen of the Western World. He actually *liked* when I got aggressive in bed, he was one of those guys who liked to be dominated but didn't want anyone to know it. So I called him all kinds of queer, loud enough for people to hear and then I said, "Why don't you just fucking kill me, faggot?" I was wired like that, I had kamikaze swagger. (I must have been blasted out of my skull too.) You know, you can get away with stuff for a long time. Luck's a big part of it.

That night, my luck ran out.

He grabbed me by the neck and I felt a sting. I remember it was freezing, a freezing wind like a knife itself. I wasn't wearing my coat . . . I was cold, then suddenly warm. I smiled at him. I don't know how or why but I knew it was the end. I was very calm . . . he smiled back. It was impossible to know what he was thinking, why *he* was smiling. In the slow-motion madness of it all I looked up and saw my namesake constellation. Really seemed to have the time to look—and it was upside-down. Did you know Cassiopeia is topsy-turvy half the year? She is, that was her punishment for sacrificing her daughter. It must have been like only 10° but I felt so warm, so sort of strangely . . . *groovy*. I thought he must have given me a hot-shot, spiked me somehow. And I kept having all of this time to stare at the sky . . . I was looking at one queen, he was watching another (me). Then I got *so cold*—talking about it now, it's so vivid! I can *feel* and remember *so much*. Everything but his name. And I hope to fuck I never do. I've tried to before but it's just *gone*, erased from the memory bank. One of those amazing tricks the mind's so good at. I don't *ever* want to remember it. Not ever—

My theory was that he had trouble in bed because he didn't fuck with his cock, he fucked with his *knife*. The thing that excited him most was holding a blade to my neck during the act. That was the only way he could orgasm. Like a bad B-movie, isn't it? Some deep Richard Widmark weirdness from the '40s. What was that flick where he pushes an old woman in a wheelchair down the stairs? He'd make cuts on my neck while we made love, little crosshatches. Boy, I'm glad I don't know you better or this would be too embarrassing! If I knew you any better, I don't think I'd ever even have opened my mouth! Obviously, that excited me too—the knife— Jesus, *what* a sick puppy. O! Check this! You'll like this detail: I wasn't *completely* crazy because I always held his wrist when he came. Because there was always that possibility in the back of my head that he'd get overexcited and give me a *slice*, not really meaning to, you know, one nip to the carotid would be all she wrote. *Finito.* Over and out. Though he probably wouldn't have stopped there . . . Hey, if you've gone that far, why not take the whole head! I could just picture his cronies (who weren't very fond of me anyway) hustling him to a safe house before shipping the sonofabitch off to Central America or wherever.

Okay, the parking lot: later, I heard a whole mob was out there, but right when it happened it felt like we were totally, spookily alone. Like the scene in *West Side Story* when Tony and Maria are at a dance and suddenly everything spins and goes dark? And everyone disappears except for them? He got down on the ground, on top of me. I'd fallen into shock, staring over his shoulder at the upside-down Queen. His hard-on felt like the handle of a whip. He was rubbing it against me. Nice, huh. I mean, kinda thoughtful—who *wouldn't* want a little *frottage* before dying? The familiar rhythm of his breath told me he was about a minute away from busting a nut. Sorry. That was crude. I'm getting drunk. Anyway, he was real quiet. Which, as I said, was *not good.* Didn't ask me to look in his eyes like he usually did when he was gonna come, he was too far into the kill. I was pretty much gone anyway. You know, starting to merge with the jet-black majesty of woozy sky. He was good at what he did. (With a knife.) The weight of him on me was a comfort . . . then I felt this *tug,* but its meaning failed to register . . . then another—pinpricky tugs that sent me farther into the upside-down Queen's palace.

In his trance, he'd taken two fingers. I didn't know this at the time—they told me a few days later.

[points to a constellation, almost directly above]

See? Can you see her, Bruce? That's her throne. See? See it? Tonight, she's right-side up—all's well with the world. Back on her throne where she belongs. As am I . . .

Okay, back to the parking lot!

There was this *gust* out his mouth—a stench—then he started spewing waste like a broken pipe. I probably thought he *was* coming . . . in my hallucinatory state. He lifted himself. Floated above me then stood straight up but as if not by his own power. It was eerie, like a crazy puppet pulled by unseen strings, something superhuman, something *abominable* had plucked him off me. I can still see his mouth as the body was dragged off, that septic mouth, smiley face *crapmouth* unleashing a torrent of bright, brackish blood. And that, my friend, was that. His invisible predator retreated to the lot's far corner to fuss over its exsanguinated prey while someone wrapped something around my hand. That would be Kura. He used his shirt as a tourniquet, leaving him bare-chested in the cold, a *very* Kura move, the swashbuckling touch! I'm sure he knew I wouldn't be able to appreciate the gesture but he did it anyway. (That, my friend, is *style*.) I know I smiled at him. I was smiling at everyone, especially Mama Cassiopeia—I was already pinned up *there*, clueless, to the topsy-turvy night.

Then upside-down *I* went, and fainted dead away.

I awakened in a too-bright room that smelled of ether and fast food.

Loud voices, laughter, shushing. Kura hovered close to Coat and Shabby Tie, who gave a tidy running commentary on my needle tracks—I had an abscess on the inside of my elbow—and couldn't stop throwing up. Blood-soaked compress on hand and under rib . . . those *cigarettes* he was smoking—not Kura, but Coat and Shabby Tie—the ones that smell like weed and incense and cheap Egyptian perfume—*clove*. Oh, and Coat and Shabby was most assuredly a *doctor* because I knew my doctors. This one was pasty, late 40s, an abortionist-type out of Faulkner, with the missed-train look of one who'd burned his adrenals for a middling cause at too young an age. Or a tragic one—maybe on a balmy summer night, he'd backed out of the driveway and run over his kid.

Apparently the boyfriend's knife found a relatively safe spot under the ribs and I'll never know if the Nameless One missed the arteries and vital organs on purpose. Probably. He was a *precise* motherfucker, would've been a helluva surgeon in another life. I'll never know what the Abominable Puppeteer did to him either, surgical-wise, once he got him to the far side of the lot.

Coat and Shabby stitched what was left of my fingers and did a pretty good job of it if I do say so myself. I must have been in that weird little private ER for two days. They transferred me to a chic Old World clinic, an upgrade from the other place to be sure. When I got my wits back, I discovered it was the Drake—that's high-end hotel living for ya. The puncture seemed to take care of itself. The main concern was my hand, because bone infection is never a good thing.

I was there a couple of weeks. It was Christmastime. I had a 24-hour nurse. Every few days, a huge Samoan looked in on me. No way you couldn't feel safe around that man. All of the people around Kura had heart. I knew they'd take a bullet for him, and probably had—or worse. My minder never spoke, which made me feel like an utter fool. Five hundred pounds, with a Cheshire grin. I had the feeling he was close to Kura, and when in his presence I made sure I *behaved*. I even acted repentant, though for what I wasn't sure.

All I did in my perfect, stately cocoon was eat club sandwiches and listen to *The White Album*. Lots of room-service hot fudge sundaes, lots of doodling and drawing, *lots* of journaling about my White (Mocha) Knight. I had become fairly obsessed. Because after all, I'd seen him just twice—once, when he stripped off his shirt to stop the bleeding and the other while being patched up by Coat and Shabby, which was kind of a dreamy corollary of the former, with more dope and less blood—so his messianic absence made a perfect breeding ground for my hormonal, father-starved, junkie-Rapunzel imagination to run wild. In my head, my mysterious savior was pure *Thanatos*, with a heavy dollop of Eros on top.

So there she was, Eloise with a social disease (gonorrhea, and cured, courtesy of Coat and Shabby). Fidgety, depressed, and packin' on the pounds . . . feeling deserted by all her witchy-woman powers. Like a doomed prisoner, awaiting reprieve—I *still* held out hope that he'd gallop up and swoop me onto his saddle. And now I remember one of the things that tortured me. They never bothered to station a guard at the door of the suite to prevent my escape, at least *I* never saw one. I didn't know which freaked me out more: that I could leave anytime I wanted, or if other people could *enter.* What if my ex's posse was hunting me down? (Not that anyone gave enough of a shit about my ex to avenge him—not to mention they would already have ascertained they were brutally outmatched.) In my worst moments, it boiled down to Kura not caring less. But now I know *exactly* why they—*he*—Kura—didn't feel the need. Because it had to have been so obvious I wasn't going anywhere, not as long as there was the slimmest chance of a rendezvous with the Big Boss. That was plain as the stumps on my hand . . . O, they must really have gotten a kick out of stringing me along! No, by the time I left, I was convinced I would just have to leave it all behind: my savior, the Samoan, the Norwegian nurse, the room service—ooh, *that* was going to hurt!—goodbye to all that. Everything but the mason jar of Darvons that Coat and Shabby had prescribed, to wean me from the heroin.

On the morning I left, I had all sorts of conflicting emotions. I was in way over my head but what else was new? I was weak and angry and weepy and paranoid. For a while, I thought Kura worked for my father! The Samoan probably disabused me of that notion somewhere along the line. But I couldn't piece together why—*how*—Kura had been there to save me nor could I understand why I was being looked after—*cared* for—with such painstaking, tender deliberation. At checkout time, the futility of my serious convalescence crush, the intensity of *yearning* for my patron came home to roost. I longed for him in every fiber of my broken being. Estrogen and Electra coursed through my veins like lava. I fantasized us having a life together—preposterous. The greater my yearning, the more crazy-insecure I became. (I suppose I haven't changed too much.) I decided to make an "overture" but was paralyzed by anxiety. What if I was rejected? Laughed at and humiliated? Another problem was—and there were moments when I flattered myself by thinking it was the *only* problem— that I was sure he knew by now that I was underage.

My mocha knight on a hijacked black tar horse . . .

All packed and dressed—it breaks my heart to see myself as that sad little girl, with her poor bandaged hand!—I held my nurse, utterly inconsolable. In the last week, I'd painstakingly composed a pitiful, "noble" letter of thanks to he who had rescued me. Lord, if only I'd kept that. I handed it to the Samoan as I prepared to go, eyes downcast, then hugged that great tree of a man while bursting into tears.

I had no idea that Kura had left the morning after the murder.

The Samoan patted the top of my head, then said, "He wants to see you."

* * *

I don't remember much about that trip to Paris (I was too happy, too stoned), other than being in possession of a passport that carried a name and DOB that weren't my own. I traveled alone. The Samoan gave me a backstory—O! *Now* I know where that story about getting my fingers chopped by a propeller came from. That was part of the original script.

Saved again!

When I got to Kura's I ran to his arms and kissed him on the mouth but he pushed me away. I was confused, embarrassed. Maybe he *was* working for my father! Or maybe he *was* my father, long lost, and we'd been reunited under the terms of a noir, a *Nouvelle Vague*. He actually asked if I wanted a tutor! You know—to be homeschooled, *s'il te plaît*. I wondered what I'd gotten myself into. I had a few tantrums and when the storm passed, we settled into a sunny life, *très sympa*. I grew up living in a mausoleum; one of my father's estates had its own police force. But *this* . . . I'd never seen such casual opulence, such riches, such beauty. He had the *most* exquisite apartment in the Marais. Well, it wasn't exactly an apartment, it was what they call an *hôtel particulier*. Effing spectacular. People came and went, all very respectful. To me, I mean. And Kura never discussed business. *Ever.*

I don't think we slept together for at least six months. It was like he needed me to be quarantined, physically *and* emotionally, before we became intimate. I turned 17. I loved having my own bed, and sleeping in *his* without fooling around. (That was a new one.) It felt safe. Incestuous, romantic—*très français!* And while I may not have been capable at the time of admitting it, I'd been through some pretty profound changes. I wasn't the girl I used to be . . . I should probably say we weren't *completely* pure, maybe a little closer to Elvis and Lisa Marie when they were courting. You know, heavy petting optional. He was in love with me from the very beginning, but I didn't know it. But that's what I wanted to believe. I was so young and so vulnerable, especially after all that had happened. I probably hoped he was just biding his time, waiting to see if his feelings held. (They held for *me*.) I wanted to ask all about it when we met up in Delhi but never had to, because he confessed to everything before I had the chance.

He had his own plane back then and we struck out like pirates—Casablanca, Tunis, Istanbul, Corfu, Gstaad . . . we were bonnie companions and that was major because Kura always said if a man and woman couldn't travel well together, there was no hope. I was a feral cat and incorrigibly ignorant, his punk Pygmalion. He read aloud to me and made charming little study plans. He was always interested in the . . . spiritual. I don't know *what* kids aspire to these days but Kura knew his destiny early on. He'd make himself into a great criminal, the greatest of all, a *dejamiento*, a saint! (In that order.) The real turning point came in his early teens when he discovered Milarepa. The legend of the murderer who became a great *siddha* was irresistible. Kura was sold.

But he would have to become a killer first.

As his reputation for ruthlessness grew, so did his fixation on the mystics. His nightstand booklist reeked of incense, shamanism, esoterica: Gurdjieff, Ouspensky, Jacob Boehme . . . Pico della Mirandola, Castaneda, Hermes Trismegistus.

And of course, *The Book of Satsang*—which the rest of my story is really about.

Hey, you know what? I'm tired.

I guess it was that homicidal trip down memory lane. Hadn't thought about it in a while. *Ugh.*

I'm gonna take a nap.

Let's take naps.

Then we'll have a lovely dinner and begin again. K?

* * *

I took a long nap then availed myself of an offered massage. A few hours later, I was summoned back to the tent. Queenie looked radiant.

Over dinner, she told me about her current travels—her quest for the "Lost City." Turkish coffee and sweets were served and we settled around a fire to resume.

Where was I?

Ah, yes: *The Book of Satsang.*

In Paris, I soon learned that a thick, well-riffled volume "written" by an Indian saint known far and wide as the Great Guru occupied prime real estate on his nightstand. It was Kura's de facto bible, actually a collection of edited transcripts of what is called satsang, a gathering wherein a holy man imparts wisdom, not just to students and adepts but everyday people. *Sat* means "truth," *sanga* means "company," i.e., the company of a guru. (I googled it today when I woke up.) *The Book of Satsang* was the best-known and most beloved of all the Great Guru's bound teachings that had been released in the handful of years before—I think it was first published in '65—Kura had copies of it stashed *everywhere.* And *this* is interesting: I later found out he was carrying it on the night he killed Douma—*Douma! Whoa!* The name just came back, isn't that funny? The brain is such a strange thing . . . Lord Jesus. "Douma"—doomsday—could anything be more perfect? Okay. Deep breaths. Anyhow, the Great Guru's public talks were simple and conversational, down to earth, free of the sunny dogma and endless scriptural name-dropping that clogs up so much of what's out there. So the book gives you a real flavor of the man. The editor did an amazing job (more about him later—a *lot* more) because the text very subtly, very *cogently* reflects the Great Guru's personal characteristics and peccadilloes. It leaves you with an eerie feeling of having been present in the room where the talks were held, a tobacco shop in Bombay that was kind of famous even then. The Master was a tobacconist by trade.

Each morning, from 9:30 to 11:30 (the shop opened at noon), he gave satsang to visitors from all over the world. Typically, about 30 people crammed into that neat, clean space, redolent with the aroma of cigars, cigarettes and all those other identifiable and unidentifiable smells of India—

Douma . . .

Hold on a minute. *[She closed her eyes]* I need to do a little voodoo here. *[She took deep breaths then suddenly shook her head rather wildly, eyes still shut]* Neutralize that fucker with a little spell. *[She shook her head a final time, then opened her eyes. Lit a joint, took a deep hit, then smiled as she exhaled]* Okay—the deed is done!

The copy of *The Book of Satsang* that Kura was carrying with him at the time of the murder—he had it on his *person*, in the large outside pocket of his peacoat—became, for him, infused with nearly supernatural qualities. Its pages were tea-stained by my blood and probably that of he who'd been executed on that freezing, starry nightclub night. Kura was always urging me to read the thing in its entirety, specifically that exact copy. (Which creeped me out.) He had the idea it was some kind of omen, that "the Source" had pointed out the *Book*'s life-and-death importance by spattering it with my "Four Humors." I laughed when he uttered that archaic phrase, yet there really wasn't anything funny about it. I'd examine the *Book*, weigh it in my hands, dip into it here and there, but only the leafs that were corroded by my *humors* finally, perversely held my interest. (But never for too long.) Back in the day I had a real block when it came to reading, just terrible A.D.D. . . . God! Kura tried *everything* to get me to sidle up to that book of *The Great Guru's Greatest Hits*. He'd bribe me with Hermès and Chanel. I'd say, "Yes, please!" but never held up my side of the agreement. After reading a while, I always failed the pop quiz.

He was patient. I was audacious enough to believe I was the center of his universe. (I came to learn I was partially right.) But Kura had enough expertise with the suicidal character to know that, as much as I loved him, it would be risky to apply too much pressure. So he played it *pianissimo*. Sometimes he read to me from the *Book* in bed, before we made love—or after. Probably during! I think I was maybe a little jealous of that guru but I was also puzzled. If the holy tobacconist was alive and well (which he was), why hadn't Kura made the trek to Bombay?

One day I blurted out as much, point-blank. He winced and made a funny face, as if he'd been waiting for someone to ask the painfully obvious.

"Because I'm a fucking dilettante."

Was he being serious?

"Do you think he's going to judge you?" I asked.

He went rigid—I'd found a weak spot. Oh, I was *haughty* . . . a spoiled, haughty, entitled bitch on two wheels.

"Well, if he does, he's an *asshole*, Kura. And not worthy of your time."

I thought I'd get a medal for rushing to his defense.

"Don't be a stupid girl!" he roared. "This man does not *judge* . . . this man is not even a man!" He literally foamed at the mouth. "And don't *ever* use that word for the *siddha*, I won't have it! Save it for your ridiculous friends—save it for the men who wish to take you off this earth, or the parents you dishonor with each breath, those who gave you life! Why don't you look in the mirror and fling that word at what you see *there*, like a monkey throwing shit! But *never* in connection with the Great Guru . . . *And learn not to speak of things you know nothing of.*"

Well, I couldn't—speak—for about five days.

I got truly frightened. Because as close as we'd become, his coruscating rage demonstrated for the first time that it was possible for him to say goodbye without looking back. That he had that in him. Which might sound naïve; but perhaps you know a little about the power that a young and beautiful girl can hold over a man. Or the power she sometimes *thinks* she has . . . On the last day of my silent retreat, I apologized. I don't think I'd ever done that before, not to anyone. I remember stealing into the den where he was reading beside the fire and telling him how sorry I was. He didn't look at me. Then I dropped to my knees and clutched his ankles, hair hanging down while my forehead brushed the floor. We'd been together about ten months and *finally* I thanked him for everything he'd done. (I wasn't sure he'd ever seen the note I'd composed at the Drake but that couldn't have been a proper thank-you.) I thanked him for all that he was and all he'd *become* to me. I thanked him for saving my life and looking after me while I healed, thanked him for daring to bring a crass, selfish, obstinate girl (*underage!*) to Paris at such great expense and even greater risk. I thanked him for protecting me, for teaching me—

I thanked him for loving me.

He bent down to lift me up. I was crying. We embraced and then he made tea. We drank it in silence; he'd learned how to make a perfect cup of English tea from his mum.

"Do you want to know why I haven't visited the Great Guru?"

His voice was deep, with sparkly, dancing notes. A cognac voice. Something inside him went still, beyond my reach. His mood and tone were elegiac.

"The reason I've not gone to visit the Great Guru in Bombay is—would you like to hear the truth? The reason I've not gone is . . . *because he is the only man I've ever been afraid of in my life.* The *instant* he lays eyes on me, he will *know.* It shall all be over! And where will that leave me, darling Queen? Where! And what then?"

* * *

So of *course* I got on that plane when he called—to Delhi. I'm afraid that's the best segue I can manage at the moment. It's hard getting back into it after a break.

Tell me, Bruce, how badly am I fucking up? Have I "come a cropper," as Kura used to say? I probably *could* be telling the story much better. But you can change things around later, no? With the editing? You can sand down the rough edges . . . I'll pick up steam—you'll see. I'll try to be more articulate. You don't know how much I've been reading *[her old journals]*! There's *so* much freakin' material. You know what I *can* do? I actually *can* try to—I'll try to do a little more editing in my head. Edit the thoughts before they come out my mouth . . . O? You think that's a mistake? I don't mean *edit*-edit, I'm not too good at that. I just mean be a little more mindful.

Anyway, we'll see. We shall see, said the blind man. To the deaf girl . . .

The Roller arrived at 7:30 with yours truly toddling out half-an-hour later, just as the sage predicted. Following Kura's script, a chauffeur in full livery smoked a morning cigarette whilst leaning against that fleshy part between bonnet and withers. Once I came into view, he flicked his butt to the curb and snapped to attention. We barreled down 110th Street and the sheer movement coupled with the ineffable mystery of wholly unexpected adventure shot little sunbeams through the clouds of my depression. Travel has always been my drug. The stubborn gloominess shifted, like items in an overhead bin. In my experience, moroseness grows in direct correlation with the time spent gazing at one's own navel—and shrinks upon fixing one's gaze on another's. I was already thinking about Kura and our imminent reunion, which further brought me out of myself.

We drove straight onto the field. It was a big plane, maybe *too* big. (I know my doctors and I know my jets.) Not gauche, but *gosh!*—pure Kura. Two pilots and a "hostess" waved from the top of the stairs. I felt like I was entering an old photograph of some starlet having her moment; I got butterflies climbing the airway.

I retired to my cocoon-ready cashmere bed straightaway, the cabin ringed with orchids. (I never did see that elusive doctor, until we landed.) She brought tea then left me alone. I nestled in to ruminate. Taking off, I thumbed the nubs of my two fingers and something about the whole situation made me laugh out loud . . . I never thought about the cause *or* effect of my mutilation anymore—I'd been running from those memories for 30 years. *The ruined hand of a cowardly witch.* I was closing in on my fiftieth year: twitchy, witchy, barren and bitchy, out of season and out of swords. I wondered how many flatfoots he put on my tail, anyway. They call that "intel," don't they? "Show intel" . . . *show 'n' tell*. Well now I'm just getting silly. (I should cut back on the wine during these sessions.) Do you remember? That he said he knew something no one else did? That my heart had been broken by a woman? O Bruce, my heart has been breaking for 11 years! She thought I'd betrayed her—then vanished. But I *didn't*. Betray her. Not even for a minute. Though I *do* believe I know how she got that deadly idea . . . a horrible, *terrible* misunderstanding. If I can just tell her the *truth* of what happened, maybe all can be forgiven. I've been searching for her ever since.[1] I told you I was getting close. Every day, a little closer. I'm not on this bus for my health. I *told* you what I'm doing, you *know* what I'm searching for. I'm searching for *her*—

* * *

To be honest, I thought he died a long time ago.

It was obvious that Kura had done well for himself though I doubted he was still in the drug trade. At his level, careers lasted about as long as a star athlete's. Someone younger, hungrier, crazier—someone luckier—always came along.

He was 62 now. The enormity of it—of *everything*—struck me like lightning as I hurtled toward him, an arrow shot through Time itself. Something he used to say popped into my head. "With your bow and my arrow, we could really go places." I remember that I said that out loud and started to laugh. And before long I was bawling, keening, blubbering, exhorting the gods to do I don't know what. I didn't want the

---

1   Briefly referred to at the end of the short preface

stewards to hear (there were three of them), even though I knew they'd been trained to ignore the random, spectacularly uncensored outbursts of the very rich and their hangers-on. I didn't want that doctor rushing in with a hypo, either.

I needed to get a grip . . .

I wasn't hungry.

I didn't feel like listening to music. That might make me cry even more. So I took a ferocious shit, crawled back to bed and swallowed a hundred milligrams of Seroquel.

Awaiting its effect, I tried to visualize what the contemporary Kura might look like. Softer, probably, like the best cotton gets. Maybe thirty pounds heavier. 20? 50? Twenty pounds *lighter*? Thinned down from a rare blood cancer or some sort of nonsense . . . *Variations on a (Kura) Theme* floated past in the jiggly aspic of my mind—still *charismatic*, that would be without question, in the Savile Row suits that gave him a rakish, pioneeringly shabby look. Being the equal opportunity masochist that I am, I climbed into *his* fantasy of how *I* would look, before realizing he must have already *known*. I'd always been camera-shy but whomever he sent on my trail would have provided him with a portfolio of telephoto headshots, surreptitiously taken in the streets by hired men. *Not fair.* Yet none of that mattered, of course, not really, because any current or even not-so-current images would be overruled by the nubile iconography of my 16-year-old self tenderly entombed in his own private amber. The Darwinian default—oy! Still, I prayed he wouldn't find me too repellant. A depressed, childless, perimenopausal woman, unlucky in love, with a shelf life of self-esteem long past its expiration date, I presumed I would throw off a medley of scents: a potpourri of moribund pheromones, burnt adrenals and brokenheartedness.

But what if—what if he was *attracted*? What if when he saw me, what if we *both*—O!

And what if he'd already arranged a grand wedding in Jaipur at the Palace of the Winds?

Team Morpheus warmly invaded, with molecule-soldiers of Seroquel and that other (non-FDA-approved) drug called *love* . . . I pinched myself with a rhythmic *no no no* because I couldn't afford to carry over the feelings I had for *her*—even in paler disguise—to my dear Kura, whose devotions I was in the midst of rediscovering. *She* was my cold case, not Kura, and nothing in me wanted to solve *him*. My love for her was real; my love for *him* was as one might feel toward a childhood curio found against staggering odds, at a yard sale. Perhaps it best remain in memory . . . I needed to convince myself this latest fantasia involving Kura, whatever its form, this so-called "romantic" (heavy quotes around that!) development was nothing more than the heart's and body's response to the fear, loneliness and isolation of depression—a trinity whose siren song banished all reason. I *mustn't* surrender, because to decide to love another risked losing all I had left, the tattered, star-dusted remnants of that *real* love I still carried, *would* carry, forever—one I still fully expected—*expect*—still—to end in happy-ever-after. *Yes* it was fun to flirt with rekindling what Kura and I once had or at least some version of it. And *yes*, he'd lifted me up—saved me from myself—with the perfectly timed request to accompany him in the solving of an ancient riddle . . . *but so what?* Was I so weak that a call from a man I hadn't seen in decades was all it took to set off a chain of fantasies ending in marriage? I admit that when I allowed myself to go down that road there was something about becoming Kura's wife that was inexorable, almost too perfect. Another

part of me knew, at least *hoped*, that this old-fashioned foolishness of mine would end at first hug—in Delhi.

I remember thinking: "Well, it *better*."

Still, I loved him. *God* it felt wonderful to love. And feel
loved again!

* * *

I can't remember how long after Kura's confession it was—
when he confided his fear that the Great Guru would peer into
his cupboards and find them bare—or how long it was after
he'd raged and scared the bejesus out of me—but one day we
were in Barcelona when he announced, "We're going."

"Going where?"

"To Bombay."

I was thrilled.

Could not *wait*. See, I had a mission—to seduce the old
swami and reveal him for the fraud he was. *[sings]* "He's just a
man . . . and I've had so many men before, in *oh so many ways* . . .
he's just one more!" I was determined to smash the false idol
and destroy my lover's illusions once and for all. Thus, Kura
would be forced to admit that *I* was the Great Guru, *I* was his
teacher—and *nothing* could compete with what I had between
my legs. O, I am telling you, Bruce, I was the most awful girl!

I'm *still* awful. At least, I *hope* I am!

The *hegira* began as a straight-ish shot but our course kept
deviating, for reasons unrecalled and unknown. I think we
came in through Karachi—don't ask. We arrived in Bombay
about a month after leaving Spain. This was 1970. From the
moment we landed, Kura was quite ill. I thought he'd acquired
some legendary Indian malady but since we'd only been in the

place a half-hour or so it wasn't too likely. I forgot to add an important detail: for the first time, we were traveling alone. That was how Kura wanted it and his posse reluctantly agreed. Not that they had a choice.

No arrangements had been made for a car to pick us up at the airport. So there I was, plunged headlong into the middle of that amazing LSD trip called India—thank God I was acid-free at the moment!—with the *padrone* fading fast. My 17-year-old Great Mother instincts kicked in; finally, I got to take care of *him*. I have no memory of how we got to the Taj—our hotel. All I know is that for a few days I was a pint-sized Patton. A real rite of passage. *Man*. We were up half the night. Kura's temperature was crowding 105° but he refused to see a doctor. I fell back on junkie survival skills and rang for ice. The bellboys brought up bucketsful—they were all in love with me. O Jesus, by the time I left Dodge, I had that hotel *wired*. I whined and wheedled and finally shoved Kura into the bath. He whinged and whinnied and threw mini-tantrums, fought me all the way. That did the trick though. His fever broke at last.

Satsang was at 9:30 in the morning. It was already dawn and neither of us had slept a wink. When I suggested we put it off till tomorrow, Kura had a hissy fit. I argued my point: the Great Guru did his "questions and answers" seven days a week, year-round. What was the rush? But he was adamant.

Our car never showed. (Of course it didn't.) We hung around the lobby like resentful drunks, half-hypnotized by the remorseful staff's honeyed apologies and assurances this grievous error would soon be rectified. The longer we waited, the deeper we sunk in the comic quicksand of penitent, sacred hospitality. To save us from being swallowed up completely, I demanded a cab.

I know madcap taxi rides through India are an awful cliché but *that* one I'll never forget. On the other side of my window there was some kind of full-tilt Halloween/*Carnaval* goin' on: a blurry burlesque of the undead, hands outstretched for flesh and candy. Whenever we stopped to make our way around some road-blocking cow—the latter apparently being the only living thing the municipality gave a shit about—the zombies pressed against the glass anew like bacteria multiplying in a Petri dish. Kura compulsively checked his Patek, the perfect way to remain oblivious to our motorized rampage. I'll admit my mordant fascination with the hairsbreadth escapes of those on the street whom the driver seemed determined to kill caused me to drop the ball on consulting the map the concierge had painstakingly notated. In a short time, we were lost. Kura sat as if frozen to his seat, his forehead too-warm to the touch. Soon we ground to a complete halt, with nary a cow in sight. I couldn't help but ask the driver why, knowing his answer would be as meaningless as my question.

"Accident," he said, through a jubilant slash of a mouth. A chorus of bobble-headed Ganeshas on the dash shook in exuberant affirmation.

Without warning, Kura bolted out the door, through the protozoa and into the festive ooze. I threw sodden rupees at the driver and gave chase.

I yelled after him but the *padrone* didn't respond. When by some small miracle I finally caught up, I shepherded him into a grimy cafe. The return of his fever rendered Kura somewhat docile. I begged him to stay put while I went for directions. I paid the harpy who ran the place for a Coke twenty times over, for which she expressed time-sensitive gratitude. It was like some fucked-up hockey game—I'd probably bought about 15

minutes of bench time for Kura before heading back to the ice
to get my nose broken.

I lurched into the street. I had no intention to seek help
from pedestrians (if that's what one could call them) and
decided my best chance was a soldier standing in the middle
of the street. He wasn't directing traffic; his main function,
it seemed, was to sweat and scowl. He had a machine gun
slung over his shoulder. I got in his face and pronounced the
name of the Great Guru. His response wasn't so much cantankerous as outright hostile, with the implicit threat of pending
violence to my person. I wondered if he harbored ill feelings
toward the *siddha* but concluded it more likely that I'd violated
a cultural code with my pretty young Western thing's pushi-
ness. I wound up back on the sidewalk, where pleas for money
crashed against me like insects on a windshield.

Hangdog and defeated, I rejoined my man. Kura was nurs-
ing a cup of tea our hostess had thoughtfully prepared—and
why shouldn't she have? She smelled a tip that might conceiv-
ably cover a few months' rent. I *was* glad to see Kura hydrating
and my only hope was she'd kept the kettle on long enough to
evict the tap water's microbial tenants. (Though I figured what
Kura already had was probably enough to kill whatever was in
the water anyway.) I was about to announce the plan: to call it
a day and return to the Taj for a much needed rest. Tomorrow,
we'd have a proper car and driver and bring a porter along to
make sure we reached our destination.

Then he spoke, for the first time all morning.

"The proprietress knows how to find him."

He looked at her and smiled. She smiled back, like they'd
become engaged while I was gone.

"Apparently," he said, "his shop is just round the corner."

A freakish serenity overtook him as we ambled onto acrid Mogul Lane, for we'd entered a world of myth that belonged as much to Kura as it did to Bombay. His eyes dilated and the color returned to his skin. We strolled along the broken spine of a vendor-choked passage already so familiar from the photographs that graced Kura's collection of books by and about the Great Guru. He walked stealthily, almost regally, to his destiny—toward the man he hoped against hope would consent to become his teacher. The man he was certain would see through him, then see him through . . .

In the years leading up to our sojourn, Kura spent countless hours in his library inhabiting the jostling panorama of Mogul Lane, memorizing—*memorializing*—all its parts, re-creating shadowy and sunlit corners, summoning smells aroused by the baked-on heat of the Indian sun, flipping back and forth from *The Book of Satsang* text to the tattered visual archive of the boulevard's temples and buildings, loitering amongst the shapes and forms of his pictorial montage with enormous patience and *intent*, so when at last he found himself in the actuality of it (en route to the tobacconist's) he was like an avid child dropped down to Narnia, in hot pursuit of Aslan's lair.

And as in a fairy tale, there came that time when the road took one no further. For today, all of Maharashtra seemed congregated in that mangy Mogul corridor and the throngs blocked our passage. Kura was undeterred. I held on to his coattails while he employed that extraordinary assassin's energy, feinting and dodging his way to nirvana. In just a short while, we'd cut to the head of the line of the shop with the TOBACCO sign (in English) . . . but we were still outside, VIPs without backstage passes. Two weaponless military men graced the door. While their presence seemed mostly ceremonial, entering the shop didn't look feasible. It was so crowded in there, it may not have been humanly possible—I doubt we'd have been able to squeeze in, even if the guards themselves gave us a shove.

Something was wrong with this picture but we were just too frazzled and sick to notice. (My turn to be feverish.) The Great Guru gave satsang every day, which by anecdote and definition was a dignified, orderly affair. Then how to explain the unruly, chaotic scene that presented itself? Kura's investigations had informed that no more than 30 to 35 devotees showed up on a given morning; the energetic integrity of a true Master saw to it there were never too few disciples, nor too many.

But *this* mob was off the hook.

I watched Kura intently. I'd seen that look of laser-like determination before. He espied a pole and sprang into action. He ascended about 10 feet before stopping short at the bottoms of the bare feet of a gaggle of men who clung at the top like monkeys on a swizzle stick. Like them, Kura could now peer over the heads of the storefront lookee-loos and straight into the shop itself. I read his lips: "His chair!" he said to himself, in transport. *"His chair . . ."* I wondered if the fever was returning and I suppose it was, in the form of obsessive devotion. He was utterly fixated on storming the sanctum sanctorum. I saw the algorithms of egress play across his face, rippling its features . . . when he signaled, I met him at the base of the pole and we exchanged places—and thank God, because all I wanted was to get to higher ground. In that moment I remember acquiring that itchy, creepy case of nerves one can catch in a faraway place on too little sleep. I shimmied up, found my footing on some sort of electrical box, then turned my eyes to the crush of spectators. They didn't *look* very spiritual—*au contraire*. Not like seekers and disciples, anyway. The way they were decked out, they might as well have been auditioning for a Bollywood musical. In the photo montage Kura put together in Paris, the pilgrims of Mogul Lane wore a wide array of costumes but the emphasis was decidedly on the modest, the simple, the austere. *Some* were "dressed," but we're talking Sunday best, nothing glam. You didn't need Emily Post to tell you satsang etiquette skewed toward less is more. (Bless is more?) But *these* folks . . . *these* folks were bejeweled, bedizened egos on parade. Of course the Great Guru never wore anything but a threadbare kurta—at least he didn't wear a *nappy*, which definitely would *not* have been okay! *[laughs]* Not a big fan of the Gandhi look. What I'm saying is, to sit at his feet dressed to the tits was gauche. You're in the man's *home*, for crissake, not the parliament building. And even then. At the time, the discrepancy meant nothing to me. I was just a decadent trespasser, a cultural interloper, a wannabe seductress—a pole girl!—an American expat junkie runaway with three kinds of VD by the time she was 13. But I'm sure I found the fashion show enthralling. I must have interpreted all the finery as part of just another holiday. You know, *Indian Holiday #6,342.*

Below me, the untouchables were being pushed, whisked and twirled into the street by fresh packs of snappily dressed cops. I'd seen many soldiers in the short time since we'd arrived but now it seemed like whole dragoons were being summoned to Tobacco Road. Jostled from multiple directions past women in glittering saris, the disenfranchised surged to the sidewalks where they received further prods from handsome householders in gold-embroidered sherwanis, the goal being not just to herd them from the shop's entrance but to whirl them out of existence. In the midst of my surveillance, I saw a figure improbably squeeze through the bottleneck at the door of Satsang Central. *Kura!* The bouncers missed him completely, as they were busy hassling with a clutch of urchins that delighted in a game whose main objective was to make a big show of rushing the door and then swiftly retreating just in time to elude the authorities, a maneuver which scored the most points if finessed without being kicked, grabbed, molested or otherwise apprehended. The most adroit of these mischief-makers found time to brazenly ape the look and mood of the policeman who had given chase or whatever fancy onlookers expressed disdain. To escape capture, the dirtball scalawags took impressive, flying leaps into a mosh pit of their peers that extended into the street, ruffling a few feathers and unraveling more than a few *dhotis* of the hydra-footed gorgon of perfumed devotees waiting peaceably on line.

I redirected my gaze. The sun no longer reflected on the glass. The inside of the shop, abrim with those awaiting satsang, was totally visible. To my astonishment, Kura had already reached his goal: breathless and illumined, he stood before the Great Guru's humble throne, beautifully surrendered. He brought the palms of his hands together in prayerful salutation, touched them to his forehead and crumpled into a lotus, neatly filling the spot that only seconds before barely contained the fidgety blob of an obese woman who, in a seizure of urgency, had decamped to answer nature's karmically ill-timed call. Kura's assured, brazen, somehow dignified arrival caused nary a stir. Befittingly, he now had the best seat in the house.

I will never forget that princely, boyish head swiveling, eyes trying to find my own. He squinted through the window, scanning at street level before remembering where he'd left me; his gaze lifted and caught me on my roost. A sunshine smile split open his face because he knew I'd bore affectionate witness to his mystic, acrobatic victory.

I still think now what I thought then—in spite of everything that was to happen, Kura had come home.

* * *

The next day, we ate a late lunch.

"Wasn't that delicious? The chef's from Morocco. Are you sure you had enough food? . . . I know it's cold, Bruce, but I'd rather do this outside. They'll bring heaters and it'll get toasty right away, I promise—and some coffees and candies . . . Esme? Can you bring two cappuccinos? And a shitload of agave . . . some fruit and cheese? And those faboo little pastries? And more wine! Thank you, Es!"

After settling, I gave her a précis of where we left off. She excitedly dove in.

As it turned out, there would *be* no satsang, for . . .

. . . the Great Guru was dead.

Pretty dramatic, huh?

At the end of that first day, we learned he had shuffled off this earthly plane just a few weeks prior—around the same time that our earthly, *private* plane was being diverted to Algiers. Needless to say, word of his demise had never reached us. This was a century before the Internet, when news traveled at a more civilized pace . . . though I do believe that as renowned as he was, if the Great Guru died *today* it would still be likely that his death might slip through more than a

handful of news cycles. His was the kind of passing that obits
generally reserve for retired diplomats, African bishops and
former child stars, i.e., ones that can be reported later than
sooner. (Scratch former child stars—enquiring minds want to
know!) That his life and teachings would eventually be widely
written about and even popularized was never in doubt. Time
has borne that out.[2]

Adamant that at any moment the saint would take his
rightful seat, Kura and I were oblivious to having stumbled
upon what was essentially a vigil. Meanwhile, I watched from
my maypole aerie; sitting before the Master's empty chair, my
lover's childlike anticipation lent him a radioactive energy.
Now you may think I'm setting the stage for a dais of eulo-
gizers—after all, I've just told you the *siddha* was dead. I said
"vigil" too but if it *was*, then what—*whom*—was everyone
waiting for?

This is where the American comes in.

* * *

Kura's belated words on the phone, some 30 years after we
met—"I've found him"—are the basis of the story I'm telling you. Understood. But before I can properly introduce the
American, I need to talk about the American's *teacher*.

It was 1997—27 years since I last saw—*left* him—in
Bombay. There I was in my zillion-dollar apartment, minding

---

2   Cf. *Shri Padodaka*, M. Cidandamurti (Mysore, 1983); *Caranamrt
    Ramayana*, Dvarkadas Parikh (Mathura: Sri Bajarang Pustakalay,
    1991); *Tobacco Saint*, David Gordon White (Berkeley: University
    of California Press, 2003); et alia.

my own business, hangin' with the gargoyles . . . remember? I get the call from Grandmaster Flash and suddenly I'm on my way to Delhi. *Whoosh.* While airborne in my cashmere cabin, rope-a-doped on Seroquel, I start to retrieve all this—*data*—everything I'm telling you now—I'm busy *downloading* because I haven't thought about *any* of it in absolute ages. I mean not really, not deeply, maybe *never.* Strange or funny or bullshitty as that may sound. But it's true. There I am on the jet, cramming for my exam—filling in the potholes of a life that sometimes, *most* of the time, didn't feel like my own. Because in that chunk of years after I left him there in dear ol' *Mumbai*—from 1970 to 1997—well, dysthymic depression, shitty chemicals and general lovelornness ruled the roost, and sealed off *so* many rooms—all the bric-a-brac and most of the furnishings were in the lost and found. So now I'm eight miles high, on my way to Delhi, freshening up my frontal lobe . . . bear with me, honey, because I want you to be as *prepared* as I can make you before we touch down—and we *will*, and *soon*, I promise! I promise we're landing in Delhi soon! I just want you to be able to give Kura your *full attention* when you finally meet him. Because if I don't talk about what I'm *about* to, it'd just be *rude*—like blowing off the first act of a play and just bringing you at intermission. *[sings]* "Eight miles high! When you touch down . . . you'll find that—it's stranger than known . . ." The Byrds! Roger McGuinn! O my God! Get my granny glasses!

All right, I herewith present: Queenie's *A Brief History of the Great Guru.*

Are you with me, bubba?

By the late '60s, the enlightened tobacconist had achieved a level of fame commensurate with Ramana Maharshi and was informally admitted into the League of Superheroes of

Nondualism. His followers—or shall I say far-flung legions of the desperate, the curious and the dilettantish, not to mention the usual pastiche of pop stars, paupers and spiritual tourists—traveled at great expense to be in his presence. He was genuinely delighted to greet them (the *rishi* could be downright chatty) though to call him gregarious would be naïve. Still, the question remained: Why was he so relentless in his public teachings if his philosophy defined quote-unquote enlightenment as a state of being that was not only impossible to earn or solicit but one that could only "happen"? (Or not.) He was known to say that a fly was as likely to land on shit as it was on honey, meaning, the *rara avis* of satori found its way to the shoulders of vagrants and birdwatchers alike. It was his view ("My *concept*," as he used to emphasize) that all the meditation, chanting and scripture studying in the world meant nothing, *including* a trek to Bombay to sit at the feet of the Master. Because all was predetermined.

At the end of the day, I suppose the Great Guru gave satsang simply because he enjoyed it. Such enjoyment was "already written," and part of his nature. He was in full agreement with the *Bhagavad Gita*, which advised that action was the thing, not the fruit of one's action. He was also fond of telling disciples he was busy "fishing." "I am looking for that big fish," he'd say, a waggish glint in his eye. "The one that swims faster and deeper than the rest." This cryptic declaration never failed to make him giggle; if his dentures fell out, he laughed even harder with what he called his "beggar's mouth." By this remark, one could wrongly infer he was trolling for a successor, but a proper saint has no interest in the tropes of lineage and continuity. Indeed, it might be said that a common thread among enlightened men was a certitude that none of their students had ever understood a word they uttered.

The loneliness of the long-distance bodhisattva . . .

In 1963, the Great Guru's fishing pole received an enormous tug on the line.

While visiting a dentist in Miami, a blond, middle-aged gentleman picked up a *Reader's Digest* with a wealthy woman's account of her passage to India to meet a renowned "tobacconist saint." He was intrigued. Gossip had it that for one week the American ruminated intensely on the article before tragedy intervened. Apparently, he was in the middle of an ugly divorce when his wife murdered their two young children. She attempted suicide but survived. During the trial, he left the States for good.

He was 48 years old when he landed in Bombay.

The Great Guru immediately noticed something different about the new arrival, a quality transcending the cold anarchies of grief. He knew he'd found a true adept, one whose self-realization was foretold—satori *a priori!*—just as he, the Great Guru, was predestined to be his guide. But it would take some work. The American's behavior was erratic. He'd vanish for days, sometimes weeks without notice, before reappearing to claim his usual spot at the foot of the sadhu's chair. Sometimes after those mysterious layovers, he was disheveled and disoriented. The Great Guru would order the Kitchen Cabinet—those roly-poly sister-aunties—to bathe and feed the Big Fish, spruce up the aquarium if you will. Other times he alighted from his travels impeccably dressed in linen suit and tie, as if fresh from Hong Kong, Johannesburg, Genève. After months of obliviously submitting to his artful guru's grooming, the American at last steadied his course.

In the year it took for the arriviste to settle, the Great Guru's focus on him never wavered. The proprietary denizens of the inner circle dug in their heels, girding for the long haul, cynically reassuring themselves that teacher's pets came and went and the newbie would be no exception. Others laid down odds the American was "next in line" and began kowtowing early. Through it all, the old sage cackled with delight. The idea of cultivating a *favorite* tickled his beggar's mouth pink, because it was no longer possible for him to have a personal relationship with *anyone* he encountered along the journey. For he had ceased being a person.

None of which meant he wasn't delighted upon learning his *chela* was a racetrack bookie on the side, nor that the two couldn't regularly share a glass of whiskey in the cool, early evenings. Nor did it mean he wasn't grateful for the acumen the American lent to the fledgling publishing enterprise on Mogul Lane. It was the expat who had suggested satsang be taped (it would have been reel-to-reel back then) and transcribed for wider dissemination. The Great Guru was enchanted by the idea and impishly rebuked his minions for not having thought of it first. How he enjoyed stirring the pot!

Sorry to interrupt myself but I probably haven't said enough to set the scene. I know I'm all over the place . . . maybe you can clean it up when you—I really *do* think I should get a little into how things worked. Not that it was all that mysterious, it's just that people really have no idea about what goes on in the life of an ashram. Mogul Lane wasn't really an *ashram*, strictly speaking . . . I promise this won't take too long.

You see, the Great Guru had been a householder and family man. Two of his five children died; his wife and him had 12 grandchildren and a ton of great-grandkids between them. She was a piece of work. Her three sisters—the "aunties"—did all the cooking (hence, the "Kitchen Cabinet") and had final say over any controversies that arose among the extended family, which occupied the two floors above the shop. All the tenants had been with "Baba" in excess of 40 years, loosely comprising what I've been calling the inner circle. *Mrs.* Great Guru kept a firm hand on the finances, which were robust on account of the steady stream of rupees donated each satsang day from attendees and local merchants; sent through the post, and so forth. A second ring of the inner circle looked after Baba's daily needs—laundry, grooming, medicines, that sort of thing. Last but not least was the outer ring of enthusiasts living in rooms scattered across the city, the typical patchwork of loners, zealots and malcontents who wash up on any *rishi*'s shore. Each ring was needy in its own way, the wife and aunties being the scrappiest, most demanding of the lot. The Great Guru took pleasure in every skirmish he secretly set in motion—

Hold on a second!

It just occurred to me you might be wondering how the *fuck* I know so much about the Great Guru—*a man I never met.*

Okay: it's an informed pastiche. Isn't that what life is anyway? And I'm really not being cute. Everything I'm telling you or am *about* to tell you was taken from notes of my conversations with the American himself. Because remember, I spent four rock'em sock'em months on Mogul Lane before I fled; the Great Guru had been dead only a short while and the American talked about him nonstop. Talked to *me*. The rest I'm filling in from things Kura said when we hooked up in Delhi—we are *getting* to Delhi, Bruce, I swear, don't you worry!—you know, things Kura told me as we headed to our momentous destination. Just *trust*. That everything I'm telling you—*everything*—has been drawn from my diaries and Kura's memory, and the so-called qualia too—remember "qualia," from school? (Maybe you weren't a philosophy freak)—sifted through contemporary consciousness with what *I* perceive to be *minor* embellishments, which in my opinion is a totally valid approach to telling a hopefully seamless tale, particularly one in which the narrator brings so much of her own life experience to bear. A story, *by the way*, that I'm uniquely qualified to share, taking into consideration not only my intimate knowledge of a key player but the quantity and quality of a lifetime of "meetings with remarkable men" . . . Liken me, if you will, to a gifted translator who couldn't possibly give you the literal text (no one could) but *can* approximate the rhythm and flavor, the *moods* of the original, and the true or *truest* sense of what the poetry evoked. The mother tongue. I'm the mother tongue motherfuckah.

In other words, have faith. I have no doubt you will. I can't imagine you've got a different strategy, doing this as long as you have.

Scheherazade sings for her supper.

Bathroom break, please?

* * *

We resumed three hours later.

Well, all rightie then.

Those satsang tapes were a brilliant success. The American had an entrepreneurial streak that was, well, very American. And the Great Guru *loved* American energy! The rookie was on a roll: from the tapes sprung the collected transcripts that comprised the golden calf of Mogul Lane Press, *The Book of Satsang*. (Up till then, I think there'd only been a few pamphlets and chapbooks.) An entire library rose, elucidating what the sadhu preferred to call his "concepts." The compilations benefited enormously from the American's elegant edits and translations. His fine ear was matched by a finer eye; he designed the book covers and even the typeface that was to become an MLP trademark. The ingeniously simple logic of it—satsang-to-tape (or cassette or whatever it was back then) -to-book—vaulted the Great Guru onto the world stage. The American was *very* shrewd when cutting distribution deals for his teacher's catalogue of essays, Advaitic homilies, and whatnot. His prescience was uncanny when it came to discerning who would work with him, and who would work against. He knew that if he was to succeed he had to imagine business dealings as a game, albeit one with serious consequences. He was sagacious enough to know that if ever he acted out of greed, the jig would be up.

Naturally, the books found their way to the States, where they piqued the interest of artists, singers and poets. Allen Ginsberg and Gary Snyder made a pilgrimage and stayed a few months, maybe in '63 or '64 . . . which actually might have been before the *Book* was published. (Peter Orlovsky was with them too.) Toward the end of my Bombay tour of duty, I remember being shown a photograph of the four of them— Ginsberg, Snyder, the American and the Great Guru—staring into the lens with "fierce grace." By then I was already beginning to resent Mogul Lane and the dominion it held over Kura. Still, I looked at that group shot and felt a pang of envy that *I* hadn't been there too . . . that funky old un-*"be here now"* feeling! And, oh: I can still see the framed page that hung on one of the grimier walls of the kitchen, torn from *The Lion, the Witch and the Wardrobe*: "There's nothing that spoils the taste of good ordinary food so much as the memory of bad magic food." No idea how it got there.

Now, back to that first day in Bombay.

1970. The Great Guru's dead, but Kura and I don't know it. Kura's sitting on the floor in front of the Master's chair, in excitation. Me? I'm halfway up a pole on my lookout, smugly surveying the scene, too green and/or discombobulated to ascribe any meaning to the fact that satsang was coming up on an hour-and-a-half late, a delay that would have been off the charts for a legendarily punctilious guru. And heedless of other signs too—the superabundance of flowers, the images of Baba glued to the paddles of hundreds of gyrating sticks held high in the air like bidders at an auction, the menagerie of musical instruments, their disparate songs in discordant competition amidst the general insanity. Nor did I take note of the ululating voices that rose and fell in an entangled, sometimes annoying ecstasy of mourning. Schooled in Western culture, it all seemed very rock star to me—weren't gurus the rock stars of India? Besides, what for-real rock star was ever on time?

A sudden implosion of quiet engulfed the shop, its shock waves spreading to the street and beyond like a silent alarm. The aggressive stillness stopped the urchins in their tracks, which said a lot. I shiver just remembering. It was unearthly . . .

—then *he* appeared. Not from the upstairs rooms, as would have been the tradition of the pandit, but from a side door . . . stepping gingerly through the multitudes as they parted like the Red Sea—I never thought I'd use that horrible platitude but nothing else can describe it, Bruce! (And incidentally, making his way along the same path my intrepid

Kura had blazed.) He was white, with blond, thinning hair and an aquiline nose. Tortoiseshell glasses. Early 50s? (He was actually 55.) I'm horrible with descriptions. Fairly bland though not unattractive. Very composed, very cool. *Lithe.* Had one of those lithe walks, a "supple gait," like a jaguar. A slight smile. Simple white kurta. I remember thinking he must be some sort of staffer who "ran" satsang. Probably'd make a few announcements before introducing the Main Event. But when he turned to face everyone, he didn't say a word. And oh! That otherworldly *silence* kept falling, the *sound* it made was deafening! Why was everyone so quiet? That sound . . . like flurries in a snow globe.

He was standing in front of the empty chair.

Kura watched, head arched back in a pose of tranquil curiosity. He too was expecting to hear preliminary—introductory remarks.

Then, the oddest thing happened:

The man sat down.

In the milliseconds that followed, I pegged him as a prankster, a rodeo clown using the sacred chair as a slapstick prop to keep the impatient crowd at bay, perhaps to soften the blow of the announcement that the star attraction was ill, and satsang would be postponed until tomorrow. A sonic boom interrupted my fantasia. A delirium of *voices*—like the reversed film of a building that was demolished, rising back up, a demolished *cathedral*—a great edifice of rising voices knocked my freakin' *socks* off. Outrageous decibels shattered the snow globe, ruptured my eardrums with joyful noise, blistering and rapturous. My reptilian brain reflexively commanded me to join the uproarious *Hosanna!* and I did.

Only Kura's throat remained still. I know, because I never took my eyes off him.

His song would come later.

* * *

I've searched my mind and can't remember a single thing the American said during satsang on that historic morning. But here's what I know about the death of his teacher:

Usually, the old man would awaken at 4 a.m. and retreat to the den to offer benedictions to the saints who came before him. Lost in prayer, he would bow to the Source itself and meditate until seven. But on the day he left this world, he forsook routine . . .

The American had a routine too. He arrived at the tobacco shop each morning around the time that his teacher was finishing up. He made tea and chitchatted with Baba about goings-on at the track—this, that and the other. After a while the American would excuse himself to go downstairs, where he effected the gentle transformation of the lobby into a room suitable for satsang. He fetched the daily flowers left *gratis* on the sidewalk by vendors, placed them in vases then carefully swept up. Pulled flat pillows from a closet for attendees to sit on. Put up the altar, arranging coils of incense and sepia portraits of the toweled and diapered Masters of Advaita. Lifted the Great Guru's well-oiled oak chair from its berth behind a display case, placing it front and center. Positioned a small table within the sadhu's reach. Set a glass on the table then filled the pitcher with water, covering it with a linen napkin.

On a counter near the entrance he laid out the beautiful Mogul Lane Press editions of the Great Guru's books, plus tapes of prior satsang, for sale. (I remember the volumes had the faint smell of cigars.) One of the last things he did was to set up a tape recorder and mic and make sure they were functioning properly. In the time remaining, he meditated, his awareness focused by street sounds and the quality of changing light. He took care to notice his breath and the soft, jostling shadows of wayfarers already gathering outside. Their heads merged and migrated, like elephants in a herd.

At around 8:30, he let them in. The American could be warm or distant, depending on his mood. There were always the needy ones with inane questions: What time does satsang start? What time does it end? Is there satsang on Sundays? and so on. He tried accommodating those who wished to buy books or tapes but most transactions happened after the Q&A.

Close to 9 o'clock, he would return to the mezzanine. The American always had oatmeal, prune juice, and toast with jam. Usually his teacher was already seated, dipping hunks of bread into a glass of hot chocolate. During breakfast the Great Guru rarely spoke though he wasn't above ribbing his tablemate's devotion to prunes by letting loose a cognoscente's barrage of farts. The American would smile but always managed to suppress a laugh, inciting the saint to new heights of gaseous devilry. As this was the designated time for the disciple to bring him up to speed on sundry household matters, the Kitchen Cabinet's attendance was compulsory. The ladies were loath to endure these noisome bull sessions but that was how Baba, in his infinite wisdom, had arranged it. While the oompah-pah of cosmic flatus grew more flagrant (not fragrant!), the Cabineteers clucked like chickens, kneading their brows and wringing their aprons in protest, looking

generally miserable. At quarter-past, with exaggerated polite-
ness, the Great Guru would excuse himself to make his toilet.
When at last he emerged rejuvenated, two of the heftier cous-
ins assisted him downstairs. By then, the American would
have taken his customary place at the foot of the chair. After
a few bows before the altar, the Great Guru lowered himself,
and satsang began.

But on that fateful day, the American overslept. It was the
first time this ever happened and he reasoned that his body
must have needed rest. Lately, he'd been more tired than
usual; maybe he was coming down with something. What
with his bookmaking—which referred to the horse and publishing enterprises in equal measure—and all the other jobs
and duties thrown his way, he was stretched thin. Then he
realized something with a start: he only *dreamt* he overslept. It
was actually four in the morning and he lay in a pool of sweat.

He closed his eyes again and pushed himself to remember fragments of a dream . . . *they were running on a track—
the American and the Great Guru. His beloved teacher was being
kicked by horses. Turning toward his disciple, he wore a spooky smile
that the American had trouble interpreting. Was it an expression of
transcendent equanimity? Or a plea for help? If the latter, his hands
were tied; intuitively, he knew any offer of rescue would be turned
away. Still, he wanted at least to make a face-saving gesture—in
the dream, he felt responsible for his teacher's suffering—but didn't
know how. The feeling of impotence, and the collateral violence,
was nauseating. The horses kept kicking and kicking. He heard the
sound of the saint's ribs snapping, breaking through the skin . . .* He
smothered any further recollections by promptly sitting up.
It was just too mortifying, too painful to know such brutality
swam in the shallow, primordial waters of his consciousness,

that he could claim ownership of a dream scenario that sponsored such sadism toward the man he loved above all others, the only being he would have died for! Such sadness and remorse . . . unbearable.

He leapt from drenched sheets to make tea but there wasn't any—he'd forgotten to buy. Which seemed like another bad dream. While rifling the drawers and cupboards, he resolved to visit an acquaintance for counsel, a venerated Sufi healer who lived on the street. The dream was of the type that aroused atavistic fears and superstitions and the American wanted to learn if it was an omen; perhaps there were steps he could take to counteract its unsettling, cryptic prophesy. He decided to have tea at the tobacco shop—a perfect antidote to his anxieties. The presence of Baba would be a comfort and help ameliorate the aftershocks of his vision. The *siddha* would just have begun morning prayers.

The American knew he was ill. His sweatless skin wanted nothing to do with the sweet, pre-dawn air. Yet the worse he felt, the greater his relief—at least sickness offered an explanation for those schizoid racetrack phantasms.

Just a fever dream . . .

By the time he reached Mogul Lane, he was winded. He made sure to softly close the door behind him (not that he ever closed it any other way), mindful not to startle his teacher's attendants—those from the second ring of the inner circle whose duty was to stand at post in the kitchen should the Great Guru call out for hot water with honey. Stranger things have happened, but a break-in was nearly unthinkable. Throughout the years there had never been an incident, not even of tomfoolery, nor had a single stem of the thousands upon thousands of roses left at the shop's door been absconded with.

In crept the American . . . to darkness, much darker than he imagined. His eyes stung from the inchoate virus. Immediately, he saw the furry outline of his Master's chair.

That's odd. Did I leave it there? Could I have?

A wave of nausea. He closed his eyes and steadied himself. He thought harder—*no way* would he have left it. The chair was his responsibility and his alone. At conclusion of satsang, there wasn't any question he'd have moved it back behind the case, where it normally lived. But at this moment, the American was unwell and lacked the clarity to be certain. The easy, confident relationship to reality that we take for granted, the ability to observe and process simple sensory data, to parse memory, had begun to decay. His mind whirred. Was it possible that at the end of Q&A, distracted by a rush of book and tape sales, he'd somehow forgotten to return the chair to its recess? And that the Great Guru, amused by his student's rare show of absent-mindedness, puckishly ordered it to remain in its derelict locale? The thought did seem a bit convoluted, far-fetched . . . *all that*, just for another little something to laugh about at their gassy morning kitchen klatches. Strange hijinks . . . to keep the chair there—more *peculiar*, than funny—

He tried to recall yesterday's events. He'd been at the track taking care of some bookie business . . . but *had* he returned to Mogul Lane? Had he come back at all? Because surely *then* he would have seen the chair and moved it—though he wouldn't have left it there in the first place so what difference would it have made if he'd come back? Suddenly he questioned which came first, satsang or the visit to the track. Well, satsang, of course . . . but *had* he? Come back? (Now it was more about the sheer, arduous remembering.) Perhaps not—perhaps he'd gone straight home. Maybe he still *was* home! This morning, he dreamt he overslept; it would make things so much easier if he could still be dreaming. Still in bed, and deathly ill . . .

Something superseded his tumbling thoughts—

What's this?

A pile of blankets on the chair—*no!* He startled and retreated, his wobbly investigations literally coming to a head. He skittered to flip the light switch, then heard a woman's shriek: his own. The Great Guru sat upright in his chair, eyes closed in mid-sip of the elixir of Eternity, illuminated from within as if by a swallowed ceiling bulb. How bizarre! The *chela* drew closer to regard the face. Its dentureless mouth bore the inviolable smile of those who die in peace and struggle no more. (Of course, the Great Guru stopped struggling long ago.) The American grew calm. He listened—it occurred that no one heard him cry out. Strange . . . He sat in meditation with the body until the first rays of dawn penetrated the shop's window. He lit incense and candles and draped a blanket across his teacher's lap. Upstairs, bodies and voices began to shift.

Bedlam ensued, and wild disarray.

Everyone went out of their minds. The inner circle was confounded by anguish, waylaid by grief. The widow was the first to stabilize and the others raggedly followed suit. In misery, it remained vital to eat. Hence, engines were stoked—the Kitchen Cabinet was in full throttle, adhering to an ancient tradition mandating all mouths be fed from the ovens of the house of the holy man who had merged with the Godhead. Vast amounts of foods delivered round the clock were ceremonially recycled, simmering long enough on the stove to be stirred by the Great Guru's ladle; the neighborhood's potluck and covered plates revolved with speedy, solemn ritual through the upper apartments' quarters, their turnaround point being the den, the room said to be the most heavily imbued with the perfumed breath of the departed. (Even his bathroom was mined for hairs he'd shed, nails he'd clipped, for ambergris of earwax.) A host of activities, sacred and banal, carried forth amidst unthinkable, unmendable loss. When agonies reached a fatal pitch the brain intervened, reflexively enforcing time-outs, moratoriums on weeping and wailing, impromptu cease-fires—after all, tears needed to be replenished—caesuras in the song of suffering that allowed shattered devotees time to sleep, to eat, to bathe. The grief-stricken looked forward to such stupefaction the way workers do a holiday.

The stone of such a catastrophic loss makes ripples in the water like rings in the trunk of a mighty redwood. (Sorry for the fucked-up simile.) Mortality's clock ticks so slowly—then so quickly—that every hour of each successive day circling the ground zero of his death seemed to form a generation; so that within the week, when the body was burned on the Ganga, decades had already passed since the event. By the time Kura and I were finally informed, whole epochs had come and gone, civilizations fallen and risen again.

The American was well equipped to deal with postmortem concerns. He knew his logistics but more importantly was able to mask his turmoil of emotions with an assuaging air of almost sunny indifference. In his years with Baba, he'd become deeply enmeshed in the ashram's business and the widow trusted him implicitly. Normally, details of the funeral and other attendant decisions would redound to her; those responsibilities were summarily dropped in his lap. To the larger community, a number of arguments supported this wisdom. Many believed the unseen forces that awakened the American from his fever (and cleared his cupboard of tea) were the same ones that had guided him with invisible hand to Mogul Lane—in essence, he had been "summoned." How otherwise to explain his teacher's baffling behavior? Why else would he have been downstairs at 4 a.m., instead of singing supplications in the den? Why would he have pulled out his chair and sat waiting, on *this* morning, if it was not because he had chosen to die? It was obvious: the Great Guru carefully set the stage before invoking his favorite student to see him off. *A final satsang for an audience of one!* Any way you cut it, to discover the body of a saint is a fateful honor of inescapable import. And that he chose to meditate beside his beloved teacher was universally thought of as a magnificent gesture, which undoubtedly eased the Great Guru's passage through the bardo of death. To say the American's status rose higher each day would be an understatement.

But the most "auspicious" sign of all was the nightmare he had of the *rishi* pursued by demons yet lightheartedly impervious to assault. He'd instantly regretted recounting his dream to the widow, an indiscretion he blamed on fatigue and the vulnerability of the moment. Too late . . . she took it as a further sign of providence.

The guru was out of the bottle and would soon be hellbent on granting a wish—whether it be the American's or not.

After the cremation, after the flowers and feasts and gutted candles, after the bitter herbs of death metamorphosized into the nectar of gratitude to God for having graced all of them with the privilege of having known and loved such a saint, after the frozen river of tears thawed enough to restore hearts and minds to the modest homes they'd decamped, after everything, came The Question that hung in the air like a fiery harvest moon obscured by clouds. A storm of a question, whose distant rhetorical rumblings would soon be exchanged for lightning, hail and thundered demands: *Who would sit in the Great Guru's chair?*

* * *

The American slept little in the weeks following the death.

He no longer went home at night, preferring to lie on a straw mat on the floor of the shop. He felt beyond exhaustion.

And what about the chair? The widow ordered it to be left exactly where it was found. The American would stare at it before drifting off, almost against his will, his imagination at play in the shifting chiaroscuro. If he squinted just right, he could trick himself into seeing a seated figure; with another sleight of eye, the chair vanished altogether . . .

Though sometimes a chair was just a chair—the saddest realization of all.

During this in-between time he thought about the future but the farthest he got was trying to envision a life without his teacher. The prospect took the wind out of him.

Not long after, the widow invited him into the den where her husband used to meditate and sing morning devotionals. She got right down to troubling business.

"*You must take the chair!*[3] It is your *time*. God *willed* it— even *you* cannot challenge the events of that morning. They were *preordained*. And who is there better than you for the job?

---

3   Queenie's impersonation of an overbearing Indian matriarch was deliciously venal, complete with bobbing head and comically fractured syntax.

If you know, *do* tell. You must *listen*. Twas *you* who sat at Baba's feet for years. Twas *you* who helped spread his teachings wide and far—you know them cold! Your *body* is knowing them too, not just your mind. This you cannot challenge! What I am saying, you have an *obligation*. You have a *duty*. That is what I am saying. He that is immortal *loved* you. He invited you to the far corners of his heart, and *other* places, where *no one* has traveled, not even *myself*! I beg you to consider! There are many good reasons to take the chair other than those I enumerated. The ones I am giving you now are the *best* reasons, the most *obvious*, for they are rooted in *simplicity* and *common sense*. But I contest there are *many others*, and some among them which are *more* than quite pressing. Surely, you are naïve to what I'm referring? I am telling you first to *consider*—then *reconsider*. You must take the chair! Now, *good*. Go! We shall talk again."

That night the American slept at home.

You must take the chair!

He wanted to talk back, but what could he say?

You must take the chair!

It was like being warned by a gypsy or getting advice from a consigliere in a cheap mob drama . . . she made him feel like a hoodlum. And in *that* room, no less, that room of prayer, his *father's* room! He found himself fantasizing about leaving Bombay, something that never crossed his mind until now. He hadn't yet visited Benares; it was said all men must go to Benares at least once in their lives. To die in Benares meant to escape the cycle of suffering and rebirth and gain direct admittance to nirvana. A vision of himself in that ancient city grabbed hold.

For the next few days, the American went about his business on Mogul Lane. Millions of rupees had rained down since the Great Guru's death. All *dana* needed to be carefully logged and accounted for; such scrupulousness seemed more important now than ever. He was glad the "books" were in order, no small thanks to his past efforts. The Kitchen Cabinet toadies continued to unnerve, sneakily lobbying for his surrender to promotion to *chairman*—though he knew they were simply doing the widow's bidding. The American cauterized the wounds in his heart with his contempt for her sleazy proposition. He knew it was only a matter of time before she cornered him again yet whenever he mentally composed a vicious response to her entreaties, he pulled up short. "What am I doing? After all, this is the woman my beloved teacher chose to marry. The union the Source smiled upon!"

Soon he was back in the den. And this time, the widow wasn't fucking around.

"The situation grows *very dire*. I think you do not have a full understanding of what is at stake! As you Americans say, *let me lay it out for you*. Through *intermediaries*, the member of a very powerful *family* has expressed keen interest in buying the shop—*lock, stock and kaboom*—for a sum even *you* would not believe if I told it to you straight to your face. It seems this *family* member, who shall remain *nameless*, was a *devotee* who did not *emerge* from the closet *as* a devotee until *after* Baba's death . . . for this, I was given no reason. So be it. This *family* member is, at the current moment, working through the *most arcane* of municipal channels—apparently, the *family* to which he belongs has a *raft* of local politicians firmly in *pocket*. The *intermediaries* of whom I speak have *roundly expressed* this family member's *wish*, should he succeed in his efforts to become said property's owner, to transform the *entire block* into a *spiritual amusement park*—your guru's *tobacco shop* being the tour's crowning terminus! But I was told by the *intermediary* not to *worry*. You see, the intermediary has *virtually guaranteed* that the *family* member has given his word: my husband's *'boutique'* shall be strictly maintained up to *'current museum standards.'* Why, the *intermediary* even suggested the *siddha*'s chair be placed on *display* behind *bulletproof glass*!

"My American friend, I won't say the money isn't *tempting*. No. I am not so foolish to make such a proclamation. As you know, Baba did not care a *whit* about it, money's merely a *tool*. The princely sum—*kingly!*—offered by this *intermediary person* would allow me to set up house very nicely, in a neighborhood even *more* pleasant than this. Because here there are no trees and I have been missing them since I was a girl. I am no martyr. I refuse to cling to appearances!—'Guru Ma, widow of the Great Guru,' and so forth. *If* I accept his monies, quite a *bit* would be left over to service the impoverished. *More* than quite a bit, so *more's the pity*. Make no mistake: I *am* your guru's widow but rest insured I have no qualms standing upon the neck of ceremony! Because when I am naughty, it does occur that an 'Advaita Museum' might even cause Baba a few grand *guffaws!* But herein lies the *problem*, my American friend: this arguably *grotesque* proposal only stands up for limited engagement—I am hearing the political bosses are already working *hard* for the intermediary's *money*. And *if* they succeed, there is a *distinct chance* I shall have but *no choice* in the matter. The offer shall expire . . . and I shall be forced to sell for a song!

"An interesting *alternative* reared its hind legs not just *three hours ago*—I tell you, things are flying fast and furious! It seems a man of *shady origin* expressed the desire to *buy us out* for the sole purpose of providing a place for his harlot daughter to bed down. The pair came to see me. The air is not yet clear of their stink; not even the fattest of Baba's cigars could conceal the rank smell of flesh and greed left in their trail. This *seedy* character had the amazing gall to say he was not merely an *acolyte* of Baba but an Advaita scholar to boot! He took me aside to confess it was his sincere hope that whichever 'essences' of the venerable saint remained—the hissing pronunciation of the word was revolting!—that whichever *essences* were left behind might have a *'salutary effect'* upon the disease-ridden prostitute he calls his daughter. 'Dear sir, spend your money in buying a clinic instead! One with a good supply of penicillin!' I held my tongue. Meanwhile, the miniskirted *rodent* paced the room as we spoke, looking this way and that, like a decorator who stepped in shite. To put an end to our whispering, which she didn't like at all, the strumpet sashayed over—hardly dressed at all, my friend!—and began prattling on about Oxford and Cambridge! Sheer lunacy! She spoke more nonsense than her father. And how she turned on the slutty *charm*. As if *I* was her next conquest!

"You might ask my motive for inviting them in. And I'll *tell* you . . . I agreed to *rendezvous* for one reason, and one reason only: I was intensely curious to lay an eye on the man who had *doubled* the offer made by the aforementioned intermediary, which in *itself* was a king's ransom! To make things even more interesting, no one at the banks or newspapers had ever heard of him!

"But these stories amuse. I'm quite certain these fools can be handled. What I am *next* going to tell you is an animal of a *different* stripe. It is far more pertinent, as it involves your personal welfare. So you must listen very *carefully* . . .

"You are aware you've always been envied, true? From the beginning! O yes . . . I know this sort of question makes you

uncomfortable, you must not answer, there is no *need*. It's rheto-
ric. You see, the personal trait of yours Baba admired most was
that you made no *investment* in the spiritual world. He extolled
very much that part of you which would not feel *betrayed* if one
day he were to *close up shop* . . . that would not feel *fleeced* or
cheated of his rightful profits. O he used to tell me this about you
with a gleaming eye—yours is an attitude *not the norm*, I insure!
Because in the end, all seekers desire for a profitable enterprise,
a pay-off, a dividend! They want to be in the *black* . . . You yourself have seen the type of person who is attracted to Baba and
his teachings. Cast-offs of the Earth—as it should be. You were
one too, no? A somewhat broken man when first you arrived,
I recall . . . ashrams are *filled* with the miserable, the tragic,
the befuddled. But let me say: the courage that gets them here,
and watches over them on their long journeys, the dogged sin-
gle-mindedness of *purpose* is also the very thing that makes them
available for nobler pursuits. Other than saving their own hides,
which of course is a natural inclination. Do you know what I'm
saying, sir? *Here's* what I'm saying. There are certain amongst
them—amongst the so-called *advanced* echelon who've been
here a while—there are certain amongst them who have their
eye—have *had* their eye, for years now!—on the guru's chair.
O you would be *surprised* at who fancies himself a candidate.
Sergei, of course . . . he's always been outgunning for you. And
Ludmilla! Ludmilla from Romania! Barely with Baba for three
years, but who knows . . . lady *siddhas* are suddenly *in vogue*. She
might just be voted into that chair by popular demand.

   "The plotting is worthy of Shakespeare! And *you*, my
American friend, have been *spared*—for the moment. Because
you are *top seed*! It's all sport, I liken it to tennis that way—did
you know Baba and me used to travel to Wimbledon? We did,

oh yes, when Baba taught at Oxford. There are many elimination matches before sudden death . . . but this should not concern you, not *unduly*. Like my 'window shoppers,' pretenders to the throne may be *handled*.

"You have *other* problems, friend, believe in me!

"I know you are a worldly man. You have *guts*, and would never have gotten so close to Baba if that weren't the case, he simply would not have *allowed* it. The stars would not have let it *happen*. Yet I must tell you: about *some* things, you are stunningly naïve. You spent years under the protectorship of your munificent guru. You stared only into *his* light—precisely as it should have been—which made you blind to other *influences* at *work*. But you have that protection no more! Bombay is a metropolis of saints and sadhus, my friend, but it is also a city of rogues, of *thuggees* . . . many so-called holy men are one and the same! They are indistinguishable! There are *networks* of gurus in rule of *whole sectors*, each with the iron hand of a *warlord*! *Swami mafiosi* . . . and these are dangerous men, not simply because of the counterfeit nature of their teachings. Many have followers who know *nothing* of their greed and violent ways and hold them in their hearts with the innocence of children! With the same loving regard as did you your precious guru . . . These *criminals* give satsang, sit cross-legged on great stages *groaning* with flowers. It is not *manna* one smells in the air, but *manure*! They hold forth to the *limpets*, the *lampreys* and the *sheep* in stolen words pried from Baba's mouth—cribbed from his books—*your* books!—rolling the pirated phrases 'round in *shit* like pigs in mud till the sentences fit their mercenary temperament or whatever the mood of the morning.

"Let me get to the point: there are *two* who need watching out for. They wish to collect Baba's *legacy* as if it were some sort of *payment due.* There is a long-haired thuggee, a *murderer,* who is chauffeured here and there in a Rolls-Royce wearing silken pajamas. *He actually believes he is our long-lost son!* His attorney forced me to give a sample of my blood, it was of course no match but still he *persists*—such are the delusions! I am telling you, American friend, this is all very serious! The thuggee believes in all his diseased heart that I am Mommy and Baba was *Daddy*, the man has his flock of sheep believing it too! A murderer and a fool! As long as your guru was *alive*, they never came near. Naturally, these men had nothing to fear from Baba, but fear him they *did.* And let me inform you of something you seem not to know: *they are now ready to take what they are most certain is theirs!* Only a *single thing* still prevents them from storming the palace—a slender thread—because what ecstasy to at last be moguls of Mogul Lane, you better know it! It is the jewel in their crown! The only *single thing* that still prevents them from staking their claim is the very *real hesitation* in the face of those loyal masses who did rightfully worship our Baba. They are keenly aware those devoted *masses* are a sleeping giant best not awakened! Do you know what these *cads* fear most? Humiliation! Defeat! Loss of *face.* It would not bode well for their reputations, to be chased out on a rail! That would be a terrible *misstep*, serious enough to threaten their entire operation! General besmirchment and bloody turf wars would ensue.

"I have one more thing to add. I know you are worldly enough to understand there is always a *corker*—a mad one, more barbaric than his brethren—there is always a lunatic looking to make his mark. The corker's advantage—in tennis, this is called 'add'—is *recklessness.* And I, my friend, through a *skein* of intelligence maintained by Baba loyalists, am now privy to the identity of our greatest threat . . .

"This is the longest and shortest of what I am saying: *You must sit in that chair.* Swallow your stubborn pride and muddle through a month of satsang until you have sea legs! Accept the momentous responsibility of that which has fallen upon your shoulders by divine plan! If you continue to give weight to cautious indecision—which as you know has its roots in that distinctive American trait called *neurosis*—if you continue to fly in the face of *your guru himself*, you shall find there is a terrible price to pay. I tell you the guru-thuggees are out for blood! When your fanny hits that seat and not before shall you be safe and under *new protectorship*: that of the *masses*. Already, the guru-thuggees know who you are—oh yes! They have been *boning you up* for some time. Have you not seen them, hanging 'round outside your apartment? Of *course* you haven't, why would you be looking? You're *blissfully* unaware. Not a care in the world! A little *baba* in the woods . . . well they are *not* interested in your autograph, sir. We've *all* been looking, all but you! They *know* you were Baba's favorite; they used to *fear* you. But each day they fear you less and less!

"Let me be frank. We're both well aware Baba had no fixed ideas on the topic of successorship *per se*; he was of a mind the whole business was *poppycock*. But it is imperative you approach any ideas you have about what your guru would have 'wished'—you must approach any such fantasies of 'knowing' what actions he may or may not have taken if he were still with us—you must destroy this notion that something about you is so *special* that it is actually *possible* for you to apprehend his *philosophies* enough to speak *for* him—you must consider this entire line of thought to be purely chimerical. The *certitude* that accompanies, sponsors and endorses *any* thought, no matter how trivial that thought might be, must always be thoroughly examined and approached with *great caution*. And then that certitude must be *vanquished*. For the mind is the enemy, my American friend! Guard against arrogance! If a person *ever* imagines it possible to know the mind of his guru, that person has set himself on a course to Hell! To believe oneself privy to a pandit's thoughts—if one may even call them 'thoughts'—it seems to me that to call them *anything* is another presumption—to believe one can truly *know* the 'mind' of a living master, let alone a dead one, providing of course that the guru is authentic . . . *that*, my friend, is to enter perdition. A triumph of Mind and nothing else. This is not to say one can never have a *feeling* or *energetic inkling* . . . but to suddenly be in prideful *possession* of such inklings or feelings is as delusional as the belief one has *full knowledge*, for the mind interprets them in the same way. To have *inklings* about one's guru's *intention* is a meaningless obscenity! Far better to admit to knowing nothing! At least with the latter, one lays claim to an ethical morality. The guru is *not* your friend! To presume *intimacy* is the sheerest of vanity. This is not America! The guru is not your Daddy nor is he your *bro'*. He ain't your 'buddy' either . . . *You*—*all* of us—are simply *unfit* to interpret the concepts of the Great Guru, who lived in *Silence*, who was—*is*—unknowable! Dare to indulge such presumptions and you are no better than the guru-thuggees! True, one feels an aching closeness to his teacher and misses him grievously when he is gone . . . that cannot nor should be denied. Yet in the shortest time, the mind transforms sorrow into the Cyclops of narcissism. You believe your hesitance to sit in the chair is indicative of humility, to 'refuse the mantle,' but the opposite is true! You're wearing your obstinance like a peacock!

"You hesitate to *sit* because you have the notion that some-how your guru would not *approve*. But there is a fly in the anointment of your logic. My husband was neither politician nor strategist so how would it be possible for him to get lath-ered over this *figment* now causing you such distress? He is no Dear Abby in the sky. Because I know what you're thinking, I know the *beggar's mind*, you have the idea he would not *approve* of you taking the chair, or worse, that you're not *worthy*. I say 'worse' because of the monstrous egotism involved in such a sentiment. Need I remind you what intrigued Father most was energy *itself* and how it manifests, which is precisely why the *Source* 'arranged the dance,' and why he was so *tickled* by your presence. And don't forget! It is the same Source that designed the predicament you are in today! *That* is the cosmic joke, my American friend! Baba delighted in your *energy*, plain and simple. He knew that if your energy could be disciplined, con-tained and manipulated, you just might have what he called 'the chance of a chance' . . . to be liberated from the Wheel!

"Look. There is no question you're a charming fellow. You've been a careful, obedient student. You are a practical man as well, and know how to make yourself useful. But surely you cannot have thought he kept you around for your skills! Do you believe he considered you indispensable? The Wizard of Oz behind the drapes of the tobacco shop, riding in on his horse to save the *hi-yo-silver* day? That he wrung his hands and cried to the gods, 'What would I do without him?' No! He did not give a *whit* and a *hoot* about the books you made, the ponies you played, the women you consorted with, or anything else! Surely, you *know* this—and if you do *not*, I shall be quite surprised and disappointed. Though I've been surprised and disappointed before . . . but I am telling you *now*. Baba had no need of friends, favorites, *cohorts*. If you don't know this, then you know less than nothing! He was no longer *human* that way. He certainly didn't need *followers* . . . Your guru gave satsang out of filial piety to the Source whence he came. In weaker moments—human ones!—he allowed himself a small, trembling excitation upon encountering those whose energy delighted him—such as you—with whom he might brush against the bodhisattva's dream: *to free all sentient beings from their cage of suffering*. Usually the ones he felt an affinity toward never stayed too long on Mogul Lane. He never thought *you'd* stay but you *did*, and that was a *bonus*, a very unusual occurrence! That was why he kept you close, because your energy was *familiar*. Fraternal. Unrefined yet similar to his. And it tickled him that you never had a clue what was 'in your wallet'!"

The widow stood, signaling she was nearly done.

"Each time you pressed Baba's feet at satsang's end, it was confirmed in the most *captivating* way. He would tell me your touch never failed to convey the 'congeniality' of your energetic configuration . . .

"I *warn* you, dear friend, do *not* make this more complicated than it is! Take your place in the chair! Do not be bothered that most of them will have need to declare you were appointed by royal decree! Six puffs of smoke from the roof, from Baba's favorite cigar! They shall see it through the crudest lens, they always do! Your challenge will be not to believe it, any of it! Making you feel *special* is not the devil's work, it's the *mind's*. The mind will summon you to its bloody battlefield . . . a clarion call not easy to resist. To hell with how it will *look*. In time all will come 'round, I can assure—

"Think it over, my American friend, I urge you! *Carefully consider* why you flee from your destiny. Your life is in certain danger! There isn't much time and I shan't come begging again. For all is *predetermined*! But mark my words, soon enough all will shout: 'The Great Guru is dead, long live the Great Guru!'"

* * *

I've been telling this story as straightforward as I can but it's convoluted by nature. Shall we do a timeline?

That last scene (hope you enjoyed) occurred roughly a month after the Great Guru's death and some 48 hours before Kura found his place at the foot of the chair—a position, by the way, he would occupy for seven years. (As it happened, his apprenticeship to the American lasted precisely as long as the latter's under the Great Guru.) Now we circle back to a question: When Kura and I first arrived at Mogul Lane just what the hell was going on? With that insane and glittering mob?

You see, mornings had become especially difficult since Baba's death. As the hubbub of bereavement began to recede, the void once filled by satsang became a continuous reminder of the Great Guru's absence. By unspoken rule, the lobby was off-limits between 9:30 and 11 when he would have held forth; its use as a walk-through vestibule or nostalgic loitering place felt disrespectful. There was a new wrinkle—devotees still gathered outside as they used to, only much earlier. Occasionally the satsang-less queue outgrew the sidewalk, snaking into the street with dangerous nonchalance. The police delicately brought this "hazard" to the attention of a Cabineteer, who brought it to the widow, who brought it to the American, who was only annoyed by the bureaucrats' bogus distress. As far as he was concerned, the whole of India was a hazard. That was when he made a brilliant decision to open the doors to the Master's house for what he privately referred to as "ghost satsang."

They filed in like it was a cathedral, festive young voices abruptly stilled by the humble oratorium. Attendees, lost in prayer and self-reflection, were so quiet the unexpected sight of them invariably startled this or that auntie passing through on official business. The American was touched by their earnestness. Now and then he found himself discreetly joining the throng near the shop's entrance. It was more séance than satsang but if he shut his eyes the presence of his beloved teacher could most definitely be felt. At a few minutes before eleven, when the Great Guru would have begun closing hymns, the voices began to whisper, a chorus of throats gargling with *sutras* before joining in song as one. It gave him gooseflesh. Naturally, they asked after the Great Guru's books and tapes. The American put a disciple in charge, a solitary Norwegian woman who moved to Bombay fourteen years earlier so she might give her life to the saint. Each morning she laid everything out.

And so it happened that all appeared unchanged, except for the absence of he who once presided—though it must be said that the empty chair, dramatically indifferent in its *thing-in-itself*-ness, proved a worthy stand-in for its vanished occupant.

Word of *ghost satsang* spread. In time, the early morning pilgrims (whom the American wryly dubbed *tobacconistas*) were joined by the simply curious. The shop began to groan under the weight of lurid mythology. Pop-up folklore had it that the Great Guru's emanations radiated from the chair but were only visible to those of strongest faith. Another claim promised visitors to the shrine a spectacular rise in income, if not an outright windfall within the year. It wasn't long before the infirm of body (there were already plenty infirm of mind!) hobbled and rolled onto Tobacco Road. The rich sent servants to keep their places in the queue in order to secure a coveted spot near the empty chair. The widow took the American aside, pointing out the ponytailed thuggee she'd warned him about. By the time the dangerous guru reached the door, the shop was filled to capacity. He implored to be let in but was sent gloomily packing. "Good riddance!" she said, adding that he'd merely come "to case the job."

A command performance limned by an understudy (the chair) nonetheless became the hottest ticket in Bombay. In lieu of demanding VIP treatment, local politicians made a great convivial show of waiting on line. As elections loomed it was important to demonstrate they were men of the people, if not *for* the people. Once inside, the burdens of municipal business fell away, allowing a pause for prayer not less than three minutes nor more than five. These enterprising gentlemen made the most of their time, shedding tears for "our Baba" and receiving imaginary blessings. On taking leave, they cavalierly waved away constituents' offerings of handkerchiefs to wipe wet eyes blinking above wetter cheeks. The same politicos soon found themselves on the horns of a dilemma. Three aficionados—one Canadian and two Englishwomen—were fatally struck by cabs in as many weeks. Even worse, a cow was hit, and perished. (*Not* a good omen.) Pickpockets were rife as rats. Initially thrilled by the Great Guru's promisingly lucrative afterlife, vendors began to fight amongst themselves over choice sidewalk billets, the closer to the tobacconist's the better. Mogul Lane became *the* up-and-coming destination for tourists led by irreligious guides. These scruffy docents spoke into microphones as they drove, delivering nonsensical lectures about the concepts of the Great Guru, his rumored wealth, the speculation he'd been poisoned and whatnot. They delved into the spiritual, in cocksure possession of an hermetic knowledge of the liminal, subliminal and sublime. Meanwhile, the governor was harassing the mayor to bust things up—to restore the neighborhood to relative sanity and let sleeping gurus lie.

Election time—a sticky wicket!

What, then, finally pushed the American into the widow's camp and the chair itself? I think it was attrition as much as fate. Because it was *my* impression he was bully-proof. And I *never* thought him capable of abrogating his integrity by servicing a brand-name legacy—nor could I envision the American plotting against those who might wish him harm. He was tired, he was grieving, he was *noble*, and had no fight in him. He just wanted to be left in peace. But instead of his teacher's death providing a reflective respite, he suddenly found himself absurdly challenged. *Aggressively* so. It was a bitch of a conundrum . . . the whole business was wildly inconvenient. He kept reviewing the widow's words. Whatever her flaws, stupidity wasn't one of them. It was true that the American's *concept* of his guru's opposition to so-called successorship had hardened into dogma. The widow's assertion that her husband had spent his life battling the perceptual policies and prejudices of man neatly overturned the American's reasoning. She was right and he knew it. The old *siddha* wasn't for or against *anything*, including someone taking out the chair for a spin. To see it any other way would mean that he'd wasted years at his guru's feet. *To sit or not to sit?* became the burning question that his egotism, laziness and outright terror threatened to ignite into a conflagration. To answer it would take everything he had, everything he'd learned in the last seven years and more.

On just such a day, in the midst of a lot of Hindi hoopla, did Kura and I make our famous entrance—duly orchestrated by the Source. May the trickster gods rejoice!

Graduation Day for us all . . .

I can't recall a word of the American's first Q&A. (Though squawk boxes strung on the outside of the shop gave broadcast.) I think I already told you that, didn't I? You know, I might be getting a little punchy—let's stop soon and have supper?

O . . . there's something I *do* remember that's important not to forget.

When any satsang ends, not just the Great Guru's, one "presses" the teacher's feet in respect. An ancient gesture. Devotees jockey to get there first. You know, "If I touch the feet before all others, that makes me special." The human being is stark raving mad, don't you think? Absolutely *wired* for hierarchy, we do hierarchy in our sleep. Kura was in the catbird's seat, or in front of it anyway. So *he* was the first. I had a perfect view from my pole . . . He prostrated himself then pressed his forehead to the floor. Remaining thus, he extended his arms for their short, deferential journey, that gentle, timeless laying on of hands. What happened next was as horrifying as it was baffling. The moment contact was made between Kura's hands and the American's feet, well, the man in the chair went *rigid*. I swear, his eyes shone with something that looked like *apocalyptic dread*. His mouth hung slack like an idiot's and the rest of him—I'm not sure I can properly convey! He looked so *startled* and *confused*, like he'd jumped from his skin . . . then came that *weird* silence again, remember how I was saying that in the moments before he sat down there was this *eerie silence?* Well there it came, no one breathed, not a soul, that behind-the-snow-globe silence I thought I'd never hear again in my life. The collective breath hung in suspension as I went about my lightning lucubrations to explain the reaction: Had Kura pressed too hard? Was there something wrong with the man in the chair's feet? (I say "man in the chair" and not "the American" because at this time you see we really had no idea who this simulacrum was or what was the meaning of it.) Was he about to have some sort of *fit?* A flurry of colorful thoughts followed: *What the fuck am I doing in India? Kura doesn't love me anymore, he never did . . . I want to go home now, how can I get home? But where* is *home?*

Just then, a coquettishly simian grin bloomed on the fellow's face as he sat bolt upright. He looked gemütlich and hyperalert. This time though, the effect was radiantly comedic, his countenance Chaplinesque. He began to mime a convict sizzling in an electric chair, not scary but *delightful*, his ticcing, twitching face pelted by the most wonderful hailstorm of expressions that morphed from an obsequious smile to the rictus of a silent scream (and everything in-between) as if to deftly convey a mission statement to the tribe: "I am not the Great Guru! He *cannot* be replaced . . . Yet I ask you to fear nothing, you are still in his hands! Have patience, I beseech you! I beseech you to trust! It is impossible for *energy* to err, of that you can be certain! Mysterious forces have brought me to this chair! All is *predetermined* . . ."

Thus, at the tail end of his inauguration, as a fillip to the substantive, wittily learned, deeply satisfying nature of his responses to the audience's questions, did the vaudevillian Vedic scrum swing from the sublime to the ridiculous then back again, celebrated by a communal roar of approbation.

The American had gambled with antic play, the same his teacher had usually confined to the kitchen table. It was a brilliant stroke. The maneuver forced skeptical seekers to challenge their reactionary resistance to change. He was *their* saint now (at least in this moment, for mobs are notoriously fickle) and had gained more than a toehold on their ardor and respect, perhaps even on their fear . . . Many pairs of hands followed Kura's. The American's face became inscrutable while he received further benedictions, which seemed befitting. For he was the American no more.

He was the Great Guru.

* * *

As I said—this I know I *did* tell you—Kura remained on Mogul Lane and environs for seven years. During satsang he could always be found in the exact spot he alit upon that first morning. He became fluent in the same duties the American had been entrusted by his own teacher.

Me? I lasted about four months, four very *long* months—I was young, and bored with the company. The ashram die-hards and devotees were either putzes or major dicks and that last category included women. I did some fooling around (I was an equal gender employer) but Kura didn't seem to give a shit. He'd lost the urge. I tried not to take it personally. After the head rush of Bombay wore off, I grew restive. He had enough sense to give me a long leash. He was too caught up in the annihilation of the Self to be bothered.

I went through a manic month of buying rare fabrics. I became addicted to the markets that sold them, whole cities unto themselves where transactions were conducted over dreamily aromatic tea in hidden rooms looking out on acres of silk, linen, cotton, muslin. I made day trips in search of obscure ayurvedic treatments, though what I really wanted was a massage that would never end—I wanted to massage my way to nirvana. The longer I stayed, the stranger my pursuits. I uncovered an infamous cult of sacred prostitutes who taught me their bittersweet songs. (That's another story.) Day trips became overnights, overnights turned into weekends, weekends into extended stays. I actually loved India but discovered I didn't enjoy traveling by myself, which was a new one because I so cherished and protected my autonomy. Now I see what I couldn't see then: I was furious at the American for stealing my man. I could handle the abstinence part but not having him in bed with me was a bear. He insisted on sleeping alone, something having to do with his "subtle body." I think I was probably going through withdrawal because sex with us was *definitely* a drug. I kept our suite at the Taj and Kura rented a disgusting little room much closer to Mogul Lane. Each time I returned from one of my forays, I fantasized he'd appear at the hotel to apologize for his behavior, and come to his senses by announcing we were leaving for Paris *at once*—or Morocco, Ibiza, Timbuktu—*if* I'd have him. (At this point in the fantasy, he was still down on his knees.) In reality, he was sullen and displeased. Which was immensely disconcerting to a wild child like myself who was accustomed to a man's affections compounding in ratio to the amount of time I'd blown him off. I'd always heard that gurus were notorious for taking their students to bed, but my efforts to seduce the American were a dismal failure. Finally, I worked up the courage to tell Kura I wanted to go home. Wherever that was . . . the Marais I suppose. I didn't get the reaction I'd hoped.

One day, he showed up at the pool while I was doing my club sandwich thing. (I always order triple-deckers at hotel pools, it's a Queenie tradition.) I was on a chaise longue fooling

around with a rich kid whose parents had taken the train to
Goa without him. Out of nowhere Kura grabbed my arm. The
boy hightailed it—so blind was Kura's anger I don't even think
he noticed. He began to shout about how he'd made a mistake
bringing me there, how I was an albatross around his neck,
that at long last he found what he'd been searching for and
was hereby firing himself from the job of *nanny* . . . I kept a
stiff upper lip, not easy under the circumstances. I said I was
happy for him and didn't *need* a nanny, thank you very much.
I must have been talking through my tears but it wouldn't
have mattered. He wasn't listening. He said he wasn't going
to waste his time on a spoiled little cunt doomed to perpetual
adolescence and that I was "spitting at God," flushing my only
chance at self-liberation like so much *shite* down the toilet. In
mid-tirade, he grabbed my hand by the wrist and raised it up
as if to present its amputated fingers to the jury as Exhibit A.
I recall a jolly waiter striding triumphantly toward us with my
club, fries and sundae held high on a tray. When he saw what
was going down, he neatly swiveled and departed. I was still
seated and Kura was standing; he held my wrist so high that
my shoulder flirted with dislocation. As hurtful as it was, and
as poorly handled, I understood where Kura was coming from.
His life had been dislocated too, in the most gorgeous way,
and he'd generously wanted me to have the same experience.
I had my doubts about his new relationship. At the time, I felt
he was determined to meet a guru, *any* guru, it just turned
out that the American was the *handiest*, with the best prove-
nance. I never thought it would last—and believe me, when he
crawled back to me I wasn't planning on being there to pick
up the karma. So I pretty much handled his rage-out, until he
said something that wounded me to my core.

"Why didn't I just let you die?"

O, Bruce! I think I *did* die—right then—died *again*—as I searched the eyes of my killer—my killer by default, or do I mean omission?—the killer I loved before knowing what love is—searched his eyes for a sign of mercy . . .

I held his gaze but none was forthcoming.

He came to my room while I was packing. I thought he was going to hit me. That's how far from love we had come. He gave me $25,000 worth of francs and enough damp, stinky rupees to buy myself a soda at the airport. I went back to Paris and stayed at the George V for a month. I was *not* in good shape. Had a wicked parasite too, not to mention a few stow-away demons of lower caste.

That was the last I saw or heard of him until that day he called my apartment in New York, seven years ago. There are so many "sevens," do you notice? Sevens and elevens . . . they really do seem to come up more than other numbers. O! Now I remember his last words to me in Bombay:

He said, "I shan't be saving you again."

I was dreaming of New York, in quiet conversation with a gargoyle, when the voice of a stewardess whispered, "We're beginning our descent."

I nudged the drape aside to look out the window.

The great orange dust cloud of Delhi lay before me.

* * *

We resumed the following day.

What happened next is a blur.

I debarked into those rioting molecules of shit, perfume, death and rebirth that belong not just to Delhi but every Indian necropolis. Two golf carts raced toward us on the tarmac, holding porters and customs officials—and Kura with two bodyguards! He hugged me and I almost fainted dead away. How my old lover looked! And my tear-streaked *self* watching *him* watch *me*, seeing how *I* looked! We took each other in, sizing up like tailors for our three-piece eternity suits— that magnificent *ache* that embraced all coming-togethers and coming-aparts, and touched the exquisite sorrow that is the shadow of existence itself.

His smile was big as a catcher's mitt.

He looked strikingly presidential in his Muga silk threads. Arms intertwined, our whole beings clutched, fussed and melded as we rode to the hotel in the small motorcade. We hardly said a word. Kura had a flair for the grandiose; the other cars were carrying "muscle." (And the elusive doctor.) I was tongue-tied except for the powerful, almost jokey urge to ask how the hell he made a living these days. But I didn't, discretion being the better part of valor. However the saying goes.

We had dinner in one of those dark, gaudy, empty restaurants that tend to live on the ground floor of 5-star Indian hotels. Wait a while though . . . did we go to a private club? Why am I thinking of this particular club? Maybe that was Bangalore . . . or Bangkok. Or Chicago! Memory's failing me . . . a club? I actually don't *think* so—no, probably not. Though he kept the details mysterious, Kura implied we had quite a journey ahead and I doubt he'd have wanted to trek off-campus on the eve of our departure, because we were slated to leave the next day. Though it *is* possible, more than possible that we took our meal in his room. Or should I say rooms, in that they occupied the entire penthouse. The Presidential Suite, indeed.

I told you this part was blurry. Starting the next morning, everything sharpens.

We had breakfast at a corner table in the coffee shop off the lobby. We'd slept well and allowed ourselves the exquisite luxury of enjoying each other's company *in the moment*, unencumbered by the odd circumstances of our reunion. We were brighter than the day that was about to enfold us, we threw off sparks and made spunky prayers of thanks to the gods of Whatever for arranging things thus. Kura had gained a bit of weight but not too much—some whiteness and thinning of hair—a slight tremor when he lifted his glass. Yes, he still had the *hôtel particulier* in the Marais on the Rue Vieille-du-Temple. (Glory be!) Yes, he was single. (*Hmm.*) His father was dead coming up on twenty years but his mother had just celebrated her 100th. When British citizens reach their centennial, the Queen mails them a congratulatory card; an anti-royalist all her life, Mum secretly ate it up. As for his current line of work, he knew I'd be curious and threw me a bone—"I am in the recycling business." I almost laughed, because it sounded so mafia.

We spoke in shallow generalities, packaging the broader strokes of our lives and exchanging them as gifts. At the end of the preliminaries, something shifted in him. He looked positively ancient—more battered pharaoh than beleaguered king.

"I remember everything about the day you left Bombay . . . a horrible, *terrible* day. A day that hurt me—as they say—more than it hurt you. I *flogged* myself for treating you so shabbily. Please accept my belated amends. 'It's been a long time coming, it's going to be a long time gone.' Do you remember how we used to sing that song?

"After you departed, I realized something I had been unable to voice or admit, even to myself. *I was in love with you.* There! I said it. O, how I suffered, Queenie! How I grieved. And all the while, I told myself such torment was unavoidable, that it was the anguish of the old, attached Self, an unhealthy aspect of the 'me' I was struggling to snuff out for good. After all, I had just begun my love affair with *the renunciate's way*, my foolhardy fling with enlightenment. Ah, but enlightenment turned out to be a bigger tease than you ever were!

"As soon as you returned to Paris, I became very, very ill. Do you remember how sick I was when we first arrived, the night before going to Mogul Lane? *That* was merely a foreshadowing, the appetizer if you will. The entrée came after you'd gone. Looking back, it's clear I'd acquired that sickness unto death diagnosed by a certain melancholy Dane, the fear and trembling that accompany the realization the Self must die—this walking, talking collection of vanities, addictions and absurdities calling itself 'Kura' must die. As you may well know, my love, one has never been truly ill unless one has been ill in India! You lay in your sweaty bed of nails, riveted by the ceiling stains, scanning them like tea leaves for meaning—and none of the outcomes are good. One's mood becomes quite dire. The American sent two ladies of a certain age to take care of me. The fever raged for two weeks. I hallucinated freely—mad dogs and midday sun but alas, no Englishmen. I was certain I would die, which in effect I did. Between visions I thought, *What fatal idiocy to have journeyed all this way!* I'd traveled thousands of miles to reach here—*you* traveled with me—to finally meet the Great Guru, the man I

dreamed would consent to be my teacher. Astonishingly, I'd
failed to give any credence to the rather ominous detail that
I'd pinned the tail of my spiritual aspirations on a corpse! The
aunties sponged me down with cold rags while my troubled
mind wandered this way and that, like an imbecile in top hat
and tails on a serious errand . . . and all of it came to nothing. In the end, I stood before pride's funhouse mirrors and
took my full measure. What reflected back was my obsession
with the goal not the journey—ergo, finding my guru—and
in that febrile moment, it became painfully obvious the adventure had been doomed to failure. My fate was sealed! How
could I have been so blind? So you see I couldn't very well
run away and follow *you*, not after all the metaphysical ruckus
I'd raised. I was like a mountain climber so close to summiting that he defies that inner voice telling him the weather has
turned and he must descend if he is to live—the devil take it,
he summits anyway! Now it was too late. I was near the summit, freezing, without oxygen . . . dying in a cheap room in
Bombay, far from Paris, far from anyplace called home, far—
oh *so* far, my Queen!—from the realm of Pure Land Rebirth.
The fever raged, scorching the earth of the American, when I
had no reason to fault him—not as yet. Fire and brimstone!
I surmised that it was not a mountain I had tried to summit
but a *mountebank*—and an American one, to boot! My descent
would not be to the foothills but down, down, to the hell of
Hungry Ghosts! And to make things worse, if that were possible, I'd chased off my lady. Whilst casting about for false gods
I had excommunicated the *real* one, the yogini in front of my
very nose! I tell you, Queenie, those were miserable times!

"When the fever receded, I lay seared in my bed, a shell-
shocked soldier after furious battle. Weak but clearheaded.

I don't think I've ever been that lucid in my life—I no longer pined, nor did I mourn you, but *celebrated* your existence without remorse. I thanked the Heavens that our lives had intersected for the brief and beautiful time that they did. *Upadana*[4] left my body. Like dye entering water, my gratitude extended to everyone I'd ever loved and to everyone I'd ever hated too. My anger, fear and consternation, my seizures of longing became those of the world and the world gave them back; and somewhere in that process, gold was spun. My guru—'the American' as you like to call him—later said I'd experienced metta, an instantaneous if temporary *bodhicitta*.[5]

"After a week of convalescence, I attended my guru's satsang and—how to convey—he smiled at me from his chair and all seemed right with the world. A simple smile that encompassed everything! O, Queenie, I had the strongest feeling—quickly ratified by my guru himself—that he *knew*, knew *exactly* what had transpired. He saw the change that had taken place within. That was when he spoke to me so tenderly of *bodhicitta* and the Six Perfections. He said how humbled and grateful I should be for having had the experience and not to let pride carry me away.

"I never looked back. It took some doing but with the help of a blood-brother—the Samoan who watched over you at the clinic, you knew him as 'Gaetano'—with Gaetano's long-distance help, I pulled off the trick of disengaging from various *undertakings* (there's a deliberate play on words there), both legitimate and illegitimate. He saw to it that final debts

---

4   Clinging or grasping—attachment. *Sanskrit.*
5   Awakening of mind or consciousness that strives toward compassion for all sentient beings.

were paid and collected too. A large sum of money accrued to a Swiss account for ready access should the need arise.

"I applied myself to the concepts of 'the American' with indefatigable resolve and rigorous intent. I kept a close eye on him, my Queen, to be sure! There was still a touch of the cynic in me, vigilant in its search for a chink in the armor, a flaw in his assertions, a sophistry in thought and action. But I failed at finding one. The harder I looked, the more convinced I was that the Great Guru's reluctant successor was also a reluctant saint. I repledged my fealty and devotion. The truth being, each day this blond enigma loomed larger and more difficult to parse. I suppose it didn't hurt that there was an ease, a 'naturalness' between us—at least I imagined there was!—as if we shared an agreement of some sort, one that transcended Mind. 'The Fifth Column'—that's what he called Mind. O, he didn't think very highly of it at *all*, which was mildly ironic, in that one needed a very *fine* mind in order to have had such a thought in the first place. But he thought it a saboteur of the first rank . . .

"I craved being near him and gladly paid the price. For my guru was exhausting to be around . . . it wasn't that he was 'intense,' which of course he *was* though not in the way we define the word. No, there was something about his *energy*, a heaviness, but an openness and lightness too. Like an inverted bell . . . I know I'm not explaining it too well. Perhaps you've met such beings in your own travels on the path? Anyway, it's my understanding that such a characteristic—this heavy, dominating energy—is shared by any *muni* worth his salt. These men are not sweethearts! Another consequence was more personal. The more time I spent with my guru, the more likely it was that he'd pounce, cudgeling me for an idiotic or glib remark, some inanity he'd found worthy of teasing me about for months! Which was actually of great benefit though it never felt that way in the moment. He was a *wonderful* mimic—it's not easy to watch oneself be eerily caricatured, especially in front of a large group. But always instructive . . . With public shaming, he disassembled your ego and pride, forcing you to examine your behavior, actions and beliefs. One had to be very much on one's toes. When he focused on you, look out! He saw right through me. Do you remember my fear? That the Great Guru was sure to *have my number*? Well, that worst fear came true after all! In spades. The best teacher, they say, is the one who tells you what you don't wish to hear. Unpleasant truths . . . 'The American' was no pushover. In the beginning, his admonishments sent me to bed for a week. He never raised his voice but the sting could be felt for days, like a scorpion's. Yet he was capable of *unutterable* tenderness. If one despaired, he poured nectar on the wound. At the same time, he was completely without pity.

"The years fell away. I didn't miss my old life. Isn't that something? Did not miss being a *player*. I did miss *you*, my Queen—well . . . a little, anyway! The Mogul Lane clan felt like family though I was careful never to make the mistake of being *familial* with 'the American' . . . Slowly, I assumed the same tasks he'd performed for *his* guru—book publishing, distribution of audiotapes, all the sundry financial affairs. As you know, I was uniquely qualified to take the reins, by virtue of the profession I'd given up. It seemed the only activity I *didn't* inherit was making book on the ponies! You see, dear Queenie, my challenge was to be thoroughly *engaged*, to take on as many responsibilities as I could handle without becoming self-important or feeling like the 'linchpin.' My guru would have picked up on that in an instant—then out on my ass I'd go! Not really . . . I doubt he'd have been so merciful as to send me packing. No, he'd rather see me twist at the end of my own rope. I avoided such a pitfall by keeping busy (a glorious way to quiet the mind), doing service, immersing myself in the river of my guru and the tributaries of all the workaday *apparatuses* that kept Mogul Lane afloat. No time to ruminate! That was my *samasti sadhana.*[6]

"I tell you, Madame Q, I became *unrecognizable* to myself in the best sense! I channeled my sexual energies into the yogas[7] and yearning for God. There were no rules against sex—'the American' didn't give a rat's ass—but I wanted to see what might arise after subtracting—then transmuting—the predatory obsessions of the flesh. I hadn't anything to lose; in a word, I'd already fucked myself to death. The game had gotten very old. Nothing to prove anymore on that particular front. It was difficult at first but in time became second nature.

"After four years, I disclosed to him the atrocities I'd committed in my long career . . . the wanton breaking of spirits, the taking of human life. Twas a high number of murders, my Queen, as you would have guessed. To this day my confession remains the most onerous and courageous of all my

6   *Sadhana* (literally, "a means of accomplishing something") refers to a practice whose goal is liberation, be it enlightenment or freedom from the cycle of birth and death. *Samasti sadhana* is the highest form and most difficult path, impossible to perform without a guru.

7   *Karma, bhakti* and *jnana* yogas were first introduced in the *Bhagavad Gita.* ("Yoga" generally means spiritual path.) *Raja* yoga completes the "Four Yogas," or paths to God, each chosen according to one's temperament: the active, the emotional, the mystical, and the philosophical.

acts. I shall never forget the kindness, the *elegance* of my guru's response, and that's all I have to say about it. I'm committed to being honest about everything—at this stage, secrets would be pointless, even harmful—but in this one area, I'm afraid the books are forever closed. I know you'll understand.

"As the years went by, I had a stunning revelation. My previous life—life before Bombay—suddenly made sense! It presented itself as nothing more than the preparation for a crime, the crime of all crimes: *I was in the thick of planning my own murder.* My guru said there are many vehicles to take us to where we're going but human weakness is such that we imagine we'll know what such a vehicle *looks* like. And yet more than not, one finds oneself in a car bearing no resemblance to that which was imagined—no power steering, too fast or too slow, uglier or prettier than we had dreamed. 'The American' said that if one is *very* fortunate, the vehicle is pointed in the direction of one's destination. But that is the exception, not the rule. The Self makes terrible decisions! Its relentless drone of *me, me, me* can run a man right off the road or advise him to ditch the thing entirely when it doesn't drive to his expectations. The *hegira*, he said, took *guts of steel*—'All roads most assuredly do *not* lead to Mecca!' O, he scared the hell out of us when he talked that way . . . twas my worst fear to reach the end of the road and realize I had taken a wrong turn in my youth or middle age, and now it was too late.

"And so, my dearest darling, I came to see that it was my *destiny* to jump ship—like *Ben-Hur*!—to leap from one chariot to another—from the Great Guru's vehicle to that of 'the American'—nothing short of an audacious *cosmic stunt* was required to keep me pointed toward the finish line. I was with him seven long years, seven years of such incomprehensible grace and mystery that even now, knowing all that I do, I wonder if I could ever be convinced to trade them away . . . But at the end of my sojourn, something happened that undid all the splendor, undid everything I'd learned or *thought* I had, plunging me into suicidal despair. I used to fear my guru would see through me, but such a fear was child's play beside what happened.

Only the flutter of an eyelid betrayed his emotions. "I arrived at a dead end. A wrong turn had been taken, and it was too late to go back."

After a dramatic pause, Kura said:

"My guru vanished into thin air."

* * *

I didn't mind being left with a cliff-hanger. I knew more would be revealed, and soon. (And I should probably add that I already knew a little about the American's disappearance through gossip I'd heard over the dharma grapevine, and from the New Age rags too. But I never had the desire to do follow-up.) As we set upon our journey, I felt like a character in a story being written in real time. I could *smell* the pages we nestled in—tea-stained, dog-eared, bloody as his maiden copy of *The Book of Satsang*, and redolent of cigar smoke too. The passing landscape seemed like a dusty, petrified forest of Words. I was glad Kura had brought me up to speed before we left because now I was free to enter that delicious contemplative state evoked by *Wanderjahre* into unknown regions.

The convoy motored past the ecstatic, messy diorama of India while our knees jostled against each other; sometimes he took my hand in his. In close quarters, the tinted windows were defenseless against a world shot through by a midday cruelty of winter light. Kura looked frail, mortal. The sky was cloudless, its cupboards looted by katabatic winds . . . the profoundly unprofound thought occurred that even one day *he* would vanish, for good, as would the memory of all loves, old and new, as surely as "the American" had, never to be found nor perhaps meant to be. What's that poem of Dickinson? "Because I could not stop for Death, he kindly stopped for me. The Carriage held but just Ourselves"—while Kura looked out from *our* carriage, I studied him with involuntary vulture's eye. The purple blossoms on the back of a hand that bespoke a recent hospital stay he'd chosen not to divulge . . . the contrived, carefree tom-tom of the carotid, a Trojan horse that one day would betray him. It seemed to know I was watching and threw everything it had into its palpitations. There was something vulgar about the skin-deep show it put on—*vein*-glorious!—as if too eager to throw me off the scent that *she* was coming, Mother Death, gunning for this 62-year-old and whatever trombones he could offer. A few more floats and the parade would be over, the majorette could lay down her arterial drum . . . An overwhelming sadness fell upon me, far and away beyond the variety to which I was accustomed. I was used to being slowly pinned in the ring, a ragtag-team of tricyclic antidepressants and MAO inhibitors in my corner—but *this* sadness was out of reach of my tricked-out, penthouse-sized, suicidal splendor. When our backseat gaze met, Kura graced me with a sweet, plaintive smile. I had the queerest sensation he was reading my mind. I know it sounds corny but that was when I had a news flash: I swore for the life of me the missing guru was *him*. I fought the urge to tell him to call off the dogs and turn the frickin' car around.

Everyone's always saying, "Find the guru within"—well ain't it the truth. But to each his own Easter hunt.

Driving deeper into the hinterland, the road grew more challenging. One of the cars in the motorcade peeled away as planned, dropping off like ballast. The subtraction felt organic, as if part of the logic of the expedition—to keep shedding our skin until we were newborns at the lost guru's door.

We ate sandwiches from little coolers. Having a meal loosened his tongue.

"When 'the American' disappeared, Mogul Lane went wild . . . an ant hill stirred by the stick of a small boy. But this time the community reaction bore no relation to the period of mourning that followed the Great Guru's death seven years earlier. The police brought their limited expertise to bear; the investigation was blasé, desultory, *laissez-faire*. They hung around the shop with long faces, laboriously filling out paperwork before moving on to the precinct where gendarmes lazily auditioned the raft of crackpots, ascetics and prognosticators who had come forward with visions of my guru's fate—he drowned in the Ganga or repatriated to the U.S. or went up in a blaze of self-immolation, leaving only crystalline relics of the rainbow body behind, albeit in red, white and blue! As the spectacle wore on, my contempt for that conniving widow and her pack of jackals went *off the charts*. I never liked her but now I did nothing to conceal it; she unabashedly returned the favor. At odd moments I caught her japing, as if to gloat that 'the American' (*she* called him that too, but always with a sarcastic twist) had finally gotten his comeuppance. In a matter of hours, my guru was purged from history, having *evanesced* under a lurid cloud of suspicion. Within days, his portraits were removed from the walls and burned; the books of his satsang I helped publish were no longer available. Even pages of the Great Guru's classic that bore the American's name under 'translated by' were torn out and replaced.

"That horrible woman! No matter that she was his earliest champion, urging him to take the chair. Something hardened her toward him those last few years. She was getting on in age, and became careless in dress and tongue. A few days after 'the American' went missing, she invited me into the very den that my guru—and his—once used as a sanctuary to meditate and sing psalms. I thought surely she was going to ask me to step into his shoes! She talked my ear off for the better part of an hour, anxious to promote the theory he'd been 'done in' by an enigmatic consortium of power-hungry thuggees, the same men, she said, who once plotted to kidnap and murder her husband. *Another* possibility lay in the realm of the supernatural. She spoke of flying yogins, skilled in the dark art of 'translating' themselves through the ether . . . then went in for the kill. 'Have you considered what I believe to be the very *real* probability that your *American guru* may simply have had enough? That he decided to return home, to find fame and fortune? He would not be the first of his countrymen to capitalize on the Source!' O, she cast her meretricious net far and wide, tarnishing all the fishies in the sea! So *base*, and thoroughly *contagious* as well—the same cheap, haughty mannerisms and grating inflection cropped up in those dastardly aunties who were under her stern sponsorship.

"It came to me in a sickening flash: *No one had understood a single word of my guru's teachings!* And Queenie, let me tell you, that terrifying insight gave me comfort. I sat with the damnable conclusion a while until I swear I caught a glimpse of the form of mankind's ignorance itself. Diabolical!

Could it possibly be true that *I* was the only one who understood that a saint had walked among us? I'll admit he had many strikes against him. After all, he was American, which cost him the lion's share of his followers from the git-go. I watched him assiduously win that share back, not through contrivance or campaign but sheer *valence*. The naysayers came to deeply respect him. Still, there were many, shall we say, opposing camps—it would have been naïve not to have noticed. I'm convinced the widow kept the conspirators' fires burning . . . the Janus-faced ones who clambered to press his feet had for a while now worked most avidly against him, whispering that his seat was a fraud and a heresy. A blasphemy . . .

"The colder went the trail, the more determined, the more *invigorated* was I to solve the invidious riddle. And I had considerable resources—don't forget those numbered accounts in Switzerland. I set up shop in a building a few miles from Tobacco Road. I employed a crew of ten—half a dozen locals with the rest flown in, individuals I absolutely trusted and had worked with before. Gaetano did a brilliant job of organizing the entire operation. I'll spare you the innovative details . . . you already know how creative I can be when an important project is at hand, no? Suffice to say I went to great lengths, some not entirely legal, to find him.

"Weeks went by and my team made no progress. I grew distant from Mogul Lane. A strange time, to say the least . . . My guru, a bright sun that once shone down on me, underwent a disturbing eclipse. Something began to gnaw. I felt like a private investigator in one of those European novels that reviewers call 'philosophical detective stories.' A portrait of him over my desk seemed to leer. I wondered if the widow was right—she so often was!—and considered expanding my search to the States.

"Approximately eight weeks after the nightmare began, I awakened from a nap to find the screw had completed its turn. Try as I may—and try I did, my Queen!—I could do nothing to alter the belief that I'd been 'had.' This new poison burned my throat, seared my eyes and became a wildfire in my soul . . . Dear heart, the fickleness of the human race is a wonder to behold. One by one my troops returned empty-handed, and one by one I relieved them of their services until finally I was alone in a suite of empty rooms, with only his photograph's sinister eyes following me 'round. I shambled about, trying to stave off what was coming—the heartbreaking realization I'd been administered a *coup de grâce*. His final teaching! O Lord. *Lord* . . . I'm ashamed to say I declared to myself *and* the world that the feet I'd washed, worshipped and worried over were made of clay. The doubts and paranoia I harbored while ill no longer seemed the stuff of fever dreams. I set fire to the portrait, burning in effigy he who once held an unimpeachable place in my heart, whose insights, energy and brilliance had sustained and transformed me. I stripped him of all laurels and medals, tarred, feathered and court-martialed him, pissed on his counterfeit spirit for eternity! I was in the grips of a kind of mania . . . deranged. A bucket of delighted, perverse fantasies watered the petals of my resentments that opened like a corpse flower in bloom: perhaps he *had* been abducted—kidnapped, tortured, killed! O be *careful*, my Queen, when the beast inside is unleashed! I hasten to add that a small part of me still remained true and watched the torch-bearing mob of Self with helpless amazement.

"But it gets worse, Queenie—far worse!

"In madness, I saw only monsters. Years of rigorous tutelage reared up like diseased horses running wild through remorseful, desolate fields. Remarks my guru had made during intimate conversation—moments I treasured, his words forming a garland I'd hoped to wear around my neck whilst crossing the final threshold of Silence—became nothing more than dirty jokes, the larcenous pitch of an obscene grifter. My guru knew the mystery of the pyramids . . . Ponzi's! O, how foolish I felt! I mention *Mr. Ponzi* only in a *figurative* sense, as no fiscal malfeasance ever came to light. Just hours after 'the American' took a powder, I knew that embezzlement needed to be ruled out. A thorough forensic examination of house finances found them intact (if anything, there was more in the treasure chest than I initially thought). My first hope—of course, this was *before* I renounced him as my guru—was to discover a theft then 'follow the money,' a process that might lead me to a suspect or suspects, the working theory being 'the American' had stumbled across *irregularities* that certain parties feared he might soon reveal. I'd be lying if I didn't say the widow was at the top of my list . . . Did I tell you about the ransoms? O my! The notes came fast and furious. Some claimed he was being held hostage, and demanded all manner of absurdities. Some were thrown right over the transom . . . All were deemed inauthentic.

"I paced those empty rented rooms, plotting my revenge. I would find 'the American' and dispatch him to nirvana myself! My Queen, I assure you I was back to true form. I gathered my wits and my Dopp kit and took a train north, the direction my very best detective said our quarry had been last seen heading. I started out as John Wayne but ended like Shelley Winters—pushy and hysterical, all over the place. I

ransacked my memory for clues the impostor may have provided, anything to impossibly, magically pull it all together.
Looking for a needle in a haystack is one thing, looking for a
guru in India quite another; I grew to covet those who sought
only needles. I was proud. My anger had nowhere to *express*
but inward. I became depressed. I concluded I'd wasted seven
years of my life and could never win them back. Not only was
the time gone but the *potentialities* it held, the way energy hides
in a bomb . . . *my* bomb turned out to be a dud. A special agony,
my Queen, awaits those who treat the Source like currency
on the exchange! Regret spread like cancer. Its skeletal hands
clutched at many things—*even you*—yet held on to nothing.

"I wadded up that whole continent, vanishing guru
included, and tossed it in the dustbin. I returned to Paris to
lick my wounds. Took up a few long-forgotten habits and felt
better for a while, reacquainted myself with old habitués and
cultivated new ones. But the thrill was gone—that's what a
wrong turn'll get you! I threw myself into business . . . *not* the
enterprise you think. No, I'd lost the stomach for that kind
of risk. I wanted 'stress-free,' so everything was aboveboard.
Assembled most of the old team and did extremely well. I
always did extremely well, except in the business of gurus! Ha!
And I must say that I rarely thought of 'the American.'

"I said 'dustbin' but if I'm to expand the metaphor, I'd say
I stuffed the whole experience into a trunk that was promptly
sealed and stored away. It lay in the attic a long, long time,
Queenie—about 15 years, in fact. Then one day I found myself
wandering up to the *belfry*. Went in and paced a while. Sat
and stared at the trunk. Eventually walked over and broke the
seal. Took two steps back. Warily circled. Lifted the lid to let
some air out and left, closing the door behind me. A year later,

I went up again. Paced, circled, sat. It felt familiar to spend time there. Opened the trunk and poked around with a stick. Walked out, shut the door.

"I had a heart attack in '92 that changed my lifestyle. I hired a vegan chef and started exercising. Though I must tell you, Queenie, the whole time I lay in hospital I was sorely preoccupied. I would close my eyes and roam around that attic . . . For you see, I opened that trunk for the same reason the surgeons opened my chest: to heal. And to my surprise, I found it held things of great beauty . . . books—*I* helped publish—smelling of incense, cigars and tuberoses . . . raiments of gold-threaded silk . . . glittering gems. Even the 'necklace' was there, the garland of my guru's words! The drought of rage and heartbreak lifted at last and in its place was a bright green stem coursing with life that broke through the skylight and reached for the sun.

"Over the next few months of convalescence, I revisited where it all began: *The Book of Satsang.* The Great Guru still spoke to me yet within its pages I saw the genius of his favorite student, 'the American,' writ large. I had not been mistaken! Still, I knew it was important to remain cautious. My conduct needed to be measured. I waited to see if my jubilance was artificial, manufactured—'postcardiac.' I wished to do nothing on impulse; I recalled with disgust how quickly I had turned on the one who was so precious to me. I needed to be absolutely certain this latest turning *toward* him wasn't arbitrary as well.

"I was still in possession of all the books I midwifed during my time as editor and putative translator of Mogul Lane Press. Some were collections of my guru's morning Q&As; others slim, elegant hardbacks filled with apothegms and parables reflecting his simple abstractions and direct truths. I unpacked the boxes and leafed through them at leisure. I had a nagging fear they'd be nothing more than 'cosmic candy' though I needn't have worried—they were awfully compelling. The beautiful little volumes held many epiphanies for the careful reader . . . there *did* seem to be a lot of them out there (careful readers). Even *after* he skedaddled—my guru taught me that word!—his book sales grew steadily each year. The unsolved mystery of his leave-taking certainly didn't hurt; hagiographies sprung up like mushrooms after a rain. Scoundrels debunked, seekers martyred, and scholars wangled over who should be authorized to be custodian of his legacy. Controversies notwithstanding, the radical breadth of my guru's concepts proved he was more than just a shooting star in the cosmology of Advaita. His place in the firmament was secure.

"A year passed. I was distracted by the profitability of my business enterprises. But at the end of each day, my fancies drifted to the missing saint . . . Along with the health of my heart, my affections had returned. *Very quietly* I began to lay the groundwork for a project as subterranean as it was quixotic. I carefully tricked my mind into believing the adventure I was about to embark upon was mere sport. I couldn't afford to be emotionally invested, which wasn't too difficult in that the chance of success was practically nil. We are speaking of a *muni* who disappeared from Bombay 15 years prior without a trace! He could be anywhere in the world, if indeed he was still alive. But you know how I am, Queenie, when I get a bee in my bonnet. The dream team assembled *this* time bore no resemblance to the farm club cobbled together in that frantic time after we lost him. The uniqueness of his features—tall,

Caucasian—might help our cause, but only if he'd remained in India. So you see, I couldn't really get too excited about the little numbers game I was running on the side and that was a *good* thing. With nearly a billion souls walking the Continent, the whole treasure hunt notion was really a joke, a folly.

"I set a ceiling on this hobby of mine at five years and three million euros. (A portion went toward *baksheesh*, from 'man on the street' beggars and shopkeepers to the highest in government.) I gave my people free rein, never asking for reports on their progress. The lot were grossly overpaid yet did not lack for further incentive: a seven-figure bonus awaited whoever cracked the code, dead or alive. (Irrefutable proof was required in order to collect.) I left them to their own *vices*, while stupidly pursuing mine. It's embarrassing to admit but during this period I reverted yet again to my dissolute ways. I exchanged veggies for red meat, took up pot smoking again, and used 'medicinal' amounts of pharmaceutical cocaine— which as you can guess, did wonders for my bypassed heart— and spent a fortune on my beloved ladies of the night. Do not judge me, my Queen. How far I had fallen from a romance with the Spirit! I hated what I'd become: an old roué, a fallen 'spiritualist' with a bad ticker and a Viagra-dependent *schmeckel*.

"It was 4 a.m. I was in Morocco. I'd been asleep just half-an-hour when the phone rang off its hook. Aside from Gaetano and Justine (my secretary), the gumshoes were the only ones who could reach me. They had explicit instructions to phone *immediately* if in receipt of important news—damn the torpedoes and perish the time zone. A man called Quasimodo was on the other end. Funnily, he was the only one whose skill I had doubted. I was this close to firing him.

"'Sir,' he said, 'I believe I found him.'

"I saw stars. I asked him to go on, *slowly*.

"A village 400 kilometers from Delhi. He's tall, white. 82 years old. He lives in a cave.'

"'A cave?'

"'I spoke to the elder—the village chief. A very friendly fellow. He said "the Hermit" showed up about 10 years ago. That's what he calls him, "the Hermit." Or "Guruji" or *jnani* . . .'

"'And?'

"'I hiked up to the cave. Very nice setup! I had both sets of pictures with me—from the ashram in the '70s, and the ones generated from the forensic model. He didn't seem to look like *either* but I'm not very good at that, you know. I'm face-blind.'

"'Now you tell me. You took a photo?'

"'No, and I'm sorry about it. He wasn't too keen on having his picture taken.'

"'Jesus! Well, if he didn't *look*—and you say he showed up ten years ago, but he's been gone for *twenty* . . . What makes you think—'

"'I didn't want to tip him—I said I was looking for a shrine. I thought he'd be standoffish but the old guy had a sense of humor. He said he didn't know of any shrines in that area, which just went to show that all roads don't lead to Mecca.'"

* * *

After too many hours and too few stops, we reached the foot of the village fingered by the hunchback with a hunch. A pair of armed men stood waiting beside a train of burros. Apparently, it was the end of the line for anything with an engine. As we mounted our steeds, one of the guards suggested he accompany us on the trail or at least partly up the hill, but was politely refused.

It felt good to have an ass massage after such a long ride. A thousand trivial things flitted through my logy, travel-loopy head. I wondered if my gargoyles missed me, and even wondered what happened to Quasimodo. Fat and sassy no doubt, shacked up somewhere on Easy Street with his seven figures (though I doubt he'd collected just yet) . . . We loped along uphill—six sherpas in front, four in back—and not a one spoke the King's (or the Queenie's) English. Kura rode ahead in a trance of monomania, eyes fixated on the dubious prize before him. I became rather fixated myself, abruptly seized by the hair-raising fear that a massive coronary would topple him from his burro before we reached the finish line. (Why couldn't we have brought the elusive doctor along?) I think what spurred that particular fantasy was a general *agita* about the man, a turmoil, a nervosity. Anyone would have been excited about the prospect of reuniting with a person who had played such an important role in one's life, that was understood, but I think Kura was fundamentally *vexed*, and not in a good way. One thing I noticed was that his reminiscences toggled back and forth between the warm, intimate "my guru" and the cooler, detached "the American," the latter even further removed by an ironic inflection of quote marks, as if borrowing not just my but the Great Guru's widow's description. What I mean to say is, his conflicted feelings were so obvious. I believe that the closer we got—*he* got—to that damnable cave, the more unresolved and bewildered he became.

I had no idea how much time had passed. We dipped then rose up the side of yet another barren ravine, crossing a cool meadow the size of a soccer field before beginning the perilous ascent of Hillock Number 17 (or so it seemed). There was no comfort to be drawn from the dearth of hints that any of these traversals were bringing us closer to our destination—then suddenly, we were there.

The sherpas helped us dismount. A few ran off, returning a few minutes later with a smartly dressed, silver-haired chap in tow. The village elder wore a silvery Groucho moustache above a crazy rack of ultra-whitened teeth.

"Mr. Bela Moncrieff!" he shouted. The elusive Quasimodo had no doubt provided the gentleman with one of Kura's aliases. At least he hadn't called him Lucky Pierre. "Please! *Come.*"

We were led to a modest home, where a lovely middle-aged woman with a bindi and a delicate ring through her nostril greeted us with a tray bearing cups of tea. She was the elder's wife. A handful of sweet morsels had been laid out as well and I wolfed two down without ceremony—I was famished. When offered, Kura waved them away.

Our host spoke perfect English. After a few rounds of social niceties, he got down to brass tacks.

"Ah . . . the Hermit!" he said with a grin. "You are his *friend*?"

"In a manner of speaking," said Kura, solemnly. "But before we go any further, I need your assurance."

"I am at your service, Sir Moncrieff, sir!"

"My man told you not to speak with anyone in the village about my *pending arrival.* Can you assure me that yo—"

"Quasimodo! *Hell* of a guy! Gave me a Macintosh *computer*! And *Frito-Lays*! And Sir Alfred *Dunhill* cigarettes!"

"You were *warned*, weren't you? *Not* to let the man in the cave know he might be having visitors? Did he tell you that?"

"It's true! But I can assure it is was a warning most easily ignored."

The remark got Kura's attention. "I don't follow you."

"If for a *single moment* I believed there was one nefarious *thing* behind the whole gambit that might possibly result in harm to the Hermit, *I would not have hesitated to warn him*, i.e., sound the alarum throughout the entire village. He is after all an irreproachable member of our community—the Hermit has quite a special status, to say the least! The village feeds and clothes him, and thanks God for the privilege. I shall reserve to make further explanations regarding my meaning at a different time, for I know you are in a *very big rush*. As said: I would certainly *not* have hung fire to *tip off* the *jnani* of *any* goings-on should I have suspected something *shady*. In fact, it would have been my distinct pleasure and honor! But when Quasimodo—one *hell* of a guy, I assure!—informed me the Hermit was your *guru*, whom you wished to make *reunion* after so many years and planned to come such a great distance to *worship* . . . my heart became full and it was a facile thing for me to then agree. So may I say: I rejoice *with* you, and *for* you!"

"Just tell me. Have you kept your word? Or broken it?"

To which the elder replied, "Sir! All that I have—apart from this village and its souls, who are my consummate children—is my *word*. I gave it to your hell of a man in complete and utter *seriousness* . . . and now give it to *you* in the very same spirit. Sir! Mister Bela Moncrieff! I will now settle it *again* so that each and every one of us are free to go about the pressing duties of our individual day. *You have my solemn assurance that I breached nothing.* The only personage who knows of your agenda other than myself is my dear wife."

He threw her a glance. After meeting it she flirtily averted her gaze, turning back to look after the soup on the stove.

"Only my wife was—is—aware that certain guests may or may *not* be—are—dropping in. *Have.* I hasten to add that in telling this woman I did not break my word. Not at all! For after half a century of matrimony, we are no longer separate people! We are one and the same."

I applauded the elder, who'd managed to put my old friend at ease, which was no mean feat. Kura rested his hands on his thighs in a posture of relaxed, fraternal fidelity. His face got ruddy and his eyes were bright.

"Your village shall receive a handsome dowry in addition to that which my man has already seen to. Such endowment is to be dispersed solely at your discretion. Now, does that meet with your approval?"

"O, eminently, sir! Eminently so!"

"Good."

The wife motioned for us to sit on two ottomans covered in ornately woven patterns. We did as she commanded. There were smiles all around. This time Kura sampled the confections. After a swallow, he faced the elder and said, "Tell me what you know."

"The Hermit arrived in the autumn of '87," he began. "He came to us as a mendicant, a *sannyasi*, a wandering monk. It is the ancient tradition of our village, as it is in all villages, to be *most hospitable* to visitors. With a holy man, such largess takes on a new dimension . . . He spoke our dialect to *perfection*. We provided him food and shelter—twas our honor and duty before God! His looks, of course, were striking; tall and blue-eyed. The sun had baked him but it was obvious he was fair-skinned. We knew not where he *hailed* from nor was it our business to ask. After a few months, he said he was *American*—a testimonial to the linguistic prowess of the man, for when he spoke to us in our mother tongue there simply was no accent *at all*. An American *rishi*—this really threw us for a loop! The very *idea* of it . . . but I've taken too much of your time. I presume you'll stay for supper? We'll catch up on everything later . . . My wife, as you can see, has been hard at work. Her soup is among the *jnani*'s favorites! *Delicacies* will be served tonight: American-style chips and 'dip'! Ha ha! I shall now suspend any more talk of the life that your guru has spent not *among* us but *within our hearts*, divinely so. For I am a poor biographer and hew closely to the maxim 'Wise is the man who knows that the line between tidings and gossip is thin.'"

"But *you* have an accent," said Kura. "I can't place it. Where is it from?"

"Ah ha! You can't see the forest through the trees. It is nothing more nor less than an *American* accent! I wished after one since I was a boy . . . and though he lacked one himself, I owe it all to the Hermit, a patient tutor, and as gifted a linguist as he is a Master of *soham*, the self-realized knowledge 'That, I Am.'"

His wife approached with plates of appetizers, to hold us over until dinner. Kura declined. Weeks of anticipation had bollixed him up; his stomach was sour. No matter—a food basket had already been prepared. When she handed me a small canvas bag with two bottled waters, the woman forever won my heart.

The hour of reckoning was upon us and Kura was coming apart at the seams. "Is he—is he there?" asked Kura. "At home? *Now?* Is he in his cave?"

"Most certainly! A hermit wouldn't be a hermit if he wasn't at home in his cave, true? The *muni* has no desires—no need to seek out *that which was never lost*. And whatever his body needs for sustenance, the village provides . . . believe me, it is the barest of essentials!"

A young boy tumbled in from outside, pantomiming guffaws while pretending to outrun the delicious torment of a phantom tickler. Then, with theatrical flourish, he stopped abruptly, stood ramrod straight and dusted himself off before extending a hand in welcome.

"Ah," said the elder, beaming with love. "You must end your foolishness long enough to carry out a very important errand." He turned to us and said, "My grandson!" Back to the boy: "You are to escort our guests to Dashir Cave without delay." To us: "My grandson *also* took lessons from you-know-who!" To the boy: *"Now,* without any nonsense! And if, while on your way, a *busybody* should inquire after where you are going, you are simply to tell them, 'Grandpa has asked me to show his guests the tamarisk tree.' Now *go.* Vamoose!"

He went to his grandmother instead and clung to her waist. She dispensed a handful of wrapped toffees; he undressed one and placed it in her hand before leaning over to nibble as a horse would its sugar cube. A most expressive, talented boy.

"Vamoose," said the elder. "Funny word, don't you think? It is my understanding it also has the meaning of 'skedaddle'—and perhaps, *scram.*" He erupted in peals of laughter as his grandson grandly bade us to follow.

And off we went.

* * *

After only a few minutes, he shouted at the boy to shorten his stride.

"Far? How far? Is it far?" Kura asked, out of breath.

Our mischievous guide turned and stared past us like a dullard, his mouth gone lax and cretinous. He briskly "came to," flashing a smile that was positively debonair. "*Not* far," he said, self-amused. He resumed the hike before pulling himself short with a staccato burst of unprovoked hilarity. Each crazed uproar sent him closer to the ground, like a cartoon mallet was pounding on his head—Sammy Davis Jr. by way of Wile E. Coyote. We followed along at his mercy.

"Do you know what surprised me?" I thought a little conversation might provide a distraction. "That Quasimodo apparently blew the mission's cover—I mean, by telling the gentleman what you were up to. I found that rather strange, no?"

"Not at all! He went strictly by the playbook. You see, as outsiders we knew the locals might be somewhat *chary*. Indeed, the village at first disavowed any knowledge of 'the American' though evidence strongly suggested he was in their midst. So we fell back upon Plan B—that I was searching for a long-lost teacher, which happened to be the truth. It was a scenario they could understand and respect."

In no time at all we found ourselves on a steady incline, a winding trail that left any reminders of the village far behind. As usual I brought up the rear, affording yet another opportunity to brood over my darling's health. It was chilly but he'd removed his coat; while he compulsively swabbed his head with a handkerchief, I watched the vertical ellipse of perspiration between his shoulder blades ruthlessly colonize the shirt's remaining dry land. We kept stopping—rather, *I* kept stopping and calling out to the boy, under pretext of having to catch my breath—so Mr. Moncrieff could catch his. My entreaties had no effect. Kura whistled at him to slow the pace but our guide grew fond of the reedy warnings and played a game of speeding up, just to trigger the alert.

Leaving Kura's physical concerns by the wayside, I focused on his mental health. It suddenly occurred to me that my dear companion might not be right in the head—that the whole business, this *obsession* with the American might be part of a bigger picture, you know, an encroaching madness, even something hereditary finally come home to roost. Maybe he was losing his mind due to some fixable but as yet undetected anomaly such as Lyme disease or scurvy . . . early dementia? I knew I was being a little dramatic but only as a way of throwing light on what deep down seemed to have a ring of truth. Let's say Kura *had* found the American (evidence to the contrary, I was beginning to have my doubts) and was about to come face-to-face. Well, what *then*? What was the point? Was he still trying to get back those seven freakin' years? The last *twenty*? Or was it simply revenge he was seeking? Could it be that the blow to his pride inflicted by the Hermit of the Cave—the Missing Link, the Grand Poobah, the whomever—had been fatal to the ego, poisoning and distorting it over the years as surely as by lead or mercury?

I was tired. When I get tired I tend to go to that "Hello darkness, my old friend" place. It took everything I had to put one foot in front of the other, trudging along in a fog of mutant hormones and garage sale neurochemistry. In that moment, I thought how wonderful it would be to transform into a burro, a sari, a rock, an ottoman, even smoke from one of the hundred trash fires burning just over the horizon. Because in the end, self-awareness has spectacularly diminishing returns (in fact, it's downright masochistic). All I knew was the responsibility had fallen squarely on *my* shoulders . . . after the aneurysm *I'd* be the one in charge of medevacing him out of some Himalayan fuckzone. And oh my God, Bruce, I *so* did not give a shit about the American! I kicked my ass with every step, not only for accepting Kura's invitation to this sucky toad ride but for ever having gone to Bombay with him in the first place.

Now it was the boy who was whistling. He pointed to a clearing, then without further ado dashed back down the mountain as if carried by the wind.

The moment was nigh.

Kura put on his coat and ran his fingers through sticky hair like a bum about to step into church. Standing a bit straighter, he walked to his destiny as I followed—the dutiful wife I never was. After a few minutes here's what we saw:

An old man in a bright white kurta, raking grass. Tall, wiry, stooped, baked by the sun. As we drew closer, he looked up and smiled before returning to his chore. He was so poised it could easily be believed someone had tipped him off (which wasn't the case). If it's possible for a human being to "grind to a halt," that's what Kura did. The shock of recognition gummed up his machinery.

A nervous clearing of the throat. Then, "It is I—Kura!"

The stilted delivery was heartrendingly comic.

"Of course," he said informally. "I know who you are."

I recognized the voice but not much else. Scarred, ravished and beatified by nomadic years of exodus, the American was still intensely charismatic. His bearing was light yet commanding. The few teeth he possessed were jagged and betel-stained. Some sort of chronic affliction—ringworm?—swelled his ankles. His hair was mostly white and gray with inexplicably random sunspots of too-bright blond.

Kura gestured toward me. "This is Cassiopeia . . ."

(I was touched by the introduction.)

"Lovely!" exclaimed the old man.

"She came from New York to be with me."

The American stared into my eyes and I shivered at the enormity of what was taking place—for the first time, I understood.[8] Without looking away, the guru said, "That's a wonderful friend." I knew he didn't remember me, and was glad. I was freer to sit back and enjoy the play from my front-row seat.

"I've brewed some tea," he said. "You must be thirsty." With that, he turned toward home, its "front door" the congenial mouth of a most welcoming cave.

"No, we are *not*," said Kura, blood up. "We are *not* thirsty, and we've brought water of our own!"

The old man bore a look of unsurprised surprise. "As you wish."

I thought Kura had been rude, then called myself out for being prim. The occasion hardly demanded politesse. Besides, I had a funny feeling the guru was pleased by his ex-student's *brio*—the manifestation of ch'i was always welcome.

"Since you are a man," began the *siddha*, "who enjoys cutting to the heart of things—a quality about you that I always admired—I shall do the same. It has been a *long*

---

8 "It wasn't until I got back to Manhattan that I realized how much I envied him this moment—for I too had relentlessly searched for the one I'd loved and lost. The difference between Kura and me was that I had given up. It was because of his example that I resumed my search, not long after his death." [From a later conversation—*Ed.*]

while since our paths crossed, but the Source has magnani-
mously collapsed time to arrange our rendezvous . . . twas
predetermined, my dear old friend. *Wowee zowee,* this is no
joking matter!

"I am one who long ago forsook living in the past *or*
future, which seem to me *vastly overrated*. Even the 'now' is
overrated!" He laughed at the small quip—really very charming. "I never bothered to consider the consequences of my sudden departure on those who called me teacher, and I'll tell you
why: *I was fighting for my life*. When a mortal man, a *man without knowledge*, already burned to the *third degree*, is in the midst
of escaping an inferno, can he be forgiven for being oblivious
to others left behind?

"But if I am to properly acquit myself, I'll need to provide
some history. In the weeks that followed the death of the Great
Guru, I found myself in a bit of a quandary. A 'pickle.' The
widow—a very aggressive woman, as well you may remember!—had virtually nominated me as 'next in line.' But why
did she feel the need for 'the lineage' to carry on? (There
was no lineage.) Certainly, it couldn't have been for Father's
sake, to 'honor his wishes,' for he had none. No wishes and
no desires! Why, then? The answer is simple: the *ape's* need
for figureheads is profound and enduring. But the trouble
begins—and it always does!—when one confounds *figurehead*
with *Godhead*. A symbol can never be the real thing, isn't it
true? Don't you agree? A symbol covers Truth as a narcotic
masks pain. Do you see my point?

"I'm going to tell you something now that to this day
makes me shudder." He mimicked a swan shaking off water.
"When I met the magical being who was to alter the course
of my life *and* my death—I refer of course to my father, the

Great Guru—one of the first things he did was to casually inform me of my Achilles' heel. He said this inherent weakness had been dictated by the stars and was so powerful it would stop at nothing short of my *total annihilation.* That was the pithy phrase he used. He said I was fortunate to have two choices: I could face the demon in battle—or I could *run.* He strongly suggested the latter! I begged him to elaborate on this fatal flaw; I was on the edge of my chair. He teased and tantalized, talking in circles before coming clean. He said the hound from Hell that was on my heels was *pride.* Pride—and arrogance, its handmaiden. I think that because he was so queerly *blithe* about it (such were the sadhu's deceptive methods of delivery), I took his warning with a grain of salt.

"Perhaps now you'll see more clearly the fix I was in when my guru—Guru among gurus!—left this world. And I am speaking *apart* from having lost the light of my life. I spent seven years pruning the garden of Self (does that sound familiar?), watched over by that holiest of horticulturists. He stood behind me, steadfast, demonstrating how to yank the very weeds that were destined to choke me. There is no doubt I was his most careful student, which made matters worse. To my guru, I was a lamb he was shepherding home; to the others, I was the 'golden boy'—quite literally, with my yellow hair! Which didn't help at all!—but *tarnished* gold. The ugly American who like a parasite had wormed his way into Father's heart. Because of me, there were whispers he'd gone senile. As the years passed, the rancor toward me softened and eventually, I came to be treated as Mogul Lane's favorite son. But I knew better, for in the Great Guru's world there can *be* no favorites. Mindful of his warning, I took this whole teacher's

pet business as a challenge. One more prideful weed to be
pulled out by the root . . .

"I never took the Great Guru for granted. The more I
drank from his cup, the deeper came my understanding that
the man was truly empty. He had achieved an optimal state of
insuperable focus and discipline of purpose. In those difficult
weeks that followed the cremation, a comment of his came
back to haunt me. 'The Universe always tests a man with that
which he fears most.' At the time, it was just a casual remark
over breakfast; only later did I realize he spoke directly to me.
For years, I'd fought to expunge all vestiges of self-importance,
that labor in the garden nonsense I spoke of. And just when
I thought I was 'getting somewhere' (a phrase of ill portent,
to be sure), they offered to make me *pope*. I would be the
'next' Great Guru, no strings attached! At first, the decision
was easy. Because I'd already *vanquished* my ego, remember?
O yes! Or so I thought. My humility was a source of great
pride, something to inwardly boast about. I was resolute. No
amount of logic or flattery could tempt me to assume the post.
In fact, my refusal was proof in the pudding of my *advanced*
state . . . do you see my point? After a while, I gained enough
awareness to view the conundrum for what it was: Father's
brilliant parting shot, a teaching that hadn't been possible
to imbue until he drew his final breath . . . and created a
vacancy! Really quite wondrous, an *exquisite* maneuver, don't
you think? In the end, the most formidable lesson of all. The
irony was that while my impulse had been to flee—hadn't he
told me to run?—an invisible force kept me tethered. Was it
ego? Or was it my guru's alternate voice, urging me 'to face the
demon in battle'? The dilemma drove me half-mad. Monday
I resolved to leave, Tuesday to stay, and so forth. *The Universe*

always tests a man with that which he fears most. My very essence was caught in a Chinese finger trap. The more I squirmed, the tighter the tourniquet!

"Almost a month passed. I lost 30 pounds. I kept no food down; my hair fell out; I was always cross. Everyone thought I'd become ill, can you recall? Acute ambivalence was killing me. Then I dreamt I was at the foot of my guru's chair, in agony. I longed for commiseration but no words came. The question *Why?* hung telepathically in the air. He answered, out loud: *Why not?* He told me that by *impersonating* a guru, I had nothing to lose and everything to gain. 'After all,' he said, 'the worst that can happen is the realization that you're a *shitty guru*. And so what? *Then* you can run.'

"The vision came just hours before my first satsang—your first too, no? Your first in Bombay? Father always admired the bold stroke and I knew it was time . . . the weeks of struggle were over. He once said that it was best to live this life with the threat of a sword hanging over one's head. My task would be to keep the sword of egotism *suspended* by serving all sentient beings. His retort—'Why not?'—was the only mantra that made sense. Perhaps *this* dream bookended the other, the one where my guru ran alongside those murderous horses. The latter, a vision of my teacher's death; the former, a rebirth on Mogul Lane. My own . . .

"I summoned all my courage and entered the shop to the awaiting crowd. It was packed to the gills, no? I carefully picked my way through. I was no longer in my body—it felt like something had seized control and was *walking* me toward my beloved's chair. To this day, I have no idea what anyone could have possibly been thinking when I turned to face them . . . My own mind could not have been emptier. And so it all began.

"At the end of satsang, I fought to remember who and where I was. I was like Kipling's *Kim*, disoriented from fever at the end of that great novel. 'I am Kim. I am Kim. But what is "Kim"?' I *did* have a small sense of relief from a vague feeling it hadn't been a complete disaster. Then I was shaken from my reverie by 100,000 volts! A *yogi* can experience his death quite distinctly during advanced meditation. It is instructive to watch one's soul depart one's body . . . which is precisely what occurred, but because I was no *yogi* as yet, it was the most painful and disturbing sensation! I heard a great death rattle from my very bones. An earthquake opened up a void, a bottomless pit into which I tumbled for seven torturous years. And *you*, dear Kura—dear *teacher*—were the instrument that *destroyed* me, yet allowed me to live!"

I didn't think it possible for Kura to pay the American any more attention than he'd been giving but with this last remark, that was what happened. As if to break the tension, the guru gestured to some shaded tree stumps whose surfaces had been made suitable for guests. To my relief, Kura sat. The American remained standing. He had 20 years on his former student though looked younger and less fragile by the minute. The telling of his story energized him.

"Do you remember the moment you touched my feet, that very first time? Think back! Meditate on the moment and you just might capture my face, enshrined in the fossilized resin of memory. At the exact moment of their tender caress, the weight of your hands stung like all the hornets of the world! Those hands, *oh my teacher*, kindled a fire that became a holocaust. In that instant, I knew: *I had made a grievous mistake.* Instead of sitting in Father's chair, I should have run, run, run! For at the touch of your hand, the merciful earth did unmercifully break asunder . . .

"In an ashram, arrogance arrives in bare feet. One hardly notices; it leaves its shoes at the door and insidiously walks in. Allow me to expand upon the theme. A fundamental method of a *siddha* is repetition. A true guru knows it is impossible to be understood by language alone; he finds ways around it, patiently working with what he has. A *sadguru* brings the word from the tip of the tongue to the throat, from the throat to the heart, from the heart to the navel. That is how he escorts you to Silence. During satsang, he may expound upon his own answer until the question is forgotten. He will repeat himself again and again but don't be fooled! These redundancies are mantras, an extension of Silence itself—what is called 'mantra yoga'—though to the ignorant it appears to be nothing more than a lack of imagination or even a *functional dementia* that must be patronized and indulged. The fact of the matter is, the endless reiterations of a *siddha* are painstakingly deliberate. The guru knows full well he must drill the seeker of truth with mantra like a woodpecker drills a dying tree! The guru watches over his students as the sergeant who supervises blindfolded troops while they practice breaking down and reassembling rifles. And so it is with the student learning the ABCs of Infinity. Anyone who has had the privilege of sitting with a most venerable Master for a week, a day, an hour—a minute!—will naturally be exposed to the repetition I speak of. God is the repetition; sound and language, the mantra; the mantra is the guru; the guru is God. The Great Guru, like a strong, kind father, demanded a soldier's homework be done, for the war against the ego is no mere battle but a massacre. Just ask Krishna!

"When I was a boy, I was *quicksilver* in body and mind. I lorded my speed over fellow students, and family too. I was shameless! I wished to show my parents how dumb they were, how much better off they'd be if they looked to their son for the answers. My father was a poor reader so I read the newspaper aloud to him in a faster than normal tempo, to throw it in his face. My mother was bad with figures so I pored over her accounts and showed her all the places her calculations had been wrong. We have a lot in common, dear Kura, dear *teacher*. When I first arrived at Mogul Lane, like you I could find nowhere to sit other than at my guru's feet. (The Source had arranged it thus.) After I'd been with him a few years, I grew restless during satsang. I became bored by those periods of repetition I spoke of. I'd heard it all before! I couldn't discreetly take my leave because my position at his chair was too prominent. Instead, I played a little mental game to keep myself from falling asleep . . . a child's game. Whenever a seeker asked a question, one I'd heard a thousand times before—the guru is not the only one who repeats himself!—I formulated a response, awarding myself points for varying degrees of accuracy. I made up little rules to keep it lively, but soon even the game was in danger of incurring my boredom and contempt.

"The compulsion continued for years, too petty and intermittent to take myself to task yet too *consistent* to ignore. I never spoke to my guru about it though wish I had, for only now do I know he could have arrested it as easily as a case of hiccups. It was nothing more than a neurotic figment of 'the Fifth Column,' hence unworthy of any attention that might validate it. To focus on the Mind was to feed it . . . this is what I told myself. If you can't beat it, revel in it! I had platitudes and justifications *galore*. How smug! What hubris! It was my distorted belief that self-awareness alone provided amnesty. I basked in my advanced *knowingness*, rationalizing the game away as a juvenile travesty, a tool with which I might 'hone' myself.

"Year after year, I spent part of satsang predicting Father's response to myriad questions. And I was often 'in the ball-park,' as they say . . . Now, I don't want to give the impression I was completely *out to lunch* for his talks, not at all. I listened quite closely. Still, there was always that moment as we neared the end—around 10:30 or quarter to 11—when I grew bored: with the game, with India, with *myself*. My thoughts flew else-where, the guru and his acolytes a drone in my ear. I'd return to my body in the nick of time to fabricate an answer to some stupid query, by rote . . . but invariably, the moment came when my beloved's response would be so far afield from the one I concocted, so wrenchingly poetic and outlandishly sim-ple, so onionskin-*unknowable*, beautiful and direct that my body stiffened with shame like a boy caught stabbing snails with a butter knife. The game would quickly be retired. For a few days, anyway!

"Here is what happened on that fatal, fateful morning. During satsang, though disembodied, I somehow glanced down to take you in throughout. You were like a small anchor attached to the chair that kept me from floating away . . . and there was something else. Your initial disappointment was easy to read on your face. (For good reason—I later learned you had traveled a long distance to sit before the Great Guru and got *me* instead!) With your desperate eyes, in your hard-won spot at Father's feet, I saw *myself*, from another time. Then, slowly but surely, my extemporaneous efforts seemed to win you over—floating near the roof, incognizant of my own words, guided by arrogance cunningly dressed in a hum-ble kurta, I was still able to acknowledge your purity, your innocence, your yearning for Truth. I watched your hard features soften . . . and it mattered, *you* mattered. I actually believe you carried me through that abominable, terrifying hour—Sri Kura! Mahatma! Baba!—and that your *attention* formed the cornerstone of the edifice of illusion I built for myself—and others—on Mogul Lane. You gave me your heart. On that morning, everyone did. It was the Great Guru who was carrying us both . . . us all.

"When I finally peeled myself off the ceiling, I remembered the game I played during my teacher's satsang. I looked at you and thought, *What if he stays? What if the one who sits where I once sat stays? And begins to play the game, just as I did?* The corollary of that supposition hit me like a gust of foul air, for I could never be expected to surprise, to *humble* the seekers as the *rishi* had done. Eventually you would be able to mimic my recycled trove of responses—anyone with half a mind could!—my personalized plagiarisms of the Great Guru's words—and win the game. *Every time.* Because it simply wasn't possible for me to usher you or *anyone* into Silence. The Great Guru had already spoken to me from a dream and told me the worst possibility—discovering the 'shitty guru within.' But there *was* something worse: *to know it and stay on!* To remain in the chair with full knowledge of the fraud, spreading the vile gospel of Self. Because you see I *liked* the chair—that was the flaw—the kid with all the answers—all the marbles—sat in the chair and fell in love. It was love at first seat!

"That insight (to know and yet remain) lit the fuse, and the bomb detonated in the *exact instant* your hands touched my feet. Because *that* was the moment I realized I would never run—nor would I ever have the courage to 'face the demon in battle.' Nothing would stop me from wallowing in *guru shittiness*, no! The rewards were too amenable. *That* moment— the laying on of hands—*your* hands, Kuraji!—destroyed *and* healed me, sealing my Faustian pact with the Mind. Flesh touching flesh was key . . . if I was still capable of staying on at Mogul Lane under such grotesque circumstances, what *else* might I be capable of? In an instant, I became no more than a guru-thuggee—my worst imagined enemy, my *assassin* . . . Do you see my point? When you touched my feet, how it burned! Remember my reaction? Think! Think back! Can you? *Turn back the page.* Perhaps your friend Cassiopeia remembers— yes, she's nodding her head. She *sees*. Return to that time with your mind's eye, old friend, and you might catch me in a petit mal seizure of the eschatological variety. I recovered quickly; I told you that little boy was fast as quicksilver, especially when it came to saving his butt. I have always been a 'trouper'—*I pick myself up, dust myself off, start all over again*—one of the quali- ties I share with my former countrymen. But at the moment I speak of I was like the actor who goes up on his lines then improvises with such alacrity that he earns a thunderous ova- tion. I covered over my torment with an elegant soft-shoe. And they lapped it up! Didn't they, Cassiopeia?

"Perhaps I've been telling my tale with more cynicism than intended. I don't mean to—I wasn't so much cynical as lost. I should have been *found* with the touch of your hands, which after all represented the touch of all seekers, all hearts. Instead, *I literally died* . . . and was born: for such brutally one-pointed *bhakti* was the very thing that, under the loving eyes of the zodiac, arranged—ordained—our extraordinary assembly today.

"For seven years, it was hell. No one could have known; such was my art. Like any good counterfeiter, practice makes perfect . . . While each successive day grew more agonizing than the last, an evolving expertise made it virtually impossible for even a close observer to distinguish false notes from true. What a connoisseur I became! After awhile, even I managed to fool myself. I was a cross between a chimpanzee and a parrot, without the integrity of either. Mind you, I was never contemptuous of the teachings I had retained enough of to pervert and drew comfort from making use of the dirty dishwater that soaked round my teacher's pots. As time went on, my respect for Father compounded—my *awe*—as did my self-hatred for having betrayed a sacred trust. The only respite from anguish came in dreamless sleep, but even then—! At night, before losing consciousness, I ruminated that there must be some purpose to it all and if only I persevered I might be pardoned . . . perhaps even emerge *enlightened*, worthy of the chair at last. Upon awakening, such fantasies were totally expunged. Again I dove headlong into the daily routine, flogging myself for the guilt I carried and for what I had become. Would you mind very much if we went inside?"

Kura blinked, flustered by a comment outside the narrative.

"I'm mindful of the sun," said the American. "I'm used to it—but it may sneak up on you." He gestured amicably toward the cave. "I assure you it's geologically sound. And Cassiopeia looks as if she'd enjoy some cool water."

He turned on his heel, marched to the cave and disappeared within. I was intensely curious and absolutely parched—both water bottles were finished, which of course he had thoughtfully noted. I got up but Kura didn't budge. He just sat there like a robot on the fritz and mopped his brow, a move that never failed to trigger heart attack head-riffs. What if he keeled over right *then*, without getting closure?

He lifted himself off the stump and shuffled toward the cave. The American's sandals were at the door. I took mine off and Kura clumsily did the same.

In an ashram, arrogance arrives in bare feet . . .

Pitch-dark. We stood stock-still inside the entrance while our eyes adjusted. The sadhu gestured for us to sit at the bench of a small wooden table. I led Kura over, afraid he might stumble. Glasses of water and cups of tea were already waiting.

"In my seventh year, something shifted," said the American. He came and sat across from us. "I began plotting my escape. I was stunned it had never occurred to me. Some part of me believed that if I took definitive action—if I left Mogul Lane behind and threw myself on the mercy of the Source—all crimes would be forgiven. Very *Catholic*, no? My demeanor brightened with the knowledge I'd begun tunneling beneath the barbed wire. The Great Escape! Can you recall my sunny mood in the months before I departed? Even my enemies—a camp that was steadily growing—noted a jauntiness in my step. I meditated each day for hours, something I hadn't done in years. My course of action, my *destiny* became clear. I likened myself to the prisoner who finishes lunch and straightens his cell before leaping from the top tier. Liberation was at hand . . . all was well with the world at last.

"I plotted that escape as carefully as a murder. The possibility that I might be apprehended by those whose open hearts I had betrayed with my 'teachings' was unacceptable. I would not have it! Nothing would be left to chance. In the years I made book I'd become well acquainted with a host of shady characters. I see now why I cultivated those gamblers and thieves—I envied the integrity of their one-pointed purpose. What a brazen, wondrous thing it is to dream of winning *by a nose*, to stake *everything* on winning by a nose! However they might be judged, those men could never be robbed of the dignity conferred by that inviolate enterprise, for it came to be my opinion it wasn't the horse they were straining toward but God Himself. It is said that this is how some escape the Wheel of Dharma—*by a nose*. With the help of my rogue's gallery, I made a clean getaway. I loved them all the more for never asking *Why?* though of course I had a ready answer: *Why not!* A report on the details of my flight would be superfluous. Suffice to say I was like one of those merchants in *1,001 Nights*, snatched by *djinns* and deposited far away from home. Only a few moments seemed to pass before I found myself hundreds of miles to the north.

"You may not believe this but I had no plan beyond achieving my freedom. I was alone and deliriously without purpose. One day, during charnel ground *sadhana*,[9] my nostrils quivered at a whiff of perfume—the intoxicating, unmistakable odor of my teacher! The Great Guru spoke through a cloud of roses and sandalwood. He said the more directionless I became the stronger his scent would grow, until one day I *became the scent itself*. With that, I began my travels to that place called Nowhere.

"After a decade of wandering, on awakening from an afternoon nap beneath a tamarisk tree, the pungent smells of my guru at last returned to overwhelm my senses. As I went begging, roadside Samaritans were stunned by my exhalations,

---

9   The ancient practice of meditation amongst human remains.

redolent with botanical attar: the field of roses now resided within. I heard his voice a final time, so loud and clear tears gushed from my eyes—tears of essential oils! He told me of a sacred place in Uttar Pradesh, on the apron of Nepal.

"It took months to make my way here. As I ascended the trail, I imagined Father leading me by the hand to my union with the Divine. Halfway up, a man with a thick black moustache (it's whiter now) appeared on the path. His smile was auspicious. The village elder—you've already met, no? I'd hardly spoken in ten years but now the words poured forth. I told him I was an itinerant priest who wished to end his days in solitude and meditation. Without second thought he said, 'I know just the place.' He led me through the meadow to this cave, the home of a leper who had passed away a few months before. A vacancy sign was blinking! I've spent every day since racing toward *emptiness* full-gallop, bent on winning by a nose! Only recently did I catch sight of my beloved again. I redoubled my speed and now my guru and I ride together, side by side."

"Do you mean to say you've achieved enlightenment?" said Kura, shaken and wild-eyed. "That you're an *enlightened man*?" The American smiled obscurely, agitating Kura even more. "I asked you a question, sir! *Did* you? Did you or did you not achieve enlightenment!"

There was something so utterly sad and ludicrous about the ultimatum.

"What I am saying," said the *rishi*, "is that now I am empty." He was quiet for some moments, allowing the echo of profundity to die away. "But the important thing to recognize is that I should never have seen the rays of *chiti*, nor would the veil have lifted . . . *shakti* could not have awakened and the words 'I am that' would have remained a mere riddle had

I not acquired a *second guru*. Of course, the teacher is always there—it is the *seeker* who is in the way. What they say is true: When you are ready, the guru will find you. I'll tell you a *concept* that is almost impossible to grasp: at the moment one finds one's guru, one becomes *truly* lost . . . until one finds another! For it is only the second guru that allows you to make sense of the first."

I will never be able to adequately describe what I saw when I glanced at Kura's face. An immemorial darkness, something primeval . . . his features dissolved before me, one set replacing another, from the fragile fear of a neurotic city dweller to the monolithic indifference of an Easter Island *moai*. I blinked hard until Kura reverted to his angry, nonplussed self. That the man who had conned him now dared to blithely lecture on the supreme importance of finding a *follow-up bullshitter* added insult to injury.

"This guru of yours, this *Guru Number 2*," he spat venomously. "I suppose he's long dead . . ."

"Why, no!" said the American. "He's very much alive."

"Then where is he?" he demanded, more tantrum than query. "Where is he! *And tell me who is he!*"

"Would you like to meet him? He's in festive spirits, *I* can assure."

"He's here?—"

"O yes! In this very room."

Kura fussed in his seat, wary of being played for sport.

"Is that right?" he said, with noxious disdain. "Well, *I don't see him*."

Kura stood. He slowly moved in the direction pointed by our host, squinting into the habitat's dim recesses. I think he was in the throes of some sort of hysteria.

"I say I see *nothing!*"

"My old friend, that you see nothing is not my affair. He's right in front of your face."

"There's nothing but a chair."

"*Correct,*" said the American. "Nothing—and everything! Allow me to be more clear. The chair does not contain the *emanations* of the guru, nor does it aspire to: *It is the guru himself.*"

The Hermit sank to his knees in front of the simple throne, prostrating himself. Now cross-legged, he looked up at the chair. "It took my entire life to find what was never missing . . ." He turned to Kura with *such love*—I know it's corny, Bruce, but to this day I swear the fragrance of roses blew straight through me. "And it is all because of you."

He wasn't done speaking though stopped short, as if knowing his guest's next move. The American's heart was open, his smile benevolent.

But I could not have predicted what happened next.

Kura bolted from the cave in a silent scream.

* * *

Mountaineers say the descent is more dangerous than the climb, which definitely applied to our return trip. We suffered four-legged and four-speeded calamities; when night fell, the driver announced it was unsafe to continue. We stayed over at an inn. Any thoughts I might have previously entertained of Kura whisking me to Paris for a little post–egg hunt R and R were pretty much dashed by the impenetrable pall that had settled over him. He went incommunicado. I knew better than to try to draw him out.

Thirty-six hours later, I was greatly relieved to be ensconced in the First Lady—Maharanee?—wing of the Presidential Suite. I called to ask if he wanted supper, suggesting we do a little recap over room service. (I already knew the answer.) After a long soak I made notes in my trusty Smythson, expanding on them when I got back to New York.

I was nodding off when the phone rang. Someone in the posse said to be packed and ready at 10 a.m. I'd never *unpacked* so when morning came there wasn't much to do but order up a carafe of lattes and chocolate croissants for extra protein. I took a constitutional around the perimeter of the hotel in the forlorn hope that my bowels might want to start a conversation; they were quiet as a grave.

I was in the lobby uncharacteristically early, befitting a depressed person in a faraway place waiting to go home to die. My eye fell on the elevator just as Kura and his retinue emerged. My main man wore a blue serge suit and a heartbreakingly sportive pompadour. He'd paid scrupulous attention to his toilet—his way, I suppose, of ending the sentence or at least dotting the "i" in Delhi. We chitchatted on the drive to the airport and I even wrung a few smiles out of him. I actually started to wonder if he *would* whisk me away, to destinations unknown.

The convoy rolled onto the tarmac but none of the posse approached the Bentley when it parked, as if knowing in advance to allow us our privacy. We stayed in the car.

"Queenie, I cannot tell you what your being here has meant. And I know I shan't be able to process it—any of it— for some time. I was going to ask you to come to Paris . . . what a time we would have had! But now that's impossible. This has been a strenuous trip and I hardly wish to send you back in worse shape than you arrived. So I've opened up my *appartements* in the Marais; my staff awaits you. An itinerary has already been customized for your pleasure, with an emphasis on the off-the-beaten-track and *taboo*. You shall want for nothing. If the idea of Paris—without your Kura!—does not appeal, the plane will take you anywhere you wish: Kyoto, Patagonia, Lindos . . . but you must promise to forgive my heavy-handed mood. You know how it pains me to be a terrible host."

"You're going back to see him?"

"Yes. I'm going back."

Had he asked me to accompany him I would have without hesitation but I knew Kura well enough to understand his speech was a farewell. I was honored to have served my purpose. He was on his own now, just as he wished.

I returned to New York and my griffin friends straightaway.

On the plane, I dawdled with completing the crossword of his plan. (He hadn't shared, I hadn't asked.) I was never good at puzzles but *was* good at tossing them aside, unfinished. Which is what I did . . . After a few months, my depression lifted, or at least became manageable. I went on about my life with the necessary delusion most of us share that we're captains of our destinies, when truth be told we have no more power over our fates than falling leaves do over a tree.

I'm not exactly sure why Kura wasn't in my head much after that strange sojourn, not substantially anyway—and I didn't feel guilty about it, either. Maybe Delhi was *my* second guru, because it helped make sense of that long-ago time in Bombay. I'm not sure exactly how I felt. Though I do remember I didn't cry when I learned he was dead.

* * *

Wow—we're nearly at the end. I think all in all it's been a good experience. (I hope it has, for you!) Just to puke everything out . . . that doesn't sound so wonderful though, huh? But you know I think it really *does* help put things in order. I mean, not that there was a dire *need*. At least I don't think there was. Who knows. So often these tremendous—*things* happen in one's life, and one never stops to take their measure or look at patterns—you know, 'the figure in the carpet.' Anyway, I just wanted to thank you, Bruce, for being such a good listener and for being so patient with my silly tangents . . .

Now of course I wasn't there for this last part I'm going to tell you so when I speak of things only Kura could have been privy to—his direct experience—I'll be channeling from *his* diaries. He bequeathed me the lot; I've been cribbing from them for much of what we've already covered. Details were taken from a notebook he kept in the last six months of his life so I guess I'll be paraphrasing more than usual.

In the moment he ran from the cave, Kura was convinced that his former teacher was stark raving mad. And yet by the time we arrived at the plush sanctuary of our Delhi hotel, he found himself in the grip of a converse *idée fixe*: What if the American was sober as a judge? Could it be that he was in the exaltedly cockamamie tradition of those legendary sadhus who attained "crazy wisdom"? Like the saints of Mahamudra who appeared as drunks and village idiots, so might the Hermit prance about his cave talking to enlightened furniture. It was a sliver in Kura's foot that had to come out.

The entourage began its return to the village immediately after leaving me at the airport. There was no mention in his journal of any sherpa-led procession up the foothills. Still, I laughed (and my heart broke for the 4,000th time) as I pictured him with deflated hair in his fancy suit, creased and soiled by flop sweat, balancing atop a burro—stubborn mules all!—an exhausted Quixote tilting against Eternity.

As they reached the meadow, he became seized by that awful ambivalence endemic to those wounded by love. One moment, he was enthralled by the possibility that the American had annihilated the Self and ascended Mount Sumeru; the next, he gloated bitterly at the prospect of the man having lost his mind.

By the time he approached the cave he was numb . . .

He called out and received no answer. He walked to the entrance and raised his voice in greeting. He paused before moving a few feet inside the doorless door.

And there he stood, letting his eyes adjust, as before.

The elder greeted him with undimmed ardor, though his easy smile was at odds with what he soon disclosed.

"You must tell me something," Kura beseeched, without so much as a hello. "You must tell me *now.*"

"Certainly! Yes! Of course!" he replied. The haunted look in the eye of his importunate visitor was plain to see.

"The Hermit—the American—*that man who's lived in the cave all these years* . . . you know him well, is that correct? He said that when he came here, you were the first person he met, and you showed him—what I mean is, that you *must* know him rather well . . ."

The smile on the elder's face was stuck; his jaw made involuntary movements, as if words were being roughly incubated.

"I went to see him just now at the cave but he wasn't there! Look: I need you to—I *want* you . . . I'd be very *appreciative* if you'd give me your opinion about something. *If you'd clear something up.* It's rather *urgent . . .* or seems to have become so, anyway. [*This last said more to himself.*] You *must* weigh your words carefully! I say this, because . . . *because my life may depend on it.*" He looked warily toward the ground, as if the abyss his teacher once described was soon to crack open the earth where they stood. "*Is this man*—this American *saint*, as you call him—is he—well, is he in his *right mind*? The question being: do you have *any reason whatsoever* to believe he is a lunatic? Senile? Sir! You strike me as a man with a level head, and a fair judge of others . . . so much so, I'd think twice before asking you for a similar ruling on myself! But sir, *if you will*—I beg of you to answer my question with as much honesty and forthrightness as you can bring to bear." A pause. "I have come to ask: *Is he insane?*"

"Yes, yes, yes!" shouted the elder in jubilation. "Without equivocation!" His smile became most natural again as it gave birth to a litter of words, the entire face assuming an expression of "all-consuming love." (Kura's written phrase, not mine.) "The Hermit of Dashir Cave was the purest, most formidable of all the *rishis* God in His unfathomable grace has ever privileged me to honor with prayer. My friend, I have brushed up against holy men for some 50-odd years! You ask if he was in his right mind. The simplest answer I can give is that he was *beyond all notion of sanity or madness*, and exists[10] far outside Time. When he came to our modest village to ask for a place he might lay his head, I could do nothing but rejoice! In my greed, I took his arrival as an augur of great tidings—which it was!—a celestial sign that our humble community might *benefit* from his presence. And we did, *greatly* so. Many miracles

---

10   Queenie later told me that, as faithfully recorded in Kura's
      diaries, his host mixed past and present tenses at random.

happened while he was among us, miracles I shall never attempt to describe, at the risk of becoming conceited or even idolatrous. (There is also the fear that by giving them voice, they may come undone.) Kind friend and guest, your question has flooded me with memories . . . and unspeakable sadness as well. But I cannot afford those luxuries at this time. For now I must oversee his burial in the sky."

The husband and wife seesawed—as he rose to leave (without adieu), she gently fell, proffering lentils. But the soliloquy rendered Kura dumb; famished as he was, he couldn't touch the bowl. "Burial in the sky" had been plainly spoken, yet eluded comprehension. When Kura finally gathered enough wits to ask, the wife confirmed that indeed the Hermit was dead.

A whole set of new emotions washed over him, if they were emotions at all. He felt surreal, bungling, disjointed.

"My husband was the last to see him. He stopped by the cave with a basket of food I'd prepared for the three of you— we had no idea your visit would be so short! You and your wife had only just left; the Hermit invited him in and began to speak . . . not at all the norm. Rarely did the holy man *chatterbox*. He preferred to meditate while his guests, mostly villagers of course, shared their hopes and loves, dreams and fears. He never gave advice nor was it solicited. Talking to him was its own reward, often resulting in great benefit. When my husband returned, he informed me of your departure and said that he'd spent a long time with the guru, just listening. I asked what was discussed but he was reticent to divulge, which wasn't like him at *all*. You've seen how garrulous he can be—my husband positively delights in chatterboxing! The only thing he divulged was that the Hermit spoke of you in a most affectionate and *animated* way, almost breathless, as if 'running out of time'—those were the precise words my husband used. And that he gave no indication whatsoever of feeling ill, to the contrary! My husband said that his spirit blazed brighter than ever."

At first blush, the news was more than Kura could bear. He'd been left behind by the American before, and now it had happened all over again! *This* time, though, came the cruelest twist. *This* time, the old man tweaked Kura's nose before rubbing it in shit. He sprung to his feet, ignoring her attempts to restrain him. *No!* He *would* not stay for the freakin' burial in the sky, whatever *that* was—he just wanted *out*, to put as many miles between him and that ogre as humanly possible. As he power-walked down those wretched foothills—those glorified mounds of dirt he'd grown to fear and detest—a raw anger displaced the spurious optimism of the last handful of hours. In his fury, a hundred yards or so down the path, he almost knocked a small boy off the road. It was the elder's grandson, bent under the weight of the burden that was strapped to his back.

"What have you there?"

The frightened boy held his ground.

"I said, *what do you have there?*"

In high dudgeon, Kura brutally spun the child around. Recognizing the cargo at once, he was stung afresh—it was the chair from the cave.

"What do you mean to do with that?"

"My grandfather told me to bring it to the school."

"Give it to me!" he commanded.

"But my grandfather said that the Hermit—"

"Devil take the Hermit!" Kura shouted. "I said give it here! Your grandfather promised it to me!" He puffed up with righteous temerity—the lie felt good and right and true. He undid the rope and pathetically wrenched the chair from the boy's back in a brief tug-of-war. "I've *earned* this damned chair," said Kura, drawing it to his chest in full possession then handing it off to the closest sherpa. *"Now that's the end of it!"*

The chair's unlikely journey ended in the Paris office, where Kura took a few mugshots with his old Land Camera.

Then he wrapped it in a mover's blanket, flung it in the closet and resolved never to see it again.

* * *

In the ensuing year, he went through the motions. He became depressed, with fleeting thoughts of suicide. They put him on lithium and Prozac—this, that and the other. Sometimes he slept on the office couch. He dreamed of the chair on the other side of the wall.

One day an unusual-looking envelope arrived in the company pouch addressed to "Sri. B. Moncrieff," in an immodest calligraphic hand. No return address. The letter was included in the box of diaries I received a few months after he passed away. I'll give us both a break and read from it directly . . .

> Queenie took the correspondence from her coat pocket with pseudo-dramatic flair. Someone poured more wine. She sniffed the glass then tasted, nodding approvingly to the server.
>
> Dusk had fallen. She read to me by the light of a beautiful lantern; the inky message bled through the rice paper, dancing among the woven threads.

"My Dearest Kind Sir/SRI Bela Moncrieff,

"I am earnest in hoping this note does most
indeed find you most well! I meant to put pen to
pencil many months ago and do ask your kind
forgiveness as to complete failure on my behalf in
that regard. While my village is a modest one and my
duties toward it simple, various pressing concerns
have the habit of being horses on the runway. Hereby
(and 'thereby' too for good measure) not long after
your leavetaking didst we villagers became unlucky
recipients of a mighty monsoon that caused a great
deal of mischief—you may be saddened to hear
me declare the Dashir Cave is now no more. The
threat of the Dengue, which arrived not long after
the waters seceded, thankfully turned out false
in its alarum. Yet in my heart I must confess to
terrible remorse for the delay of this most serious
missive. As months passed, the greater became
my understanding of the crowning importance its
enquoted words would hold for you; as they were
uttered by the Hermit himself, who instructed
they be conveyed forthwith and straightaway, at
all cost. So you see I have no excuse nor have I
defence. Again, I humbly ask your forgiveness, dear
Sri, adding that sometimes a procrastinated man
becomes a means unto himself.

"By the way, if you are wondering how I captured
your address (which would mean in fact that you are
reading this, and thus providing me with the most
supreme of blessings and lasting unction!), it was from

the direct intercession of that most loyal and most jolly fellow Quasimodo, who arrived not long after the *jnani*'s sky burial bearing the generous gifts that completed your contract with our village, a largess which has continued to make the aggregations of All Souls exceedingly grateful.

"I believe my wife did admit that after your departure I was privileged to spend a few hours in the company of the blesséd Hermit—may his memory forever be sanctified!—a time in which he shared many things pertinent to your life that have remained unbeknownst (a circumstance this note shall attempt to rectify); in fact, he discussed the very things he had planned to share with you in person, if you and your lady friend had not run off. But, all-being *mukta* that he is, the Hermit of Dashir Cave even knew you would return just as you did, to miss his death by mere hours! Alack: such was overwrought and writ by the stars. When you appeared at our door for the *second* time, unaware of his passing, you were most *fired up* and in no state to listen to anything a person might tell—nor was I in any mood to impart what I had so carefully been entrusted to pass on. (In that stage of the game, I had not even told my wife.) My plan was to relay every single one of the intimate profundities the Hermit had donated (to the best of my shabby abilities) over dinner, immediately after attending the details of his inhumation. When I came home to find you'd again taken a powder, I said to the Missus, 'This man is like a horse on fire!' I was deflated though not surprised, for the Hermit had just gotten through highlighting his erstwhile student's penchant for the triggerhair—relayed with a twinkle in his eye, to be sure!—so that I became enamored of your willfulness Johnny-on-the-spot as well, which lessened the sting. But barely.

"If you've read this far, I assume you shall read the rest, and with great care. For the love of God, I urge you with every fiber of my being to continue!

"The *jnani* conjured an in-depth précis of your histories together—such was his art (and his heart) that within the shortest while I knew more than was possible and felt too like I'd been along on your journeys! Then he told me something which really shocked me to Hell. Guruji said that only *two weeks prior* to your appearance at the cave, he had been ready to depart this Earth. And *please*, sir, *do* understand God saw fit that the village idiot— myself!—was at least blesséd with the awareness that before him stood a saint of all saints! I am certain that such a man as you—who sat vigil at the foot of this precious being for so many years—cannot be incognisant of the fact that an enlightened man has the ability to choose the date of his liberation from the Great Wheel . . . and just as he may summon death, so are the most powerful *rishis* able to *postpone* their departures as well. The Hermit averred that on the very morning he was poised to merge with that essence which is Silence—two weeks before you came to our village—a mystical Voice bade him delay. Now, the Hermit was always faithful to the commands of that Voice, as it belonged to his teacher, the Great Guru himself, and refused to manifest excepting upon occasions of categorical importance. Most charmingly, he added how there were many things he did not understand (this, I very much doubted), and what a privilege it was to still delight in the inscrutable.

"We sat in the cave not long after you had gone and he told me that when he saw you enter the glen, all was suddenly understood. 'The final veil had lifted.' Perhaps it seemed to you as if he'd been expecting your arrival, for in a sense he was. The Hermit said he went back to raking the leaves of destiny and gratefully rejoiced, praising anew the wondrous Universe and everything unimaginable Mother dared conceive. He told me his life had come full circle and the beautiful dance was nothing more nor less than *doings* choreographed by the Source. He said that years ago you freed him from that awful business of being a false sage—though I can never believe he could be such a thing!—that *you alone* were the catalyst of his enlightenment . . . and now you had come to free him one last time! Do you remember what his feet looked like? When you saw him raking? The edema? Did you know they swelled up just hours before you arrived? Guruji said it happened *spontaneously*, in 'energetic' memory of your ashram touch . . .

"In our tête-à-tête, the Hermit spoke of that fateful day he recoiled whilst you pressed his feet in tribute, each finger like the sting of '10,000 hornets.' He told me it was *your touch* that raised the curtain—then lowered the boom! And how it took seven anguished years after that to leave the damnable chair behind . . . Guruji instructed me to recount these words to you at once, upon your anticipated return, *so you too could be set free.* He said it pained him to see you suffer needlessly and that he would have waited for you but could no longer delay his journey. I repeat myself when I say I was prepared to share with you over dinner all that he had commanded me to, but you'd already *vamoosed*—again!—and one thing led to another . . . over weeks and months . . . the flooding and all . . . not that I'm looking to make excuses for my own dereliction . . . even though it might be most charitably understood, as I have written so very few letters in my lifetime . . . in fact, have *never* put pen to pencil without my Guruji making the gentlest of hints and corrections over my shoulder so to speak, for he used to guide my hand in the occasional personal missive or official proclamation . . . such are the reasons—not excuses nor defence! (Nor not meant to be, really) . . . as to my paralysis for more than half a year. I was in abject misery at the impossibility of distilling the words of a *jnani* and panicked that his message would be so garbled as to lose its irrelevance *entirely.* My hesitation only worked to compound my dread. Now, I feel only shame at my careless delinquency, and pray you forgive!

"Do you know how the body of the saintly Hermit was discovered? In the cave, on its knees before the chair, in eternal obeisance. My grandson was thus honored to discover the Beloved One poised in the bardo between this life and the Pure Land, and came running in a lather. We went back together; and that was where I saw him, his elegant, attenuated fingers frozen in a caress upon the approximate metatarsals of his unseen master! For Ramana Maharshi did say, 'The real feet of Bhagavan exist only in the heart of the devotee' . . . During the extraordinary conference I keep referring to, the Hermit poignantly avouched—it was the first time I ever saw the tears of a saint!—that he had been the first to descry the body of *his* teacher, in Bombay, the difference being that unlike the posture of the American in death, the Great Guru had taken full possession of the chair, like the pilot of a 'great vehicle' come home. Twas the Great Guru's fate to launch himself into the Unknowable from the chair, that prosaic cynosure whose indifferent 'thereness' (the exacting word used by the Hermit), analogous to Infinity itself, had been polished by thousands of satsang sittings as a stone smoothed by the sea, transformed into psalm and song. The Hermit was unbashful to inform that while it was his teacher's destiny to be carried to Silence in a golden throne, it was his own to be liberated by traveling *alongside* the Great Guru in the guise of supplicant, a pilgrim forever 'at his feet' in service and surrender. He said that in the end, whether one sat in the chair or kneeled before it, was a thing governed by stars and individual temperament, and one was not better than the other.

"The Hermit insisted your arrival was an omen that his Earthly cycle had ended. I'm afraid I'm being clumsy . . . he said it so much simpler! But hear me out—for this next is of *ultimate importance*. When Guruji told you his cave chair was the 'second guru,' it was naught but an impish lie that he couldn't resist in the moment, because you were so incensed—like a charging bull! He knew you weren't ready to hear the Truth. So he made that impish remark to defuse, but (as things turned out) had no time to rectify it—until now—through me. What he did not have the chance to impart was . . . *the second guru was you! You* were that teacher who comes along (if one is so blesséd) to make sense of the first—*you* were the one who illuminated all that the Great Guru had tried to show him, which he never fully understood. This knowledge only came to him in the final weeks of his life . . .

"How magnificent, he said, is God and his workings!

"He asked me to convey his words as best I could and to thank you by proxy. I hope to Krishna you will deign to send a reply through Mister Quasimodo, one hell of a guy, so at least I may know the letter found its mark! All of my life I have adapted to failure but could not go quietly to my grave knowing this memo had never been delivered . . ."

Shit—I'm getting a headache! Probably not a good idea to read by candlelight, huh?

Queenie set the pages down and closed her eyes, looking within. She rubbed the bridge of her nose then used both hands to rub her temples. Someone brought a pill and she swallowed it with a gulp of wine. She lit a cigarette and inhaled deeply, closing her eyes again.

Can I paraphrase the rest? The letter closed with a heartfelt apology to "Sri Bela" for not having treated him as justly deserved. The elder regretted he'd been unable to comprehend earlier that Kura was "also a saint who walked amongst us. For who else but a saint might have the power to mean so much—*everything!*—to one as glorious as the *jnani*? To have been the *catalyst* to freedom . . . and to top it off, to meet him at journey's end so he might properly return to Mother's arms! Who else but a fellow traveler could effect this?" He even asked (in the diffident way one asks of a soothsayer) if there was any meaning to his grandson finding the body in the cave—was it a sign the boy himself might become a saint? He proclaimed he'd been twice-blessed by God for arranging the divine intersection of his meager life with that of Kura and the Hermit's, then wrapped things up by extending a "standing room invitation." "The Dashir Cave shall be up to snuff within the month, jewel-hearted one! It awaits you, as do we all! We are forever in your debt and at your service!"

O—I almost forgot. And this is pretty good. He wrote that the theft of the chair—he didn't quite use that word but something thereabouts—ah yes, "purloined"! He used *purloined*—he said, "After my talk with the Hermit, your action made eminent sense." Or something like that. I'll read it to you tomorrow when I can see straight . . . the *gist* of it being, he drew enormous comfort knowing the chair was back in Kura's possession, "restored to its rightful place in the lineage of Kings." What he couldn't have imagined was that having that chair felt like a curse; that's how Kura described it in his diary. So he set about what was to become a final chore.

He retrieved the curiosity from the closet, unpacked it, and set it opposite his desk, as if awaiting a visitor. He decided that the only way to make things right—to lift the curse, I suppose—was to return that which did not belong to him. The sole person fit for the assignment was Quasimodo, who not only was well familiar with the village and its obscure location but more importantly had a warm relationship with the elder. His wishes were to be taped to the chair in the form of two notes; one addressed to "Mr. Q," and a second to Justine, Kura's secretary, informing her that the courier was to receive a $25,000 bonus upon verification the deed was done.

After outlining the plan in his journal, Kura collapsed and died.

* * *

I make it a habit never to go to funerals.

Our long goodbye ended in Delhi—Lordy, he looked so fine in his blue serge suit! Besides, I had no desire to be in Paris on a rainy Thursday, stranded and bereft. Do you know the Vallejo poem?

I will die in Paris, on a rainy day,
on some day I already remember . . .

Isn't that lovely?

And that's the end of my story.

—O! Good question. The answer is, my name and address had literally been glued to one of the diaries, along with a proviso that all volumes be forwarded to me upon his death. I suppose he must have had a presentiment. I guess there wasn't anyone in his life he felt closer to . . . and I feel really honored by that.

I've only recently begun to dip into the journals from the late '70s/early '80s, after Kura returned from Bombay to Paris. O man, he was *completely* at sea. He was using, heavily. Coke and heroin—his health was really going to shit. (He had the heart attack in '92.) As always, he had an amazing network of friends. Jodorowsky, of course. Karl Lagerfeld, Olivia de Havilland. And there was Genet . . . That surprised me—I didn't think *anyone* knew Genet. And I don't know how it happened, but he met Carlos Castaneda. In Paris. Castaneda was one of his heroes. They had lunches and dinners over a month's time. And there was this rather astonishing conversation Kura transcribed that foreshadowed the American's remarks at Dashir Cave. Evidently, Castaneda told him the same thing: that it was imperative to have a second teacher! Castaneda said that *his* second teacher was Death; that Death helped him untangle everything he'd been taught by the Yaqui Indian sorcerer Don Juan Matus. It interested me that Kura wrote about Castaneda kind of *upbraiding* him. Castaneda *admonished* that Death had been Kura's first teacher—I'm not sure exactly what Kura had divulged about his violent past—and seemed to chastise him for never having understood "a single word Death was saying." Can you imagine? He wrote that Castaneda said something like, "Death taught you *everything* and you understood nothing! When you find that second teacher, be sure to give him your *full attention*. The second teacher will tell you—*show* you— what was on Death's mind." When I read the passage, I wondered if Kura had completely forgotten about it, even after the American had said as much.

Anyway, are you hungry? Did *anything* I say make sense to you, Bruce? Let's walk for just a bit—*[We did, circumnavigating the tent in ever-expanding circles in the cold night air until we were far enough away from the fire to be enveloped in the off-putting, syrupy darkness]* I've spoken in so many people's voices over the last few days that I'm hoping you'll indulge me a few remarks that are wholly my own. What a concept, huh? *[Queenie went quiet—I presumed to gather her thoughts. There wasn't enough moonlight to see her face let alone its expression. She walked farther away, huddling into her cape and scarves. Slowly and unobtrusively, I moved toward her to catch up. She was crying]* Whoa. O!—no—I'm okay. I am. It's just that . . . I don't know—suddenly I got so *sad*. O Jesus. It just kind of hit me! I guess I've been holding it in. I guess I've been—whoa! Sorry! I'm crying like a freakin' baby over here . . . I guess there's something so—*beautiful* about it. The whole deal . . . "The figure in the carpet." I know *Kura* must have seen it too, I mean, the beauty. *Had* to have, in the end. At the end . . . 'cause he wasn't a dummy. He was *no dummy*, not my Kura! It's just so . . . it's all so *compelling*, don't you think, Bruce? No? "The gangster and the guru"—ha! Call Hollywood, somebody! But oh my god, such *anguish* in the last half of his life. The last *third*. Especially that last year or so . . . boy oh boy oh boy. And all because he thought his teacher had betrayed him! That's a hell of a resentment to carry . . . *thirty years*, that's how long it took, it took *thirty years* for the mouth of the snake to clamp on its tail and complete the circle. *[looks up]* You know, I've always loved the stars. Loved, loved, *loved*. I was intrigued by the constellations early on because of my name. That's ego for ya. Learned everything about them—when they were visible, when not, what part of the sky—knew all the myths behind them. So that's what I did with those three, from the penthouse. When I got back from Delhi . . . on one of those freezing, crystal clear New York nights when the sky looks like—a painted Jesus on black velour. Looked up and figured out who would go *where*. I conjured the Great Guru—"The Teacher"—sitting on his galactic throne; the American—"The Supplicant"—kneeling at his guru's feet. And there was Kura—"The Guide"—completing the trinity. No Catholic reference intended.

* * *

I was going to miss her, not just for the surreal opulence of the experience she provided but for her passion and intelligence, and capaciousness of Spirit. She truly was unforgettable.

I had planned to leave the next day, though when morning came, one of the staff delivered a string of characteristically charming, seductive, handwritten notes to my tent. (From the inside, one would never have known it to be a tent, such was its luxurious construction and design.) Queenie forbade my departure, insisting she still had vital information to impart. What followed came the next evening over dinner. The detail she subsequently provided—that "single, religious detail" alluded to in the foreword of this book—rocked my world, as Queenie might have said.

I have never recovered, nor hope I ever will.

I got curious about something. A few months after Kura died, I rang the Paris office to speak to his secretary. I was already in possession of the diaries; we just never had any real reason to talk until now. Justine was hired around the time he returned from Bombay so she'd worked for him about 20 years. I gleaned from his pages that they were devoted to each other. Maybe they used to fuck or maybe she just loved him. If she did, that would have gone unrequited, 'cause I was certain he didn't have any love left to give. Not that kind anyway.

After expressing belated mutual sympathies, I casually asked if the chair had ever found its way back to the village. She was perplexed. "What chair?" she asked. I flashed that Kura may have written down his plan without ever having had time to implement it before he died . . . though if *that* were true, wouldn't Justine have read about it in the diaries? She had all of the volumes at hand too because I insisted she make copies before sending (I was afraid the originals might be lost in the mail en route. I was always paranoid about that sort of thing). Maybe she wasn't the kind of gal to read her deceased boss's true confessions, but feminine instincts told me otherwise. Another possibility was that she *had* read them but was playing dumb because she thought I'd judge her as a snoop.

So I gave her a leg up by tactfully mentioning the very last page of the journal, in which her employer expressed an urgent desire to have a certain courier return a certain chair to a certain province wherein lay nestled a certain village, and so forth. Her voice quavered; she admitted to being so busy with legalities in the wake of his passing that she hadn't been able to "properly" read the facsimile, at least "not all the way through." I suppose I'd embarrassed her (not my intent), as there were only two options ultimately to be taken—at least *committed* to—i.e., to read the damned thing or not. But I'd caught her off-guard and now she risked looking like she didn't really give a shit about his posthumous memoirs. The more I downplayed my question, the more lugubrious she became. It got worse by the moment—I could hear her barely suppressed panic at having maybe taken a giant dump on her loved one's final request. Now *I* was committed, and walked her through. "Did there happen to be a wooden chair near Kura's desk when they found him?" Again, she was stymied. (The *when-they-found-him* actually provoked a cough.) I bullet-pointed that he wrote in his diary that a chair had been removed or at least a chair had been *intended* to be removed from the office closet, and so on and so forth. After a long pause, Justine said "Ah, oui!" a bit too stagily but unmistakably thrilled to be in the affirmative mode. There *was* a chair, she said, a very *odd* little chair . . . Was anything taped to it? No, she said tentatively, "nothing to my *knowledge*." The footfalls of panic returned. Well, I said, maybe it might be good to have a look? Long pause. She said the closet had been "cleaned out" and I knew she regretted the words as soon as they came from her mouth. One of Kura's pet peeves was giving too much information, a lesson she must have learned well but had forgotten in the heat of the moment. She said she'd look into it "thoroughly" as soon as we hung up.

Justine called back three days later, sounding truly distraught. She feared the chair was aboard a ship, on its way to America! She added to my confusion by saying, "It *was* in the closet . . . and that fact alone *should* have made it exempt. It should never have been *touched*. O, it's my fault, Cassiopeia, all my fault!" When I asked what the hell she was talking about, I got pitched into a primer on Kura's recycled goods empire, one of whose entities shipped donated clothes and furniture to needy countries that paid by the pound. (Yawn.) Apparently, back when it was politically unpopular, Kura had a brainstorm that the U.S. would eventually be a bigger importer than exporter. As usual, he was ahead of the curve; by the time his theory bore out he had already laid the groundwork. He'd cultivated high-level relationships in Washington for years, delivering full containers to the States at no cost (to his great tax advantage) . . . which was more than I cared to know. But what could I do? Justine was like the proverbial dog on the pant leg. She ended the conversation by swearing that she *would not rest* until she learned the exact whereabouts of that freakin', fucking chair.

Cut to: TEN WEEKS LATER.

There she was on the phone again, unbearably chipper, unconscionably French. (It was starting to feel like we'd once had a fling that ended badly.) She began by telling me that she'd at last been able to read the diaries straight through. "There was *so much* about religion that was hard for a lay-person to understand, but it was such a moving experience! *Incroyable.*" Her voice cracked. I'm not sure what it was about her that made me want to shoot myself in the head. "It just brought him right back . . . in such an *amazing* way. Like he was in the very *room* . . ." She told me the diaries should be published one day, "though of course this cannot happen, for obvious reasons." Then, almost as an afterthought, Justine said she'd managed to track down the chair. "As it turns out, Cassie, there is an *amazing symmetry* to what happened." By way of explaining her jubilance, she recapped the last part of the diary—his wish to return the chair to the village school, its destination before being wrested from the boy. While she knew the chair had belonged to Kura's guru, she still couldn't seem to grasp the significance of that final gesture. What she *did* know was that the chair had ended up in a school after all, albeit one in America. Hence, her pleasure that her boss's decree had been fulfilled "in a roundabout way."

Justine declared that she would never have learned of
the chair's Stateside migration without the "creative investigations" of "a very interesting man called Quasimodo." (It was
as though she'd forgotten I'd accompanied Kura to Delhi and
most likely would have been privy to the name.) She wound
up flying him to California, where he reported that the item
was indeed part of a shipment of five containers to arrive at
the Port of Oakland. Four left the harbor on trains, but the
fifth—the only one that held furniture—languished outside
a warehouse for six weeks before its contents were trucked to
a sorting facility. Records indicated the items remained there
another month and were then dispersed to needy schools in
the Bay Area. The resourceful *Monsieur Q* had diligently visited
every institution on the list, to no avail. He'd even come armed
with a Polaroid—Justine found the Land Camera mugshot
tucked in the pages of *The Book of Satsang*—but never had the
opportunity to compare and contrast. In the end, there wasn't
any real proof the chair had been adopted by any school at all,
but it was close enough to ease Justine's guilt. For that, I was
genuinely glad. Sometime later I received an envelope with a
final, eerie souvenir. Justine had thoughtfully framed Kura's
photo of the chair, believing it would make a nice memento.

I'd only seen it from a relative distance, swaddled in the
darkness of Dashir Cave, but in Paris, Kura had taken a picture under harsh fluorescent lights. Now that I had a closer
look, I was surprised by what I saw. Justine was right, it *was*
an odd little chair. Its shabby state couldn't hide its prove-
nance—turn-of-the-century Edwardian. (I happen to know
a bit about these things.) The armrests were high; they call
them elbow chairs. I used to see them on weekend treks with
the love that *I* lost. (She adored antiquing.) I wondered how
a chair like that would have found its way to the foothills

of the Himalayas, though I'm sure they're not uncommon in India . . . probably belonged to some Brit, a bureaucrat who sold it or gave it away, then wound up at a flea market or something—oh look, I'm already coming up with a back-story! Still, it's likely that the explanation was pretty prosaic. But isn't it always—don't you find, Bruce, that just when you think it's simple, the truth reveals itself to be so crazy-compli-cated? *Somewhat* of a riddle, I suppose . . . though not exactly Hemingway's snow leopard, is it? I'll bet *somebody* has that story. Good luck finding him.

There are mysteries upon mysteries, no?

I never asked if I could examine any of her artifacts, including Kura's diaries, but for some reason I did inquire about the "mugshot" of the chair. She excitedly summoned a helper to fetch a 19th-century Japanese puzzle box made of exotic wood. She moved a series of slats until the top slid open. There were papers inside; underneath them, a photo framed in mother-of-pearl. Actually, three photos: a large "portrait" of the chair, flanked on both sides by smaller, detailed images. The first was that of its cabriole-style leg, ending in a finely ornamented foot; the second, of an engraved copper identifier affixed to the undercarriage.

The letters were well-worn but you could just make them out—the name of a shop, with a phone number: "Ballendine's Second Penny." With a shock that hasn't diminished an iota to this day, I came to realize the American guru's chair was the very same that Ryder used to hang himself.

In 2010, Charley gave me the account of his son's death. I heard Queenie's story five years earlier, and had been haunted by it ever since; my mind had ready access to its many details. So the moment Charley mentioned the name of his wife's parents' shop—Ballendine's Second Penny—everything started to click. We can presume that the cheap-looking, provisional dog tag featuring the merchant's name fell off somewhere between Paris and Berkeley; after all, it was fastened to the cane, most of which had already disappeared by the time Kelly came across it. (God knows how it held on during its life in India.) Otherwise, I would most assuredly have heard about it from Charley. It would have been a very big deal indeed that an item from the "Second Penny" would have reappeared in such a way—like the proverbial dog traveling thousands of miles to come home . . . and an even bigger deal that Ryder would have jumped from it.[11]

As earlier explained, the chronology of narratives was reversed for dramatic considerations; in a sense, Queenie's story was the "second guru" in that (for me) it truly did make sense of the first, in ways both figurative

---

11   Rereading Ryder's tale, I was struck by the image of the shattered remnants of the chair burning in the fireplace—if you'll recall, Charley's wife instructed him to do so—and was reminded of the sleigh burning at the end of *Citizen Kane.* I could see "Ballendine's Second Penny" melting too, but it was only a cinematic reverie; while Rosebud uncovered a lost childhood Elysium, the former revealed nothing. (Or, more tellingly, Nothingness.)
  While assembling this book, I came across a passage in *The Teachings of Sri Ramana Maharshi*, and thought it germane: "Creation is like a peepul tree: birds come to eat its fruit, or take shelter under its branches, men cool themselves in its shade, but some may hang themselves on it. Yet the tree continues to lead its quiet life, unconcerned with and unaware of all the uses it is put to."

and literal. And I suppose I naturally resisted the linear approach, not only because it goes against my grain but because some key plot points—the dog tag; the chair winding up in Berkeley—might have interfered with the reader's absorption in Charley's moving chronicle, even telegraphing what was to come. The last thing I wanted was to rob anyone of a hoped-for frisson.

I often find myself musing along the same lines as Queenie. We know how the chair journeyed from India to Berkeley yet the story behind its voyage to Dashir Cave from a defunct antiques shop in Syracuse that occasionally bore a "Gone Fishin'" sign will never be known.

But as the lady said, there are mysteries upon mysteries.

* * *

These were among Queenie's last words, on the night before I left. We haven't spoken since, nor do I know her whereabouts. All efforts to contact her have failed.
She was very stoned.

Okay, that's enough.

E-*nough.*

I'm finished—*famished.* Let's go kill 'n eat somethin'. Then it'll be *your* turn, bub. Tha's right, bubba, I've decided I can't let you leave . . . just *yet.* Right *on.* No way. 'Cause you're blessed. An' I'm too blessed to *stress.* Aw, just teasin'! *You are hereby free to go.* You're probably a better listener than you are a talker, anyway. Am I right? Course I am. On second thought, you ain't *completely* off the hook yet so don't fall to pieces on me . . . O come on now. I ain' gonna make you sing for your

supper. But I *cain't* just let you *skate*. I mean how would it look?
To the ladies and gentlemen in our audience? Well you know
maybe I could but that just wouldn't do, not after what-all you
put *me* through. Just wouldn't be right. What are friends for.
Blah. Man, I am *drunk*. Guess that'll happen when you have a
72-hour nip or however long the fuck it was—heh heh heh—
was that the long goodbye or the long hello? But enough about
me, let's talk about me. Okay now *really*. Listen up. I'm gonna
ask you to perform an activity, I'll tell you what it is. In a minute. No cause for alarm. Nothing illegal or *compromising*. Well
maybe just a *little*. But I swear it won't *hurt*—though maybe it
kinda sorta will. What are friends for. Have some wine, we
need to soften you up for the kill. Ease the ol' performance
anxiety . . . *Hey*-oh! I'll bet you're the type who needs loosen-
ing up. O shit, I'm not going to have to seduce you, am I? *[calls
out to staff]* Esme? Ez? *Es-me!*—where is that girl? O there you
are. Don't mind me, I'm drunk off my ass. I'm so drunk I'm
drunk off *his* ass. And yours too. Must be the celebratory oxy.
Things go better with ox. And the celebratory weed. And the and-
the and the and-the. You know: *job well done.* I told the whole
story! *Whoa.* Kinda honored my baby, my Kura, something
maybe I never did so well in life. Though that isn't really true.
He didn't honor *me*. No, that ain't true either, he was awesome.
Sorry, Kura. Devil made me do it. Ez-honey? Do you think we
can get a fire going? Ya do, ya do, ya do? O goody. Then can
you get that together? To get a fire going? Could Miguel—can
you tell Miguel? That we want a fire? Maybe over by the tent?
Yes. Well, dig a *pit* then. Go for it, Esmeralda . . . do what you
gosta do . . . Say what? . . . Yup. *Exactamente.* Thank you, Esme!
Man, I have been wanting me a fire *all day long.* If we don't get
one going pretty soon I'm like to *shoot* somebody, and I shoot
pretty good too. From the hip! *Right.* Ha! *Hey*-oh. But seriously,

Broozer, you've talked to what, thousands of people? Okay, maybe not *thousands* but *hundreds*, right? I mean, at *least*. So don't get all modest. However you slice it, it's a shitload and a halfa people. Right? And not *everybody* has the gift of blab, *comme ça*. I mean, *comme moi*. *Non? Mais non? Mais oui?* May we? Well, pardon my French. Bet you've had your fair share of folks baring their souls in under an hour, brevity being the soul of wit and all. Speed storytelling. Oops! Then what does that say about *moi*. Enough about *toi*, let's talk about *moi*. I talk a lot but I'm funny, right? Aren't I, Brewster McCloud? Does being funny make me look fat? Don't answer that. Allow me to continue. Some of the folks who told you their stories—some of 'em probably blew lunch in an hour, maybe *less*, am I right? Course I am. So here's my little request. Queenie's gonna lay it all out for you, put *all* her cards on the table. K? I want you to think of a story somebody told you, a *single, solitary* story. Like a *beautiful* one. It can be *short*, but *hell*, it don't *have* to be. It can be *long-ass*. But the deal is it has to have stayed *with* you, plus you have to need to *want* to tell it, because—because there's something about it you just couldn't shake. K? Beautiful or haunting or crazy-funny or whatever. Do a really short one, or a *long* one, I only offered training wheels as a simple courtesy. Didn't want to jam you up. But if you're pressed for time, it can *really* be short, you can tell it, like, in a New Mexico minute. Ha. *Hey-o!* Y'all remember those "60-second fairy tales"? Edward Everett Horton. *Horton Hears a Who*. Horton hears a whodunit . . . Weren't they a hoot? Or should I say weren't they a Who. And why is it that whenever I get drunk, I start with the y'alls and the—the Southern shit. I don't *know* why, but it's been that way since when-evuh . . . *Love will keep us togethuh.* Remember "Fractured Fairy Tales"? From *Rocky and Bullwinkle*, right? Boris and Natasha! You could just tell us a fractured fairy tale, Bruiser. But enough about me . . . but I'm *serious*, I want to hear a story you *really liked*, one for the road, or at least one you think *I* would like. One for the roadies. Something *memorable*. So c'n you think on one? While I go freshen up? I guess the story's on the other foot now, *huh* babe—ha! Come on. Just think on it. And we'll just sit here in suspense waiting for the other story to *drop*. Ho ho ho. *Heh heh heh*. I *know* you can do it, babe. I know you can make it! *I know damn well . . . yes we can can I know we can can yes we can can uh why can't we if we wanted to we can can*—tell ya what. To be fair. If that big brainuh yours rolls snake eyes, then you can just *make something up!* Hell, ain' nobody gonna hold you to it, no one'll ever even know the *difference*. 'Cause nobody's even fucking listening but *me*, bubba. Man, you have got to understand, Bruce— right now I am so fucking tired I don't even know my name . . . I know I'm drunk but I am freaking *serious* about this! Get your *freak* on, Mother Jones . . . *get your free gun*. So you'll—do we have an affirmative, sir? I mean, you can wait, you can wait to tell us over dessert. Crackling fire, starry night, blah. Or you can *not* wait, you know, tell us *whenever*. Blah. Pull up a chair and stay a while. *[sings]* "Don't be shy meet a guy pull up a chair. The air is humming . . . please don't be long please don't you be very long please don't be long or I may be asleep—" . . . Tell you why—I'll tell you why I'm harping. Why I'm being so *importunate* over here, is because—because it's—it's so *weird* that this *thing* just came over me like BLAM— *right* when we finished. It is *too* fucking strange . . . because you would *think* that after three days I'd had enough. *Nope!* It just sort of dropped *down* on me, this crazy *urge*, this *need*—do you know what I'm saying? Sounds sexual huh. Wull mebbe it is. I just had a thought . . . know what it *might* be? It *might* be I'm still in my own *stuff*, you know, stuck in my head, and maybe I just want to get *out* of my head. Because these last few days we went to some *very* heavy places, my friend, I am *telling* you. And you *know* it. You little devil. 'Cause you *took* me there. Dark, heavy places—beautiful but heavy. So maybe now I just want to cleanse the palate. Does that make sense? What are friends for. Don't answer that. Why fucking analyze. Where's Esme . . . Esme? Ez! Ezzy? *Esme!* Never can find that girl. *[sings]* "Never can say goodbye, no no no no . . . Then you try to say you're leaving me and I always have to say no, tell me why . . . is it so . . . *don't wanna let you go*"—bubba, go have some wine and start googling that big brain o' yours while I freshen up. I am just so *effing tired* of hearing my own story— for three effing days!—and it's such a trip, I am telling you it was like *whoosh* right you know *exactly* when we finished like this voice was saying "No!"—this *need*, this fucking *need* washed over me, this primal *thing*, and it's not even a full moon!—like an actual *physical craving.* So Bruce you have *got* to fucking think—because I don't want—it's like it's *too soon,* I'm not *ready*—I hear this *voice*—you know I'm just not you know quite ready to—*apparently,* anyway—this voice is say-ing like *come on come on* just let me hear *one more*—blam blam *blam*—'cause I'm just not *ready* yet, Bruce—it's like a *drug,* like I'm still coming onto the *drug*—goddammit Bruce all I'm say-ing is I want to hear one more story! So just *come on,* man!— and I fucking *know* you understand—come on! *Come on come on come on come on come on*—tell me a fucking story!

END

CHRONOLOGY

1934—Kura is born.
1952—Cassiopeia ("Queenie")
is born.

1954—Kelly is born.
1960—Charley is born.
1967—Charley is molested by clergy
through 1972.

1968—Kura and Queenie meet at a
club in Chicago. A few months later,
they reunite in Paris.
1970—They visit a guru in Bombay.
Queenie stays four months; Kura
remains for seven years.

1976—Kelly becomes a Buddhist.
Her practice deepens over the next
25 years.

1977—Kura's teacher disappears
from the ashram. After months of
fruitless searching, he returns to his
home in the Marais.

1990—Kelly and Charley's son
Ryder is born.

1992—Kura has a heart attack.
During convalescence, he renews
the search for his teacher.
1997—After a near 30-year separa-
tion, Kura and Queenie rendezvous
in New Delhi. She accompanies him
to a remote village.
1998—Kura dies at 63.

*1997—Charley becomes a plaintiff in
a class action suit against the Roman
Catholic Diocese of Orange.*

*1999—Kelly's mother dies; she
and Charley are wed. Kelly takes
a sabbatical from school teaching
and tutors prisoners in the fundamentals of Buddhist meditation. She
eventually helms a popular special
education program for children. Kelly
signs a contract to write a memoir.
2001—Kelly and Charley experience
a terrible loss. Charley receives a
settlement.*

2005—Queenie tells her story
("Second Guru").

*2010—Charley tells his story ("First
Guru").*

Other Titles Available from Arcade Publishing